I'M GOD AND YOU'RE NOT

As told to
Michael Zelig

Oren
Athir
Media

Cover Photograph: Crafty Vali
Cover Design: Angelina Pateli/Stuart M. Schnapp

ISBN: 978-1-7323389-1-3 (Paperback)
ISBN: 978-1-7323389-2-0 (Hardcover)
ISBN: 978-1-7323389-0-6 (E-book)
ISBN: 978-1-7323389-3-7 (Audio Book)

Library of Congress Control Number: 2018946360

Printed in the United States of America
First Edition, 2018

Oren Athir Media
97A Hawthorne Ave
Park Ridge, NJ 07656
www.orenathir.com

www.michaelzelig.com
www.imgodandyourenot.com

Dedication

For "JoJo" and in loving memory of Mom and Dad.

Acknowledgments

"I'm God and You're Not" has been many years in the making, and to properly thank all the people who influenced and/or encouraged the writer over the years would take much too many pages. My gratitude to them is boundless.

This book might never have been finished, or at least the ending would have been much different without the support and love of some very special friends from "the Café." They are a constant reminder of the goodness that shines from certain people. Most especially I am in debt to "A," "S,"and "V" — my beloved "family," and to my son, for being my light through the darkness.

Whatever flaws are in the book are mine and mine alone.

CONTENTS

Before the Beginning – An Introduction by Michael Zelig

We were having one of our more severe Northeast winters. It seemed like every other day or so would bring another cropping of snow with its customary pleasures: Another round of shoveling out the cars only to find stalling batteries. Long lines at the supermarket as desperate hordes descend on the scene in a mad fight for yet another container of milk — as if all the cows had finally run dry and there would be no more milk ever again. Streaming every bad movie available on Netflix, over and over again — the ones you wouldn't waste a dollar to see at the theater —to the point where you start saying the lines along with the muscle-bound villain, in fact you start rooting for the villain as desperation sets in while you look out the window only to see Mother Nature dump another two feet of snow on the ground.

The warmest room in my home was my workroom, and that winter I spent a great deal of time in it, mostly working with my computer, and cruising the Internet. One day, after waiting for the latest Windows update to be installed, I was staring at the home page of my browser, wondering where to go next when the computer seemed to spring to life. My hands were off the keyboard, but suddenly the address of a new location was being typed on my browser:

http://www.god.heaven

1

And the computer screen jumped to that site. There I saw a simple white screen that said nothing more than:

GOOD MORNING

followed by a button that read:

PRESS HERE

I pressed the button.

Suddenly, there was a clap of thunder and a bright flash of light and in an instant I seemed to be outside on a beautiful Spring day. And in that thunder, I could swear that I heard someone calling my name.

"Here I am," I answered.

"Good," came the response in a deep bass voice that seemed to shake the tree and the earth around me so much that I was forced to my knees.

What's going on? I thought.

As if reading my thoughts, the voice answered out of the thunder, "Don't you get it? This is God. Jehovah, Yahweh, Allah, Ahura Mazda, Great Spirit, Brahma-Shiva-Vishnu, 'I am that I am,' the Father-Son-Holy Ghost.... I don't care what you want to call me. Listen, I've decided it's time to put my foot down. Of course, I'm speaking metaphorically since I don't really have a foot. The human race has had thousands of years to get it together, and you keep getting the damn thing wrong! That wasn't such a big deal when it only affected your own kind, but now you're at the point where this blind stupidity of yours threatens all life on your planet! So, I've decided to tell you my side of the story once and for all, and I want you to take it down."

"God? Come on, why would God talk to me?"

"Why would God talk to you? Haven't you read your Bible where it says I picked Abraham, a nothing sheepherder, to found a great nation if he followed my ways. Then there was Moses, a tongue-tied runaway from an Egyptian murder rap, to lead the Jews to the promised land, and Paul, Saul (he could never make up his mind)—an epileptic misogynist! A nice Jewish girl from a backwater town in Judah to give birth to my only son! Do you want more? The Quran states that I sent the angel Gabriel to Mohammed—a trader, a businessman, for a change! —to tell him my holy word. What in heaven's name was so special about any of them? I can pick anyone I want—saint, sinner or nebbish!"

"Well, thanks, I guess. But, don't you usually work out of places like Jerusalem? Who's going to believe anything that comes out of New York?"

"Haven't you heard of Mormonism? Anyway, why believe anything that comes out of Jerusalem? A book is a book. And look at the mess your world's made out of the Jerusalem writings, not to mention the Mecca writings, the Rajagrha writings, and so on and so on."

"Well, maybe California—?"

"Oh no, I'm not messing around with any of that New Age crap. Are you for real? Besides, the only religion that comes out of California is television and movies. No, they're too busy worshipping each other out there to pay any attention to me, though I suppose that's a little better than the politicians who are too busy worshipping themselves. Now no more arguments, let's get started."

Another flash of light and I saw a fireball come streaking down from the center of the swirling clouds to land before me. As it hit the grass, it immediately stopped burning and revealed a state-of-the-art laptop. I picked it up, turned it on, and so began the first of many sessions that make up the text of what you are about to read.

Given what follows, I must remind the reader that I am merely the conduit of these chapters. They were written down exactly as they were spoken to me on numerous occasions over a period of a year. Unlike the usual editorial processes, I have not altered the text in any way.

I wouldn't dare!

New York City
May 18, 2018

Book I – In the Beginning

In the beginning God created the heavens and the earth. The earth was a vast waste, darkness covered the deep, and the spirit of God hovered over the surface of the water. God said, "Let there be light", and there was light; and God saw the light was good, and he separated light from darkness. He called the light day, and the darkness night. So evening came, and morning came; it was the first day.

I've always liked that version of the Creation that opens the Biblical book of Genesis; it makes it sound so simple, so straightforward. Well, I must tell you that right there is the first of many times the truth is going to clash with what you've read in the Bible. It's even possible that this version I'm going to relate could wind up getting banned on some list of forbidden books-- just like the Bible itself once was! I can just see the headlines now "God bans God!" Oh well, that's all part of the problem—the assumption that once something is written, it's—you should pardon the expression— "gospel," and you should go on for eternity with blinders on. I mean, according to the different books in the Bible, I am in favor of slavery, bigotry, genocide, and animal sacrifice. *Do you actually think that I want you to go around sacrificing helpless animals to me so I can have a whiff?* We're bound to come back to it again and again but come on humanity; I gave you a brain, so I must have intended you to use it!

But, for now, let's just start with the observation that, no, the act of Creation just wasn't as simple as all that.

First of all, you have to understand that being God isn't all it's cracked up to be. First, the whole omniscience thing. You would be surprised at what a pain that is at times. I mean, I knew how the whole universal unfolding would go even before I began the act of creation. Just to really hit home here, think about the fact that I knew I would create the universe even before I ever thought about it. See, I just *know*! Which really puts a damper on the element of surprise—if you take omniscience to its logical conclusion, God just can't be surprised by anything. Oh, I can be amused, perplexed, puzzled, disgusted, angered, yeah, all that—but if I know all, you, that is the whole human race, just can't do anything that can *surprise* me—I already know what you're going to do before you do—if you get what I mean.

So, that doesn't quite work, does it? Kind of puts the whole kibosh on the free-will bit, eh?

Any one of your cleverer philosophers could quickly point out that the fundamental flaw in the concept of the unfolding of a divine plan is that if God already knows how it winds up, then it's a done deal. Why go through the whole mess — creating stars, planets, atmospheres, life; watching humans stupidly murder each other in your superior ignorance of just what I have planned or what I want of you; observing civilizations rise and fall, children suffering from neglect and starvation in a world designed to support and nourish them all; watching innocents immolated or crucified because you just can't agree over whether I am One or Three or Two Thousand Four Hundred and Twenty-Seven! — when the whole thing is a fait accompli? And then you go and wonder whether you humans have free will! What kind of madman would I be if I did all that intentionally, knowing all this in advance? "Do unto others as you would have them do unto you," indeed! Something wrong with the picture? Well, all in its time and place.

Of course you have free will! Look at the schmucks[1] you pick as leaders. Divine Right, my tuchas!

Oh, don't get me wrong. If that were all you were, all you were capable of, I would have destroyed the lot of you long ago (my supposed promise to Noah, notwithstanding). But, boy, Humanity: you really do piss me off sometimes!

And before we go any further, let's get one thing straight: I am not going to tell you how the whole thing is going to turn out—

---

[1] Just because I use the word "schmucks" here does *not* mean I belong to a particular ethnic group, or that I have a religion. I am neither Jewish, Christian, Moslem, Zoroastrian, nor Wicca. Nor am I deist, theist, atheist, or agnostic, for that matter.

7

I'm God and You're Not

I mean, you'll just have to go along for the ride. That's part of what being human is about.

I hate to disappoint you, but despite the delusion of grandeur a good number of your leaders have, you're not the crown of creation. I did not create the universe for your sake. And by heaven! how you could possibly think that yours is the only planet with "intelligent" life on it is beyond belief. I mean, really! I'm extremely fond of you for a heck of a lot of reasons, which I'll get to, but come on! Get a little perspective, humanity

In short, I'm God, and you're not!

Well, yes, I'm quite aware of how you worship me at your synagogues, mosques, churches, temples, shrines…what have you. Don't think I don't listen. Why, sometimes I even listen to your religious broadcasts—now there's a concept for you; can you even imagine that we would get television in heaven? So, I know what's going on down there. Holy, Hallelujah, Baruch Atoh, Hari Krishna (or Rama or Vishnu or the manifestation of your choice), Allahu Akbar!, whatever you want. Hey, I'm certainly pleased that you remember me, and that there is some thought to good and evil, and basic moral principles. Great. Can you take it to the next step and *leave each other alone to worship me as each of you sees fit?* I don't recall giving any of you the authority to say whom I've damned and whom I've saved, and who is blessed, and who has blasphemed my

8

name. Do you really think I'm so petty as to actually care about this? After all, sticks and stones may break my bones --again, metaphorically speaking of course-- but names will never hurt me. And as far as all you fanatics go let me tell you a big secret: If I wanted someone killed over this stuff, I am certainly capable of doing it myself. I'm God, remember? Jesus Christ!, if I could destroy Sodom and Gomorra, crush Leviathan, drown Pharaoh's army in the Red Sea, destroy Babylon the great, and – pièce de résistance! – resurrect the dead, I think I can fight my own battles, thank you very much.

I mean, do you honestly think I had nothing better to do than to create you so you could go around persecuting each other for my greater glory? What sort of sick, sadistic son of a bitch do you think I am? Or maybe you think it's like television...like I look at the Earth edition of the Universal Channel Guide and think, "Hm...there's a fight between the Sunnis and the Shiites in Syria. Nah, maybe I'll watch the starving masses in Burundi tonight...much better than Survivor." Do you suppose I think those are comedy shows?

Anyway, let's get back to this all-knowing God thing. That one was a problem. If I already knew how the whole goddamn thing turned out, what was the point of going through the whole creation bit? It's sort of like turning on the TV to watch a bad movie when you already know the plot. Boring! So, the only way it works is that I don't know all the details. Yep, I don't know everything. Nor would I want to. Kind of makes the whole thing pointless: Why put all of creation through all that suffering and pain? It's not like I can go to someone with a smug look on my face and say, "Told you so!" I know what the end game is supposed to be, but I don't necessarily know how we get there. Sort of like a detective story where you know the murderer in advance, but you want to see how the detective catches him. Hey, inquiring minds want to know!

Oops, I supposed some of you might be shocked that I would have used the expression "goddamn" a few seconds ago. I guess I just took my own name in vain. Now, I'll get into it more when I get to discuss Moses, but that old commandment "You must not make wrong use of the name of the Lord your God" (or as some put it "Thou shalt not take the name of the Lord thy God in vain" [2]) does not mean that you can't curse. Heck, it really takes a saint to avoid saying a good "Goddamnit!" after hitting your thumb with a hammer!

Do you want to know what wrong use of my name is? Killing those who think differently about what I am than you, saying that an illness, a tragedy, poverty or other misery is a punishment from me, invoking my name to justify your wars, *that's taking my name in vain*!!!

---

[2] By the way, it should be "carry" not "take" if you really want to translate the word *nacah* from the Hebrew correctly.

Book I – In the Beginning

Well, now we get to Creation. Oh, I readily admit I've made my share of mistakes in this Creation thing.[3] Hey, I was learning as I went. I mean, it's not like I had a Do-It-Yourself Build Your Own Creation book to follow, did I? Hey, even this God thing...I'm a self-taught God. Do you think I had a Mommy God and a Daddy God to tell me, "Now Son, bubonic plague was a very naughty thing to do. You go right to your room without any supper. And no TV tonight, you're grounded!"?

In a certain respect, I'm much like you. Think about yourself. How much do you really understand, really know about yourself? What makes you tick? No matter how much you think you know...in the end, the hardest thing is to know yourself. It's like .... hmm.... you have an abstract idea of what love is, but you can't really know what it feels like until it happens to you. You can't truly know what it is to be frightened, or angry, or sad until you feel those emotions. Or, the difference between reading about sex and actually having it!!!!

Here I was, knowing everything abstractly, but not having the concrete experience of everything. Knowing I was God, but what exactly did being God mean?

I had to learn how to be God!

Because why on earth would I bother to create the universe? There I was, omniscient, omnipresent, omnipotent, omni–this-that-

---

[3] Yes, I know some of you think your own human race is my biggest mistake, but let's drop that for now.

11

and-the-other, minding my own business and the next thing you know, I'm doing construction work. And, as I already said, like any first-time handyman, I learned as I went—so, I suppose some parts turned out better than others. Of course, that's all a matter of opinion, anyhow.

But, what actually made me do it? Did I wake up one morning and say to myself, "Boy, I feel great today. Think I'll go out there and invent—Everything"? Well...hold on to your hats -- because you may not like this one!

The number of stories you tell about why humanity was created is as numerous as the inhabited planets in the Universe. But, let me remind you again — sorry, Creation wasn't for your sake. You are not the perfect result of my infinite plan, although you are part of it.

And to think of the theories that were and are going around about what God is and what I want from creation!

They're all wrong, you know. Up in heaven we heard them all and made up names for them. And I and the Heavenly Hosts would just like to share with you a few of our favorite human theories about God and the nature of the Universe:

1.   **The Exispectorant Theory** - The Universe was created when God accidentally spit up a wad of phlegm

2.   **Unintelligent Design** - The world is too complex to have happened by happenchance. Some intelligent mind must be behind it all. This mind is criminally insane.

3.   **The Scientific Method Theory** - God is a scientist. The earth is contained in an enclosed sphere. Here, God performs various experiments — for example, what would be the effect of exposing human babies to encephalitis?

4.   **The "What? Another Rerun?" Theory (later called the "We've got one hundred thirty-seven creations on this thing, and we still can't find anything good to watch" Theory)** - God originally was very hands-on, creating and interfacing with His creatures. Then, He just got bored with the whole same old stuff day after day. So, He went away. The most recent version is that He's busy channel surfing other creations hoping to find one that's interesting.

5.   **The Siesta Theory** – God created the world, but the reason he's so silent lately is that He's in the middle of a good nap.

6.   **The Vacation Theory** - Because of the pressures of the job, God is currently taking a five-eon vacation on his own private planet.

7. **The Lennon Theory** – "God is a concept by which we measure our pain." — whatever the hell is that is supposed to mean! Some hold that this theory should actually be "Pain is a concept by which we measure our God." Is that any clearer?

8. **The Twilight Zone Theory** – God created the world. Then he rested. He is now busy praying to His own God.

9. **Theory Zzzzzzzz** – This is all a dream God is having. No one is sure whether God is having a nightmare or not, but please, somebody wake him up!

10. **The Black is White theory** – The universe is evil. Therefore it had to be created by Satan.[4]

11. **The Dumb T-Shirt Theory** – Frankly, my dear, God doesn't give a damn.

12. **The "I Love You, You Love Me" Theory** – God is a big fat purple dinosaur. This explains much about how the world works.

13. **The Capitalism theory– God** is money. Money is God. [5]

---

[4] For some reason, this seems to be Lucifer's favorite theory. Though he's not so hot about the evil part! And hang on, you'll meet Lucifer in a couple of pages.
[5] This happens to be the true religion of most of the inhabitants of an area known as the United States.

14.   **The "Wanna Bet?" Theory** – A particular human (call him Pharaoh, Emperor, King, Dictator, etc.) is God. Why? Because he says so. Since this human has a lot of soldiers supporting him, his divinity is taken as a matter of faith ("If you don't believe I'm God, you can take it in good faith that I'll have you killed"). There is a way to really prove whether the human is God—namely, stab him, hit him over the head with a boulder, throw him into an active volcano. Oops, son of a bitch is dead, ain't he? Good, now we can pray to him in heaven. Gee, the damn bastard seems awfully quiet now. Hm....

15.   **The Heterosexual, Homosexual, Bi-sexual, Trans-sexual, A-sexual, Sexual Theory** – Of which there are four variations:

a.   God is a man. That explains everything! (This version is advanced by men)

b.   God is a woman. That explains everything! (This version is advanced by women)

c.   God is a woman. That explains everything! (This version is advanced by men who think the world is really screwed up)

d.   God is a man. That explains everything! (This version is advanced by women who think the world is really screwed up)

16.   **The Cosmic Yoke Theory (Sometimes called the "Damned If You Do, Damned If You Don't" Theory. Also known as the**

"My God's Better Than Your God, Even Though He's the Same God" Theory). – There is one and only one God. God wants us all to love one another as brothers and sisters. Therefore, He revealed himself differently to many prophets over the centuries so that there would many different religions, all calling Him by different names, and each one claiming to have the sole and only full-realized truth about God and what He wants. And because God is Love, He wants the followers of the "one and true religion" to utterly destroy the followers of the other one and true religions, because they are damned for worshipping the one God under a different name and truth. And while that's going on, within the "one and true religion" there are variations of that one fully-realized truth — so God wants the few who really, truly understand the truth of that religion to destroy other members of the same religion who may have a slightly different interpretation of that same truth — and yes, who are damned as well.

One legend that came out of this theory is that once upon a time, Yahweh, Jesus, and Allah got together one day and decided to divide up a good portion of humanity between them. They placed bets over how long it would take their followers to wipe each other out — and which of the three religions founded in their name would finally emerge (if any) as the sole winner. These three manifestations of God spend most of their time sitting around Heaven laughing their heads off.

17.   **The "I am He as You are He…" (a.k.a. "I am the Walrus" or "What is, is; What isn't, isn't") Theory** — All living things constitute God. And the Universe as you know it is merely an agreement between all living things. Another way to put it is that merely by your existing, you have agreed to the way the Universe works. That makes You the putz who put all this together. Don't you feel like a real schmuck!

18.   **The "Oops, God is dead. Miss him, Miss. Him" Theory.** - In the beginning, there was a God. But He was so busy texting that He wasn't watching where He was going, got hit by a passing Angel in a runaway Universe, and fell through a hole in reality.

19.   **The "If I Think Too Hard About This, My Brain Gets All Wobbly and Wants to Throw Up" Theory.** – Man is but a tiny speck floating on an electron (the Earth) around the nucleus (the Sun) of an atom (the Solar System). This atom is part of a compound (the Milky Way Galaxy) that is one of many that make up a cell (the Universe). This and countless other cells makes up the body (the sum total of all Universes) of God. God, in turn, is a speck on an electron…. etc., etc., …which makes up the body of His God, which in turn is a speck…and so on and so forth ad infinitum. And within each living creature on earth is a sum total of universes that make up its cells; each cell in turn consisting of the sum total of its compounds (galaxies) which consists of atoms (solar systems), each

of which have a nucleus (a Sun) around which circle electrons (planets) upon which are living creatures who…etc., etc., and so on ad infinitum.

20.   **The "It's as Good as Any Other Theory "Theory or The "Your Guess is as Good as Mine" Theory** - The Universe rests on a serving tray. The serving tray rests on the back of a blue whale. The blue whale rests on the tail of a gigantic red rain dragon. In turn, an elephant balances the rain dragon on its four legs. The elephant's back rests on a sphinx. The sphinx rests on the back of a camel. The camel rests on a walrus. The walrus rests on the wings of a condor. The condor rests on the back of a Gila monster. The Gila monster rests on the back of a platypus. The platypus rests on the back of a boa constrictor. The boa constrictor rests on top of a flounder. The flounder rests on top of a Coolibah tree. The Coolibah tree sits on top of a slimy toad. The slimy toad rests on top of a praying mantis. The praying mantis sits on top of a cucumber slice. The cucumber slice rests on the top of a kumquat. The kumquat rests on a pebble.

The pebble wobbles a lot.[6]

So, let's go back to the beginning. And I mean that in a non-Biblical sense. Forget about the earth being unformed and void thing; I'm going back to when *everything* was unformed and void.

---

[6] That pebble business is really a lot closer to the truth than you may think!

Book I – In the Beginning

I was self-contained. All past, present, and future existed in my unchanging omnipresence. There was nothing except me, drifting in an eternity composed only of me. And this pretty well went on for oh let's say billions and billions and billions of your earth years, as I contemplated myself.

And then, I had a Thought. It was quite a curious Thought, this first Thought of eternity. For it occurred to me that in all this contemplation of myself, there was one thing I did not know: what *did I look like?* If there was nothing there but me, then this was an unanswerable question. You might even argue that it was a mean- ingless question, but still, that's what I thought. Now, you, of course, understand that there were no mirrors back then. I mean, I hadn't even created the cosmos yet, let alone even contemplate what a mirror was. So, I decided to create something that would be outside myself -- an *other*, if you like. So, I created the first thing.

Now, here's the funny thing: I had created this "thing" — for lack of a better word — but it had no substance. It was like a con- cept, an idea of something. After all, this was before I came up with matter or energy, and Einstein's theory didn't exist yet (not to men- tion Einstein). So, this thing had no form.

"Hello?" I said to the thing.

There was a momentary pause, then this thing replied, "and a 'hello' to you, too. What am I, anyway?"

"Well, I hadn't thought of that. It seems stupid to just say, 'you're a thing.' I know I'm going to create more things, different things, so I need to call your type of thing something other than just a thing or I can tell we're just going to get more and more confused. Ah, I think we will say that your type of thing is called an 'angel.'"

The thing thought for a second. "Okay, I kind of like the sound of that. 'An-gel.' Sounds like something light and airy. Now, what do I call you? What's your name?"

Name? Now, that was an interesting concept. I had no name since I never had to refer to myself before this. I chuckled.

"What would you like to call me?" I asked. "Why don't you give me a name." I was curious to see what the angel would come up with.

The angel was silent for a while. "I think," it said finally, "I shall call you 'Lord.'"

"'Lord'? Why Lord?"

"Why not? It's the first thing that occurred to me. I thought of a few other names: 'cat.' 'kumquat,' antidisestablishmentarianism,' 'Bob,' 'Microsoft,' but I don't know. I just like the sound of it: L-o-r-d!"

I chewed on this for a while. "Yes," I agreed, "that will do nicely. It does have a nice ring to it. But, now, my angel, what is your name to be?"

The angel answered without hesitation, "Lucifer."

Lucifer and I proceeded to have a friendly meeting of the minds, and I quickly grew fond of my first creation, and I did indeed go on to create many, many more angels. For instance, there were Michael, Azrael, Beelzebub, Belial, Iblis, Asmodeus, Raphael, Gabriel, Uriel — all created in perfection by my thought.

And things went on merrily for quite some time.

Book II – Creation

ut you've heard of the saying "trouble in para-dise," no doubt. Well, it does have more than a terrestrial meaning. Let me explain.

Many of you have the impression that the an-gels sit around all eternity just playing harps and singing my praises. You know, "Holy art thou, O Lord" and so forth. Sorry, but I'm not a megalomaniac. Some who claim to speak for me maybe, but I'm not. I don't have to hear that I'm holy and blessed; it sort of comes with the territory. I mean talk about belaboring the obvious! It's sort of how Goliath felt – remind me to tell you about him and David later – when people would gather down outside around the Philistine campfires and say, "Oh Goliath, boy you're big!" And he'd yawn, and say, "No shit pipsqueak!"[7] and then bash a few heads in (the guy really had a temper). Now, I'm not the one to send down a plague while someone's blessing me, but try to im-agine how you'd feel if that's all you heard day in day out – "Oh Blessed are You, Lord Holy, Holy is Thy Name." I KNOW THAT! I'm the one who came up with this "blessed" stuff in the first place, remember?

---

[7] I realize some may be shocked that God would curse. First of all, remember I'm God and, I can say whatever the hell I want. Then, go examine the Bible and you'll find that there's cursing all over the place. Just what do you think it means when it says, "God cursed…" .and so and so? But just for the record, I don't consider words like "shit" to be obscene. Words like "kike," "pollack," "dago," and so forth… *those* are the true obscenities!!!

And by the way, there's just so much harp music anyone can take! Even I like to get down occasionally and boogie!

Which begs the question, how exactly did we pass the time back then? You're probably wondering how we could have survived without soap operas, American Idol, 24-hour "news," rock 'n' roll, rap, American presidential elections, Survivor, and all those other cultural epiphanies to keep us amused. Maybe some of you might be willing to bet that that's the very reason man was created in the first place! Well, the angels and I would have long discussions about many things, like "how many angels could dance on the head of a pin" and exactly what was a pin anyway? We'd have long sing-a-longs. In fact, I think it was Asmodeus who invented the song "A quadrillion bottles of beer on the wall" – which gets really tedious after the first two million rounds or so. Stuff like that.

Now it must have been some five or six billion years ago [8] when Lucifer first asked me what it felt like to perform an act of creation (referring to his). The problem I had explaining it to him was much like the one you people have describing an orgasm to a priest— "Frankly," I told Lucifer, "if you haven't experienced it for yourself, there's just no way to describe it."

Not one of my better answers, I admit, because it got Lucifer to thinking about it more and more. So, one day, he and the boys— not to be sexist, but that's how I refer to all the angels, as "the boys," though an angel is neither male or female, actually sort of

---

[8] We weren't big on time yet.

23

androgynous, which does solve a lot of problems, such as the one we got into with that Adam and Eve thing—but I'm getting ahead of myself....[9]

Anyway, so the boys got together with Lucifer (as usual) as their Spokeangel and presented me with a proposal. "Lord," he says, "the guys and I have been thinking."

"Oh?" says I, not a little amused since I know what's about to come. "What's on your mind?"

"Well, you know Lord, not to complain or anything...I mean, we really appreciate you creating us, and taking an interest in us and all that, Lord, and no disrespect intended, but we've been hanging out like this for what seems an eternity" – which in truth, it was! "So, what's your plan? Now what?"

I thought about this for a while. "What makes you think there is a plan, Luce?" – I called Lucifer "Luce" for short. "Maybe this is really all there is." Okay, so I was leading him on a bit. Then with a smile, I added, "Well, I'm open to suggestions. You and the guys have anything in mind?"

"Well, you made *us*. Why stop there? Why don't you turn us loose and let the boys and me see what we can come up with? Hey, how hard could it be for us to whip up something really neat?"

---

[9] Since I brought it up, let's take care of this right now. I'm not going to be politically correct with this man/woman-kind bit -- we know what we mean! I can just see someone protesting now -- "God is a male-chauvinist! He's anti-this, that and the other one!" How boring! Get a grip, humanity! First of all, what's makes you think I'm male? Or female for that matter?

I thought about it. Actually, I pretended to think about it, since this was indeed part of my eternal plan (remember, I told you there was a plan).

"And, no disrespect, but, we want to do it by ourselves, Lord."

I whistled. "By yourselves?"

"Yeah. You already know how, and how are we ever going to learn with you leaning over our shoulder."

"Hey, look, Luce, you just can't go messing around with the framework of the ineffable without knowing what you're doing. Lord knows what will happen!"

"Yeah, Lord always knows."

"Oh, that was just an expression that is going to be bandied about incessantly someday. Don't give me that hurt little angel look of yours; you always do that when you think you're not going to get your way."

Lucifer pouted. "Okay, okay," I laughed, "Gather up the guys."

Since communication among the Heavenly Hosts is instantaneous, the multitude was before me as soon as I finished speaking. "So, you want to go into the creation business, eh?" A small number nodded, and a larger number mumbled denials. Some said that they had no recollection of any conversations about creation ever taking place. Some argued that since there was no agreed upon definition of the term "Creation" that it didn't exist. The archangels blamed the idea on the cherubim, and the cherubim blamed the idea on the archangels, and an ever greater number just kept silent. I should have remembered this later when Beelzebub and Magog were working on creating politicians, but you can't think of everything all the time.

"So, you want to get into the Creation game, huh?" I said, laughing, "You want to extend my work, huh? First of all, haven't you noticed something? Right now, there is nothing out there to work with. And I won't have you messing up my lovely little Heaven with a lot of failed experiments. So, we're going to have to build the External Existence.

"But, understand this: there are some elements to Creation that you angels just cannot do, only I can. That's because everything ultimately stems from me. Some of these things you'll find out later on. I could tell you what they all are now, but sometimes you have to learn from your mistakes. Besides, you wouldn't believe me anyway! And while we're on the subject of learning from mistakes—that applies to the Creation as well. What is created must be allowed to grow and find its way with a minimum of interference from us. We can push in the right direction, but we never force. Existence is learning. I want creatures that think, not automatons that merely obey.

"The first thing you must understand is this: You can't create something from nothing...You need me to lay down the foundation of Reality. Behold!"

Book II – Creation

I opened my palms, and there was a little ball of my divine substance. As the Hosts watched, it began to glow with an especially lovely blue tint. A low sound came from it, gradually growing louder, vibrating through my angels with an "Aumnm."

"This is the sound all Creation sings. This is the Note Eternal," I said. It was an E note, by the way, for those of you who wonder about that sort of thing. Think of it as a chord, played on a piano, crashing at the end of a tremendous buildup of sound upon sound, climbing up and up. [10] "And so, it begins as was envisioned in my First Thought."

The ball began to whirl, growing bigger and bigger as Lucifer and the others drew nearer, each reaching for a touch of it. The angels themselves began to chant "Aumnm," filling the air.

The ball began to flash yellow, green, red, purple "Behold!" I said. "Let there be Stuff!"[11]

The ball shattered with a roar. Shimmering lights spread out before us, new spaces in the outline of Eternity.

And the angels said, "Ahh!"

Multi-colored specs touching, spinning in my Divine Dance, joining, splitting, forming, reforming.

And the angels said, "Cool!"

---

[10] Okay, so God is a bit of a musician at heart - Did you think that final bit of "A Day in the Life" just sprang into "Sergeant Pepper" out of thin air?

[11] See, I told you. Boy, if I had a shekel for every time I've been misquoted! Well, never mind.

Solids coming together in spinning balls of fire spewing forth even smaller balls, repeating the cycle like an Infinity of movement.

And the angels said, "Way to go!"

The balls congealing into conglomerates, suns, gaseous masses twirling, flashing, the beginning of planets, moons.

And the angels said, "Far freaking out!"

Now I clapped my hands. With a tremendous whooshing sound, the entire display immediately collapsed down into that original ball again.

And the angels said, "Ooooh!"

I laughed. I do like putting on a show, you know? I suppose I am a bit of a ham at that.

I motioned them closer.

"Now take one more look into the ball of Creation."

And once more the ball increased in size, or maybe it was that this time I had shrunk the angels down to fit into the size of the cosmoses I was creating. They'd have to get used to it sometime if they wanted to start messing around with the details. And we passed into the ball. Now they could see that the ball was composed of myriad balls just like it, though these balls were of many different sizes, and sometimes were darker or lighter, displaying different colors.

"This is the sum of all Creation existing in what we shall call Time and Space. It is of my substance, but distinct and is perishable, so that the Eternal essence can rejoin and mix anew. Because it is of me, I feel every part of it. Each of these balls shall be called Universes within the great Ball of Creation.

"Uncountable universes containing uncountable ways to grow the great experiment of Creation."

And to find out what happens when perfection begets imperfection, I thought in my hidden thoughts. *To find out exactly what it means to be God.*

Ah, do I detect a question from the audience? Am I implying that the Creation is less than perfect? —a thought that a few hundred years ago would have gotten me tortured and burned at the stake for blasphemy in some religions that popped up on your planet. Still, I must admit that that whole "Crucified God" thing has a certain fascination for me. So many variations: I mean, the Norse God Odin even did it to himself (though that seems somewhat sadomasochistic to me, --- pain just isn't my thing ---- more of that later).

Is the Creation perfect? Well, let's see: starvation, poverty, torture, greed...you want more? Over and over again, you just don't seem to get it, humanity, do you? You're not doing your part!

Now I happen to think that a Supreme Being should always set a good example. None of that "do as I say, not as I do" stuff. So, even though I knew better, I realized that I needed to take an entirely hands-off approach for the time being, so the angels could experiment, learn for themselves what worked and what didn't work, and come to understand what I was unfolding.

However, I did watch, and I listened.

At first, each of the angels went off on his own to try to build his own center of the Creation. And there were endless ideas that the angels came up with to create universes: a universe of liquid which annoyed some of the angels immensely, since when we visited it their wings got wet and it's really a major pain to untangle the knots.; one that was liquid fire, [12] that was a bit annoying to Gabriel since, as it turned out, he developed a bit of a tan which didn't look at all good with his complexion....and so on and so on.

Belial, on the other hand, showed us something I don't think any of the other angels even considered. When we went down into Belial's universe, we saw that there was nothing there. I don't mean to say that he hadn't done anything with it, I mean to say that he had literally created *Nothing!* It was a center of complete darkness, no light, no sound, not a thing escaped this sense of ...well...nothingness. It was the first Black Hole!

"So, does this mean that creation can be destroyed?" he asked.

---

[12] Beelzebub, as if you had to guess.

I shook my head. "Not that easy, my lad. But here's one of the rules of the game...you can't create something from nothing, and you can't create nothing from something. The creation of one thing creates its opposite. Or to say it another way, everything contains its opposite. White contains black. Up contains down. You can't have one without the other. So, nothing is everything. And everything is nothing. Which means that your nothing actually contains something. If that confuses you, blink three times, whistle over your shoulder, drink plenty of fluids and call me in the morning. Do not pass Go. Do not collect $200.

"None of you have the vaguest idea what I'm talking about." I laughed, as only I can. The entire Creation shook with my laughter. I was having fun. That's right, fun is part of the game.

"Belial tried to create Nothing, but its essence is Something, because ultimately it comes from me. So, the essence has to go somewhere. Here, I'll show you."

We went down into the center of the darkness, and one by one walked into it. Without consciousness of movement, we were suddenly in another Universe. It just happened to be one that none of the angels were currently working with, but it was a very nice Universe just the same...still being in its raw state of Divine Essence. Really just ready to begin Cloudy areas of light swirling around, congealing into an area that seemed to be collapsing in on itself until....

"Shazam!" I cried. "Tutti-frutti-a-rudy!"

Bang! It was pretty Big Bang at that![13]

Anyway, with all these Universes being created, I was waiting for one of the angels to make the obvious statement. And so, one did.

"But there's no life!" exclaimed Astarte.

"Exactly," I agreed. "But then again, Rome isn't going to be built in a day—don't worry yet about what Rome is, we'll be hearing plenty from it eventually. Maybe building from the Universe down is a bit much, eh? How about this." I gestured around us. "This is a perfectly good Universe.... It's kind of pretty, even." I moved my thought across the ball of Creation, and it became dark except for one small triangular area. "Someday, a great thinker will say 'God doesn't play dice with the Universe,' but no one ever said a thing about marbles! Ah, what the hell!"

I tossed the ball, and it sailed in an arc into the heavenly abode. It landed, rolled around for a while, and then settled. We all looked at the triangular area, and a spiral galaxy was revealed. It was very white, so white that – oh heck—call it a milky white. Yes, it was the galaxy you call the Milky Way.

---

[13] Okay, I'm making that part up. But it keeps your scientists happy...try to measure me, will they? As if I want them to really know what's going on. Yeah, right!

You really can't appreciate how just plain pretty the Milky Way is. Photos just don't do it justice. It's just a beautiful pattern...swirling away like that with a big bunch of darkness in the middle.

I froze the ball some more until only a point of light was revealed and tossed it again. It landed somewhere near the outer edge of the galaxy and started to join it in its, well—not-quite eternal dance. It gleamed and flashed brightly as we went down towards it.

Let there be light! Indeed! Ladies and gentlemen, boys and girls, children of all ages, behold Sol, your Sun—just your average, every day, garden-variety yellow ball of fire.

"Okay, check this out!" I said. I rolled some of the Divine Essence in my hand until it was a very tiny ball, about the size of one of your Earth pebbles. With my index finger, I flicked it right at the heart of Sol. It hit head-on, and part of the edge of Sol flew off into the void in front of the star like a shining flaming sword. As it spread out, pieces broke off, little balls gradually cooling into ten planets.[14]

Now, if I were going to do it all over again, I would have just created one planet first. Because now the angels started arguing about which planet was prettiest and therefore should be used as the one containing life. Everyone's a critic!

---

[14] Yes, I did say ten!

That actually caused a bit of a problem. See, there was sort of a 50/50 split between using the third and fourth planet. The bickering that went on! God, families — know what I mean? And good old Lucifer just had to be different. He really took a shine to the second one; he kept on and on about that one, how pretty it glowed. I think he never got over it; he sort of adopted it as his own. Even today, he likes to hang out there. "Oh Lucifer, light of the morning…"[15]

We could have gone on arguing about it for eons, but this was no way to get anything done. As it turned out, the first attempt to create life occurred on Mars. That's right! Not Earth! Mars…the red planet. You got to remember that sometimes I move in mysterious ways.

And I knew very well what was going to happen when Lucifer asked to see me.

"Okay, Luce, what's up?" I asked.

"Well…we kind of …that is… here!" He placed something into my lap.

I looked at it. It sort of looked the way a black, gooey thing would look if you pressed it with your thumb and it just became more black and gooey. Except for the really gooey parts, which were even blacker. Sort of a black, gooey lump that just sat there being a lump.

"What the heck is this?"

---

[15] Just to paraphrase Isaiah 14:12 a bit.

"Well, a bunch of us got sick and tired of the fighting and the waiting around, so we hopped down to the fourth planet and put our heads together and came up with this. We call it, 'Yech.'"

"Well, what does your Yech do?"

"We don't know. 'Yechs'?"

"Okay, so you made this Yech, and now it's yeching all over my lap. Which is to say that it's sort of lying there, doing absolutely nothing."

"Well, it's a start."

I opened my hand and watched the Yech drip off my fingers and onto the newly waxed floor, making the sort of mess that would plague housekeepers for centuries to come. I wiped my hands and made a face.

"How did you come up with that?" I asked.

"Oh, we took some angel dust, a smattering of some spare eternal essence you must have forgotten you left lying around, and so —"

I smiled. I'll let you in on a secret. I have to confess that that eternal essence just didn't happen to wind up in Lucifer's way all by itself. A certain deity may have had a hand in that, if you get my meaning. Sometimes you have to lead the angel gently where you want it to go. Now the Divine Plan could really begin.

"Some start!" I mused. "I'm not opposed to your idea, but some things you just can't do by yourselves. So, tell me what your Yech really does."

"Well—nothing, I guess," said Lucifer in a small voice.

"Yes, that's right." I nodded. "Remember that I said that all Creation ultimately stems from me. So, must all entities that move, that think. The divine spark is needed, which is why you needed some of my Divine Essence even to create Yech. Now, wipe up that Yech, it's beginning to smell."

Lucifer looked really down. "Oh, come on, Luce. Cheer up. Nobody's perfect. Come here." I bent down and took up some of the dust from the planet. "Go ahead. Try something else."

I placed the dust and some divine essence into Lucifer's hand. He looked at it, rolled it around into a ball for a moment or two absentmindedly, and then started to give it a form. When he was satisfied, he put it down on the ground. Oh, it wasn't much to look at, little better than the Yech was. It kind of looked like a pancake, actually. Not much too it.

"Okay," he said. "Now what?"

"Watch." I leaned over the thing Luce had made, made a tiny hole in its middle, and gently breathed into it. As my breath filled the creature, it began to breathe in and out in time to my breaths. I let go, and it started to move.

I slapped Lucifer on the back. "And behold, there was life."

Luce looked at me somewhat dumbfounded. "Easy, Luce. I told you that there were some gotchas to the creation thing, didn't

I? Well, you just came across number two: See, you can create anything you like, but only I can give it the spark of life. All life comes from me; all life is a part of my essence."

"All life is a part of God?"

"Yes. Though I would prefer to say that God is in everything."

We brought the angels together and showed them exactly what Luce and I had done. I had to demonstrate the lesson a couple of more times, and then their enthusiasm took over.

"Okay, guys. Here's the deal. I'm giving you a free hand on this creation thing on this planet. I'll watch, I'll help if you request, and I'll provide the breath of life to anything you create. But when you all agree you're satisfied with everything, I'd like you to permit me to create one final creature."

Being a good bunch, they readily agreed and set to it.

The angels would show me what they produced, and I would breathe the life essence into each creature. On the whole, I was quite pleased with my angels. Their you-should-pardon-the-expression "creativity" was tremendous. Not every creation worked, of course. Would *you* blame the other angels for complaining because Raphael's flying shark-goat kept eating up everything around it? I thought the whole thing was blown right there and then until Michael came up with the first disease and succeeded in wiping the thing out. And that wasn't the last experiment gone awry. There was any number of failures; I'm afraid we didn't do that good a job of cleaning up after ourselves — we did leave an aw-ful lot of stuff lying around that you're arguing about to this day. Not quite survival of the fittest, but more of majority rules. Frankly, looking at the lot of you, I sometimes wonder if Darwin didn't have a screw loose anyway. In any case, I didn't always necessarily agree with what they produced. For example, I never understood why Abaddon came up with the mosquito, and perhaps in hind-sight, Ebola wasn't such a hot idea, either.

I tried to keep my interference to a minimum, though there were a few notable exceptions. Occasionally, the angles would fol-low my suggestions. I'm especially proud of trees. I thought that was a clever concept of mine. First of all, they're really pretty, and I liked Gabriel's idea of using them to replenish the oxygen supply they decided to use to keep the animals' life energy functioning since, while divine essence was the spark of life, some sort of fuel was needed to keep the 'fire' going. He truly had a sound scientific mind.

For example, take water. Have you ever really deeply thought about the nature of water? Consider the fact that water freezes from the top down, which you are familiar with if you ever saw ice float in water or done something stupid like attempt to cross a slightly frozen lake — just right by the sign that says "Danger: Thin Ice" — only to have the ice give way under your feet. Ever wonder about the reason for that?[16] Simple. If it happened

---

[16] Outside of the fact that you really should lose a few pounds?

the other way, freezing bottom-up like most liquids, all the fish would freeze to death – and, if you believe in evolution since under that scenario life began in water – oops, life would have frozen to death before it ever really got going full time. Chemists will tell you that the reason why water[17] has that unique property is due to what they call "hydrogen bonding" – in this case, a bond between the hydrogen of one water molecule and the oxygen atoms of another water molecule – with the result that ice is less dense than water and able to float. That was Gabriel's, too[18]. And if you stop to think about it, it's a huge clue that there must be some intelligence behind everything. I like to think of it as "God's Proof of His Own Existence" or "I Make Water, Therefore I Am." It's subtle, but there it is. A dead giveaway that!

And yet, there are those who would say that it's merely a fortunate accident of a non-created universe that water acts the way it does. Ha – right! The odds are about ten zillion better that a camel can pass through the eye of a needle than hydrogen bonding just being an accident

I really wanted to make this life thing a low-maintenance project; I thought that once we got everything moving, we could all sit back and observe what would happen as if it were a cosmic television show. Boy, talk about your cosmic boo-boos!

---

[17] If you remember your chemistry, the formula for water is: H_2O—two parts hydrogen and one part oxygen.
[18] With a little help from you-know-who.

So soon we had a world teeming with plant and animal life of all sorts: roses, crabgrass, bluebirds, vultures, butterflies, tsetse flies (and just in case you were wondering, yes, flies were Beelzebub's idea- where did you think that "Lord of the Flies" thing came from?), horses, hippopotami, rabbits, mice, dinosaurs, whales, sea urchins, platypuses, aardvarks, orangutans, gorillas, King Kong and Godzilla[19]. Now I admit we might have gotten a bit carried away with those dinosaurs. Actually, if it hadn't been for those little bitty brains, we'd be talking about Tyrannosaurus sapiens today, and not the homo sapiens you all know and love. And you know, for a hell of a long period of time, Azrael had a bet going that I sent that asteroid on purpose to smash into the earth and wipe them out, but nope, just one of those cosmic accidents — hey, I set up the rules, I don't break them willy-nilly, you know?

This is probably the place to point out that, while indeed we first created life on Mars, we decided to back up our experiments on Earth. This was proper experimental procedure since it was always possible that the addition of newer species (like humanity!) might wipe out older ones before we had perfected things. So, think of the Earth at that stage as a control system so that we could always recreate life before the wild card of a self-aware life form (again, that's you, humanity). Therefore, Earth had every life form we created before you. Just as a precaution, you see. And as it

---

[19] Nah, only kidding about those last two.

turned out, as I'll explain later, it's a lucky thing for you that we did so.

"So, what do you think, Lord?" asked Michael.

"All in all, a pretty good job, if I do say so myself."

I know what you're thinking: where's *mankind*? Well, you hadn't been created yet. See, you were sort of an accident at first.

Things could have stayed in this state for quite a while with us going on about it being good and all, but we were interrupted by the sounds of an argument.

It was Belial, Ezeqeel, and Suruph.

"Okay, what's going on?" I asked.

"Look what Ezeqeel and Suruph did to the beautiful pig-monkey I was working on," complained Belial. "They massed it up with the donkey-dolphin they were working on, and---well, just look."

He gave me the creature. It certainly looked a mess. It had the general build of the monkey, but the brains of the dolphin and the donkey were mixed together, with the pig part of the brain.

"We didn't mean any harm," said Suruph. "We were just playing with it. It was an accident. Ezeqeel doesn't know his own strength sometimes. We were staging a fight between the donkey-dolphin and the pig-monkey, and we kind of bashed them together."

I shook my head. Boy, try to raise an angel in the way it should go....! "Okay, okay. Let me see what I can do with this." I rolled the donkey-dolphin-pig-monkey in my hands, reassembled the arms and legs by knocking each down to two from the original ten arms[20] and legs, reshaped the skull so it wouldn't hang down below its knees, got rid of the snout, and then I showed it to the angels.

"Well, what do you think of this as my contribution?"

"Gee, Lord," said Lucifer, "I don't know. It kind of looks like a naked ape."

"Personally, I like the whales much better!" said Asmodeus.

"It's not as colorful as the peacock," observed Gabriel.

"On the other hand, it doesn't smell quite as bad as the flamingo!" replied Michael.

"What are you going to call it?" asked Beelzebub.

"Behold, 'Man'!" I said.

"Gee, what a piece of work!" said Luce, under his breath.

"Now, now," I replied, "it may not look like much, but hey, I did the best I could with the materials you gave me. But, that's beside the point. So, here's my idea. I am going to make this creature totally free, to think for itself, independent of my will. What will the creature ultimately choose to make of itself?"

"Well, but you know everything, Lord!" Luce pointed out. "If that's so, then how can the creature do anything you don't want it to do, how can it be truly free?"

---

[20] I wonder if that's why you women say men are all hands sometimes. What do you think?

"Ah, I'm way ahead of you on that one. Long before we got serious about this creation thing, I did away with my all-knowingness. I blocked that part of me away voluntarily when the concept first came up, so that man can be truly free."

Lucifer thought about this a bit. "I don't know if that's so wise," he said. "Look at what we did creating this planet…lots of goofs. I have to admit Urziel was right about a killer rabbit being a silly idea. Though I still would have liked that flying horse idea that Gabriel had."

"Oh, and who was going to go around and clean up the mess it made?" remarked Ezeqeel, pointedly.

"Point taken," admitted Lucifer.

"So," I continued, "consider man an experiment in free will. What would happen if a creature could act with forethought and an understanding of the consequences of its actions to change the destiny of the entire planet? Does it choose to rise to the challenge to create an earthly Paradise, or does it sink into the mud?"

"What if it does both?" asked Suruph.

"Now that *would* be a mess," I agreed, "certainly the worse of all possible worlds. I do have plans for humanity…but I can't, won't force it to act under my will. That would defeat my whole purpose, and if mankind hadn't the freedom to choose actions that are good or evil, and hopefully rise up from its more animal nature… heck, might have left the planet the way it was without it.

The plants and animals would get along just fine without him being there!"

"And what *exactly is* humanity's purpose?" asked a sardonic Lucifer.

I smiled the sort of smile only I can. "That would be telling! But, I will let you know this much: Without humanity, I can't truly be God."

Book III – Of Adam and Eve and Cain and Abel

dam and Eve? Okay...well, first of all, that's not even their real names. The word *Adam* means "dust," and *Eve* happens to be the English for the word *Chav* which can be translated as "life." Now, I don't know about you, but I sure wouldn't want to go around being called "Dust." Sounds like an insult to me.

Want to know the truth of the matter? Well, the first man[21] was named Chauncey, and the first woman[22] was named Mabel. But, for simplicity sake, let's just use Adam and Eve and avoid a lot of confusion in telling our story.

But, before we go any further, let's settle that stupid male versus female argument of yours once and for all. Adam was *not* created before Eve, Eve was *not* created before Adam, and despite rumors to the contrary, Adam did not have a wife before Eve called Lilith. You know, I would wonder how stories like that get started in the first place, but for the fact that I've seen what passes for investigative reporting on American TV.

The first human being was not male; it was not female, it was *both*. I don't mean to say it was a hermaphroditic creature; I

---

[21] That would be your great-great-great-great-great-great-great-great-great-great-great-great-great-great-great-etc–and-etc—" unto the first generation thereof' ancestor.

[22] Likewise.

mean it literally was both a male and a female. I said before that when I shaped the first human I reshaped the skull. What I didn't say is that I reshaped the skull, but took the faces of the pig and the donkey that were still stuck together there, rearranging them so that there would be a male face and a female face joined at the nose (if you can imagine what that looked like). And here is where I got my first lesson in the fact that nobody's perfect, because we set the human being—oh, let's call it Chimchi just to give it a name here, since that just happens to be what we called it—down on the planet, and decided to let it name the animals.

You never heard such a ruckus. The Chimchi's male side would say "Rebratium suplantis," and the female would say "petunia." Or the female side would say "robin," while the male side would say "Red flap flap." The male would say "What-the-fuck" and the female, "platypus." And so on.

Of course, neither one would concede. And the arguments would get louder and louder, until there was no peace in Paradise.

Finally, the Heavenly Hosts had had just about enough of this sort of thing. The angels petitioned me to do something about all the noise coming from earth, so I put the human to sleep and split it into two parts, sewing up the gash in the middle, and re-shaping their noses. The female wound up with a cute little nose with just the hint of an up-turn, and the male received a long, some-what fleshy one.

Now, doesn't that make a lot more sense, doesn't it seem more likely than me putting the male to sleep and then creating his "better" half from his rib?

I mean really, humanity: Ultimately, it doesn't matter *how* you were created, what matters *is* that you were created. Do you honestly think it makes any difference who came first, the male or the female? As if I had to practice on one before I created the "per-fected" other---now that's hubris, humanity! If the Bible were to list all of the myriad imperfections of each sex, it would be longer than *War and Peace*, *À la recherche du temps perdu*,[23] *Lord of the Rings* (with *the Hobbit* and *the Simillarion*) *and Les Misérables* combined!

Nor does it matter what color he/she was! I don't give out awards because of a person's race, color or creed! Besides, if you want to know what my favorite color is, it just happens to be green...and I didn't make any of you *that* color. Didn't it ever occur to you that maybe I placed a list of colors on a dartboard, closed my eyes, and let the dart decide? It very well could have been that way, you know.

The stupid things you worry about! People starving in the midst of plenty, wars being fought for countries that won't even be around in twenty-five years...and you argue over which came first, the chicken or the egg—and which side of the toilet paper goes out, which side goes in, don't you, my dear Lilliputians! And to think

---

[23] That's *Remembrance of Things Past* for the non-French speakers in the audience.

that Buddha refused to speculate on whether there was even an ultimate God or not because that had nothing to do with the problem of existence! Let me make this one easy…you really should be a lot more concerned about things that are in your power to do something about, and less on things that you can't change. Gee, what would you do if I didn't exist? Create me in *your* image? Oh, I do forget…some of you already have.

Okay. Okay. I know, I'm getting a bit preachy here. Like, who do I think I am, anyway? God or something?

Now, where was I? Oh yes, we've just created Adam and Eve. And having completed our labors, and thinking we'd done one damn fine job, we decided to take a break from our work, and after a nice, relaxing bath, grab a couple of beers, throw some steaks on the bar-b-q, and call it a day. It really was a pity that sports hadn't been invented yet.

You know how the traditional story goes. According to Genesis, Adam and Eve are living peaceful lives with all the creatures of Creation in the Garden of Eden in which I had planted two special trees: The Tree of Eternal Life and the Tree of the Knowledge of Good and Evil. Adam and Eve have a pretty good deal. There's only one rule: Do not eat from either tree. And you can recall how supposedly the serpent leads Eve into temptation to eat from the second tree, compounding the fault by convincing Adam to eat the fruit as well. Then I find out, and mad at them for breaking my rule, and—again, according to the Bible story—worried that they would now eat of the Tree of Eternal Life and become "as gods," evict them with curses from the Garden. And that's why men earn their bread by the sweat of their brow, and women have birth pain, and why the serpent moves in a winding, torturous manner on the ground, and why we have original sin and so on and so forth.

Well, let's deal with that becoming as gods thing…to suppose for a moment that there was such a Tree of Eternal Life…how does living forever make you a god? Hell, if that's all there was to it, Satan and the boys would be God, too. I don't want to recap everything I've already said about Creation and the Divine Essence, but I'd kind of like to think there's something more to this god thing besides just never dying. And this living forever thing just isn't all it's cracked up to be, either. Considering the propensity of the human race to repeat certain actions—like getting pissed off at each other over some casual remark supposedly about who or what I am, and wanting to kill everything in sight in the name of love and hope…I mean, think of your favorite movie and being locked into a room where that movie plays over and over and over again, twenty-four hours a day, for ever and ever. Give it a couple of days, and I'd bet you'd be looking for a new anything, just to keep your mind from turning to mush!!!! Come to think of it…that wouldn't make a totally bad idea for a Hell, now would it?

The truth of the matter is that, after we fixed up the two of them, Adam and Eve were pretty accepting of just being alive. Think about it—one minute, you are one person, and the next, ZAP!, split in two. Two distinct entities. Just think of the psychological adjustment that most anyone would have to make. Think of the number of popular self-help books that could have been written about this: "Two from One: Separation Anxiety and How to Cope," "Body Image or Getting to Know Your Orifices," "Self-Love: You and Your Appendages," "Men are From Dust, Women are, Too." And then, all those talk shows Adam and Eve would have been on if television had been around then ("Today on Dr. Phil—My better half *is* me!") ...

On the other hand, perhaps there is something to that Jungian idea of animus and anima, each always looking to complete themselves with the other half, after all.

And we're now getting into the ticklish area of our story. Not that I'm a prude, Heaven knows! But, since the universe itself was not intended to go on forever, likewise, it was not in the plan that any particular living thing—humans included—should live forever either. Well, actually we realized that we were putting ourselves into a bit of a bind at this point. If we left things as they were, we ourselves would have had to keep perpetually replacing plants and animals as they wore out—sort of a holy assembly line, if you like. That would never do. Not our job, goodness knows! So, that's why we came up with turning the Earth into a self-perpetuating ecosystem---things like having the plants and trees breathe carbon dioxide and exhale oxygen, then, in turn, having the animals breathe in the oxygen and exhale carbon dioxide for the plant life! Nice, smooth, very efficient. See, who says that God and Science are irreconcilable?[24] Since no one wanted to be locked on an assembly line, constantly replacing worn out creatures with new ones of the same model, we needed to have methods whereby the creatures could reproduce themselves.

We're talking S-E-X here!!!! I realize that's a dirty word to many of you, but it is a reality. So, let's put aside the prudishness — as well as the leering remarks from the other side of the peanut gallery---and deal with what is nothing more than a natural function, just like eating, or drinking, or defecating. It just happens to be the one you tend to make the most overwhelming god-awful big deal about. The idea is that I wanted to encourage you to "be fruitful and multiply," so it's designed to be pleasurable and fun. I wasn't trying to appeal to masochists (though Heaven knows you humans certainly came up with ways to get that into the act!). It wasn't, as I'll tell you, invented as a tool of the Devil to lead you into sin. It's not dirty; it's one of the best ways two people can have fun together without one of them necessarily getting killed in the process. And,

---

[24] By the way—if I can get the attention of those folks out there who think that they have an inside track to my thoughts and ways (They don't!)—this also means that stuff like climate change doesn't need more testing and that you better start dealing with reality!—though where some of you get your concept of reality from really makes me wonder—don't go blaming me for that one!

most importantly, it brings forth the hope of the future, that there will be a next generation that, God willing, [25] won't screw up things quite as bad as you did (okay, so I do have my optimistic side). Pleasure isn't something evil, you know — despite what some of your fanatics think.[26]   It's rather funny that some of you came up with the concept that I created something that you would enjoy just so that I could punish you for enjoying it! You must think I'm one hell of a sadistic bastard if you believe that one! But you do have to remember something common to a lot of pleasurable things — food, drink, scratching an itch, rubbing your toes, posting what you had for lunch on Facebook — too much will get you every time.

Okay, so maybe you all got a bit carried away in the "multiply" department at that. On the other hand, that whole thing about the "apple" and "be fruitful" leads one to note how coincidentally sex didn't happen until you were literally full of fruit.

And as for venereal diseases — no, that's not my way of trying to get your attention by punishing you! What kind of sick, little mind comes up with that stuff? It's actually rather insulting to me if you think about it ("Better not screw around, Bob. God will send a little microbe to eat out your brain if you even think of touching

---

[25] About this "God willing" stuff.   Take some responsibility, humankind. It's not up to me what you make of the world or of your lives…if that were true, you'd be nothing more than little robots running around blindly doing things without any idea of why you were doing it—Hmm, wait a second here!

[26] Maybe you need a quick review? Let's go over it again…pleasure good, pain bad! It's a very simple equation. Actually, I like to keep things simple as far as you're concerned…the evolution of conscious thinking is a slow process from your side of the fence, you know?

Gwen down there." "Hey, Cynthia, God's going to sew it up, and you'll have to piss out of your mouth if you start messing around." "Don't be touching yourself that way, Peter…your palms are gonna get hairy, and you'll go blind."). Not my doing! Not my style, I don't need some little microscopic thing to do the job. Nope, I want to get someone…one, two, three—ZAP!, they're toast! Simple, neat. I don't mess around.

Blame me for AIDS, huh? You really have balls, don't you? Would you like me to shrink them for you, huh? Look, we created heterosexuals, we created homosexuals, and we even created asexuals. It's in the genes, as you call it. That's just the way it is. We didn't put a moral judgment on it— *You* did! Damn, if you want a moral imperative, how about **THOU SHALT NOT MURDER**? Last time I checked, that one wasn't revoked! If you think that creation is holy, then everything created it in, every creature, *every* human is holy, too! Did you ever think that after something like AIDS is finished with its victims, their souls are still mine and that I might simply bring them into my presence? So, when you arrive in Heaven, [27] do not be too upset if you are greeted into my presence by a drag queen!

As I was saying, the team was brainstorming on the idea of reproduction. We did pull a couple of all-nighters on this one. Coming up with that sperm and egg idea took longer than you would think.

---

[27] That is, assuming you *do* arrive in Heaven! —if there is a Heaven at all!

"Maybe when the time came to have a new human, we could turn their legs into roots that plant in the earth and they could just sprout a new human like a tree." That was Raguel's thought.

Sarakiel suggested, "They could jump off the side of a mountain, Splat!...then regenerate as two new beings." We put the kibosh on that one right away, since we weren't wholly convinced that he was just kidding. It just sounded too messy. Besides, who wanted clean-up patrol?

Makatiel accidentally gave us a clue to the solution. "How about this?" he exclaimed. "Bit by bit, their heads start to swell up. Bigger and bigger. Maybe to about twice their size and weight. Then the skull splits open and out comes the new human."

"Come on!" Lucifer interjected. "How the heck do we fit a full-grown human inside the head of another? Talk about getting a swelled head!"

Makatiel considered for a moment. "Well...why does it have to be a full-grown human anyway? Maybe we could come up with a smaller version to come out and then grow into full size later on."

Now, this seemed an idea that generated a great deal of excitement. We debated a lot on that one. There were arguments over size and shape, how big exactly this mini-human would be, and so forth. We rejected the idea of springing it out of the head, and...

I said, "Do we want to consider one thing we're all over-looking? We've got a female, and we've got a male human. Do we want the male to give birth to males, and the female to give birth to females? Do we want each male to look identical to each other and each female look identical to each other female? How would they be able to tell each other apart? That's bound to cause some confusion down there. And for us, too. I mean, if Michael wanted to talk to Adam, how would he be sure he wasn't talking to Seth? Do we carve their names on their chests?"

Everyone went silent, as the angels usually do at first when I stick in my two cents. So, taking advantage of the lull in the conversation, I continued.

"It seems to me that maybe we want each individual to look like an individual. Creation should be an on-going thing, not frozen in a moment of time. I'd like to think that somehow what we've started can be built upon, can evolve into something greater.[28] Let's take the potential of what we've got here and let it develop. I'd like the best of both the male and female to be combined into the offspring."

So, we came up with the idea of Sex. Copulation. The idea that it should be pleasurable—why make it into a chore? Fun is good.

But we were left with one problem. Sort of the same issue you have today—and that is, sex education. It seemed ridiculous

---

[28] Uh oh, are we getting into an argument about evolution versus creationism?

for an angel or me to go down there and start giving humans lectures about procreation. And we also had to introduce the ability to procreate in the first place

Okay, so even the heavenly hosts have an afterthought now and again. Didn't I say something about learning as we went? Anyway, what on earth did you expect for a first attempt at creation?

And I probably should mention—just to answer the unasked question—that no, angels don't have sex! Since I created the angels in perfection, there's really no need. And remember that under normal circumstances angels don't die...so much as I love them, there's a definite limit on how many I want hanging around me all the time

But let's get back to the immediate question: How were we going to give you the ability to have sex and also give you the desire to have sex at the same time?

In retrospect, I'm less than thrilled with how we handled it, but given that the first man and woman were pretty childlike,[29] in retrospect, I do admit it was a bit of a dirty trick.

Now, I don't want to embarrass anyone, but I have to admit that with all the pushing and pulling, and joining, and splitting, at that time we sort of shortchanged you in the brains department. Let me see...how to explain it...did any of you see that opening in the old Kubrick film, *2001*, when that really weird music started to

---

[29] Since life wasn't so complicated then, they didn't need to know all that much anyway.

play on the soundtrack, and the apes came out, and danced up and down in front of the monolith like…well, like a bunch of monkeys? Didn't you kind of laugh and think "what a bunch of stupid ass morons" or something like that?

Guess who the "stupid ass morons" were. There was Adam, always tripping over his big feet, [30] and there was Eve, who was perfectly content to weave flowers together into hair decorations all blasted day.

Not exactly much to give you confidence in the future of the human race at this point.

We needed some way to up your intelligence and to implant the knowledge into you. So, we placed it into microscopic-sized memory chips disguised in fruit so that Adam and Eve would swallow it and, among other things — such as much better taste in art[31] — thus gain the desire for sex. And it wasn't an apple, by the way. I can't imagine how that old story got started. Nor was it a pomegranate, like some Biblical scholars claim. Come on, did you ever try actually to eat a pomegranate? You open it up, and there's a whole lot of rind, then you have the seeds, which are covered in a fruit sack. It tastes pretty decent, but it sure makes a hell of a mess on the rug. And isn't it always right after you've just wiped up the spot where little Johnny spilled the ketchup next to where the cat did its business instead of using the cat litter, too? Oh, and we

---

[30] I mean, for Christ sakes! Can't you look where you're going, you big lummox!

[31] My God, but that Adam had no sense of color coordination!

didn't use a banana, which is my personal favorite but is a bit mushy to hide anything in.

Actually, we used kumquats. So, the kumquat, you might say — to continue the 2001 analogy for a moment — was our mono-lith.

One small problem: Have you ever tried to make a child eat something that was especially good for them...kind of winds up all over the floor, the ceiling...just about any place but in the kid.

And Adam and Eve would just not eat the thing! It was pretty enough...all a lovely shade of orange, it smelt nice, it fitted into the palm of your hand, so you could easily carry it around with you for a snack...but man, humanity, are you stubborn!!!

Then, Lucifer thought of an idea, the sneaky little devil![32]

He took the form of a human, and one day, while Adam and Eve were sunning themselves by a river, he slithered up to them and said:

"Hi, there! How you doing?"

Adam jumped. Eve hid herself behind Adam. They'd never seen another human up to that point, so they didn't know what to make of the situation.

"Hello," Adam replied, hesitantly. "Who are you, stranger?"

Lucifer smiled. "Call me.... Snake. I was just walking through your lovely garden here, admiring the flowers and the

---

[32] Luce asks that I remind you not to take that thing about the devil literally.

trees, the animals, and I saw you two sitting there. Thought I would say 'Hi!'" He popped a kumquat into his mouth and chewed it – it looked exactly like the one we wanted Adam and Eve to swallow, but it didn't have the programming in it.

"What's that?" asked Eve. "What are you doing?"

"Just having a bit of lunch here." He swallowed and then smiled benevolently at Adam and Eve. "Would you like one?" he offered.

Adam shook his head. "No thanks, Snake."

"They're really good," Lucifer said, holding a couple of kumquats out.

Adam was always the cautious one. He shook his head. "No thanks."

"Nice and juicy...."

"What's juice, anyway?" Eve asked. But, picking up on Adam's cue, she also refused a taste. You really can't blame her. We hadn't invented hunger when we'd created the two of them, so they had no concept of eating.

Lucifer popped another kumquat into his mouth, chewed and then swallowed it to give them the idea of what eating was. He stood for a moment, then threw a kumquat up into the air, bowed, and then caught it in his left hand on its way down. "Hmm," he said, after a moment, as he continued to toss and then catch the fruit. "I suppose you're better off anyway. God might get pissed off."

"God?"

"Yeah, God. The big fella who kind of put you here in the first place."

"Oh, yeah," Adam said. "I remember. That's the one who breathed into my face. Boy, he has some nerve. One minute, nothing! Suddenly, bang, there I am, all these bright lights blinding me, and he drops me off here without as much as a by-your-leave. It's not exactly like I asked to be born, now did I?"

"Yeah, that's the guy. This is his fruit. I got it from the Tree of Knowledge. He'd probably get a bit miffed if he knew I took it. He's kind of possessive about that sort of thing. Sometimes, he's a bit of an old fuddy-duddy, if you get my drift. But, they really are good. You should try it."

Eve watched Lucifer as he continued his one-man game of catch. He smiled at her, and shyly, she smiled back. She looked at Adam, who looked back at her, shrugged, and also watched Lucifer.

"Hey, Adam, catch!" yelled Lucifer. He quickly tossed the kumquat over to Adam. Well, what could Adam do? Without thinking, he held out his hand and caught the fruit.

"Nice catch, you have good reflexes. But, let's see what kind of arm you have, eh? Throw it back to me."

Adam obediently threw the kumquat back to Lucifer, who caught it, tossed it up in the air, caught it again, and said "Good throw. But, let's not ignore the charming Ms. Eve here." And he tossed the kumquat to Eve, who found herself catching it and then studying it in her hand.

"Adam, here! Try to catch my fastball!" Lucifer shouted, as he pitched a second kumquat over to him. Adam fumbled it a bit, and then caught it in his right hand.

So, now both Adam and Eve had a kumquat.

"Bravo," Lucifer applauded, putting his arms around the two of them. "Now if we only had a few more of the two of you, we could make a pretty good outfield. You're both pretty good catching with your hands. But can you do this?"

He threw another, smaller kumquat up in the air and as it fell back down, Luce opened his mouth and caught the fruit with it, then displayed it with his teeth to the delighted couple.

"How about trying that one?" Both nodded. "Ready? One, two, three!"

Two small kumquats, small enough to be swallowed whole, flew into the air and plummeted back down. Adam caught his first, smiling broadly as he triumphantly showed his catch, and then Eve quite daintily caught hers as well.

Once more, Luce had his arms around each of them. "Very good. Very good. You two are just naturals." And suddenly, he closed their mouths with his hand, and, then tickled their throats, forcing them to involuntarily swallow the kumquats — much like you might force your pet cat or dog to swallow a particularly nasty pill.

A minute or two went by.

Adam looked at Eve.

Eve looked at Adam.

Adam smiled at Eve and gave her a wink.

Eve smiled at Adam and gave him a wink right back.

Adam held out his hand to Eve.

Eve nodded and took Adam's hand.

Lucifer bowed slightly, whistled, and said "Well, looks like my work here is done for now. Pleasure meeting both of you and..."

He stopped, realizing that Adam and Eve were no longer there.

"Hey, Lord, I think we've done it."

And the sounds coming from a nearby bush seemed to prove him right.

"Good job, Luce," I said.

So, no, I wasn't pissed off about eating some forbidden fruit. I *wanted* you to eat the fruit. But, this might make you wonder about that banishment from the Garden of Eden stuff. You know, where it says in Genesis Chapter 3, verse 22-34:

> Then the LORD God said, "Behold, the man has become like one of us, knowing good and evil; and now, lest he put forth his hand and take also of the tree of life, and eat, and live forever." Therefore the LORD God sent him forth from the garden of Eden,

to till the ground from which he was taken. He drove out the man; and at the east of the garden of Eden he placed the cherubim, and a flaming sword which turned every way, to guard the way to the tree of life.

...and so on, and so on... Nope, sorry, hate to burst your bubble here but no Tree of Life — it just doesn't work that way.

See, if I read that passage correctly (and obviously I do), it implies that I was frightened of you. Now, whoever came up with that one was naïve as all get-out! I am the source of your creation; I breathed life into you; and, as I've said earlier, it would take no effort to wipe out every last trace of creation — remember the Flood story?[33] — and merely by eating a fruit, you're supposed to become like me? Ha! In your dreams, mankind!

Of course, on the other hand, I know of at least one resident of the White House in Washington, DC, who has acted like he's thought he was God and behaved more as if he were the Biblical "Satan." But that only proves that in America just about any schmuck can grow up to be President.

Besides, if I had wanted you to live forever, we wouldn't have had the whole sex thing. Because if you could live forever AND we had the sex thing, you would have overrun ever damn square inch of the planet years ago—not to say that you haven't done your goddam best to do so anyway! Lord God Almighty! You

---

[33] By the way, we'll get to the truth behind the Noah story a bit later.

would think the defining characteristic of the human race was the urge to self-destruct. I said, "Be fruitful and multiply" *not* "Be fruitful and destroy everything in your path"! It's a damn good thing you *don't* live forever. Otherwise, the poor planet and the other living things on it wouldn't stand a chance at all.

And for those of you who don't believe in me or in any of this and treat Darwinism as your "rational" God—the whole Darwinian based "survival of the fittest" stuff does not mean *only* survival of the fittest, you know! Then again, you would think there is some fundamental flaw in the Theory of Evolution since so many of your "evolved" species think that the primary purpose of their existence is to line up in the pouring rain to guarantee they get the latest iPhone on the first day of release!

So, we didn't kick you out of anything. You kind of had the run of the planet in the first place. Granted, things were generally peaceful for quite some time—that whole discovery of sex kind of kept you busy for a bit, as you may imagine. And occasionally I'd pick a couple of angels—Luce in particular sans his Snake disguise— and we would come down and kibitz with Adam or Eve, and on the whole, things seemed to show we had made a promising start to everything. But, there was always room for new developments.

You know—I've always liked the image of the "lion lying down with the lamb." It's such a lovely, noble thought. However, to be honest, since the system was designed to be self-running, you had to eat. It has to do with the very fact that you are perishable. If you think of it like a car, you have to keep feeding it gas and other essentials to make the thing keep going. So, you did have to eat. For the longest time, you were indeed vegetarians...and yes, this was a result of the kumquat incident (which we in heaven call the real "Special K" [34]). The human diet was heavy in kumquats, and carrots, brussels sprouts, and – yes – apples! and so forth. And the original drink of choice was water. Yep, clear, pure, unfiltered, un-adulterated, un-homogenized, unpasteurized, un-bottled, natural water. And you didn't have to pay someone \$2.25 for something I gave to you for free – Shame on you!! Gradually, however, human-kind developed a taste for meat. Originally, the way humans got to taste chicken, or unicorn, or dragon, for example, was through the natural or accidental death of such creatures. And then, speaking of dragons, there was fire.

Boom! A bolt of lightning hitting a tree, or a dragon got teed-off at something, and voila! After you got over your initial fear of the thing, you would sometimes find that animals had gotten caught in the fire and were cooked. And of course, natural curiosity lead to touching them, finding them hot, and as a reaction, putting your fingers in your mouth, and – hey, that tastes good!

So eventually, you had the start of bar-b-q season.

---

[34] I'd apologize to Kellogg's, but we did have it first, after all.

I should point out that we in heaven have no need or desire for food, but, when we take human form as we often did in those days, we could appreciate the taste and smell of various foods.

However, I'm getting ahead of myself.

While Adam and Eve and their offspring were investigating their world, we were still experimenting with the elements of creation. I won't go into the whole thing here, but when someone came up with a new discovery—bread, for example—they would bring it up to a committee of heavenly hosts and, after final approval, we'd share it with you.

For instance, the very first thing we came up with after sex was with wine. Of course, the nice thing about being incorporeal is that we don't get drunk on the stuff.

Unfortunately, you do!

And eventually, that had to have consequences …

Well, it seemed that the kumquat implant took…for, soon we had Cain, and then we had Abel. We're going to get into some heavy stuff here—we are, after all, going to be talking about the first murder in Creation. But let me first tell you that the story as you know it is mostly the version put together by the Sheep Raisers Guild of Canaan, Local 478, during a period when vegetarianism was becoming the in thing. You know the official Bible line…supposedly the thing that set Cain off was that I apparently liked the offering of burnt meat better than an offering of grapes. Nope, not true. Actually, after a long day contemplating Creation, there's nothing like some sweet music (courtesy of Mozart, or Beethoven, or J.S. Bach, perhaps) and a nice Chateau Laffite Rothchild. Kind of gets you in the mood for a nice Chateaubriand.

Look, the real issue is that Cain and Abel were a couple of spoiled brats. I suppose that's natural since Adam and Eve were first-time parents and they didn't have any parents of their own to model their behavior on—but let's not make excuses for what happened.

Although Adam and Eve had a number of daughters as well, at the time of which I'm speaking, Cain and Abel were the only boys. Now, perhaps part of the problem was that Eve always had a soft spot for Abel, her "baby boy" as she always called him. And Abel knew it all too well and took advantage of it. While Cain would be out tending the garden and tilling the soil with Adam, Abel would be lying around with the sheep. [35] Eve would always be making him extra cookies and packing special goodies into his lunch box, while Cain would wind up with a watercress sandwich. So, Cain was justified when he would complain to Abel that "Mom always likes you best!" And Cain would redouble his efforts to impress his mother, but nope, Abel was her golden child. On the other hand, Adam favored Cain, for the very reasons that Eve did not. Adam would take Cain along when he went exploring, while Abel was left to stay home with "Mother and the girls." And it didn't

---

[35] No sexual connotation meant here, by the way.

help that both Cain and Abel had a crush on the same sister, Nemaha. So, there was always some sort of sibling rivalry between the two — who could run faster, who could jump highest, who was tallest, who could pee the farthest...

Ah, yes, who could pee the farthest. The universal issue for man[36] always seems to get back to one thing — a pissing contest!!!

Now, picture to yourself two twenty-one-year-olds, long sibling rivalries simmering just below the surface, and...

"Hey, Abel, give me a hand with this thing." Cain was pushing against a large boulder, trying to move it out of the cave that the Adam Family was calling home. Eve was doing a bit of redecorating and had decided that with a new baby on the way, they needed to clear out some more space.

"Oh, all right!" replied Abel with a sigh. He put down the one-string lyre he had been playing for his sister, Nemaha, and slowly got up. He put one hand on the boulder and pushed. "Hmm, that doesn't seem to make any difference, Cain."

"Don't be an idiot. Put your shoulder into it and push like I do." Abel got into position besides Cain. "Okay," said his elder brother, "now push!"

Abel had a smirk on his face, but he did what Cain asked. Slowly, they pushed the boulder out of the cave and let it fall down the overhang and land a few hundred feet below them.

---

[36] I mean "man" not "humanity" as a whole. Women have enough problems of their own without being caught up in the one we are getting into here.

Abel stood up, sweat pouring down his face. "Are we done now? I was writing a song for Nemaha as a birthday gift, and I'd like to finish it."

"Don't be such a wuss! Look, what say we grab ourselves a couple of sacks of wine. We worked hard, and now it's time to relax!"

"Well—I don't know, Cain. Her birthday is Sunday and all— "

Cain slapped Abel on the back and nearly sent him sprawling. "Plenty of time for that, Abel. Come on."

And after a goodly supply of the juice of the grape, Abel and Cain were feeling no pain, you betcha! However, they were feeling the call of nature.

Abel's head spun as he slowly rose. He leaned over the edge of the mountain they were on, and nearly fell over the side. His elder brother grabbed him, more to steady himself than Abel. Then they both dropped their loincloths.

"Betcha I can hit that tree over there," said Abel.

"Which tree? The one with the coconuts on it, or the one with the bananas?"

"No, no, no." Abel belched. "Look down there." He pointed an unsteady hand towards a pomegranate tree some ten feet below, which stood out on a ledge before a dangerous drop of fifty feet. "Think you can hit that?"

Cain laughed, drunkenly. "Hit it? Hell, little brother, that's nothing. Are you challenging me?" He slapped Abel on the back and let out a roar. "Here, let's see you top this."

Cain grabbed his Willy and let fly. Abel stood beside him and did likewise.

Two fine golden arcs shot off against the blue sky and down towards the tree. Cain's was a heavy one, while Abel's seemed lighter and higher.

"Ha!" laughed Cain. "Right in the middle."

"Oh yeah?" returned Abel. "It's not over yet." He adjusted the angle of his spray a bit. "There. Now we're even."

"Hey, you're cheating."

"No, I'm not."

"Yes, you are." Angrily, Cain gave Abel a slight push with his free hand.

"Cut it out, Cain."

Cain snickered and matched Abel's angle. "There. Mine's going farther."

A few more seconds and it was over. "Looks like I win," Cain laughed, self-satisfied.

Abel looked at Cain and then snorted. "Big deal. It doesn't matter anyway. Mine's bigger than yours is!" he whined.

"What are you talking about? My piss went further than yours. I win."

"I'm not talking about who's piss went further. I'm saying that my Willy is bigger than your Willy."

"No, it's not!"

"Is too! Look!" Abel pointed to his own well-endowed tool, and then to Cain's, which was noticeably smaller by a few inches. "Cain's got a small Willy! Cain's got a small Willy!" He began to dance round Cain, making his brother angrier and angrier.

"Stop it, Abel. Someone's gonna hear you. You better cut it out."

But Abel ignored his brother. "Cain can't cut it. Nah nah nah nah nah! I can't wait to tell Nemaha about this."

"You're not going to tell anyone," Cain shouted, now furious. Without thinking, he grabbed Abel and began to beat him with his fists.

Cain, the taller and more muscular of the two brothers, was much the better fighter of the two. Abel began to panic. Reflexively, he reached into the cloth pouch that he wore around his waist, pulled out the sharpened stone he always used to cut strings for his lyre and slashed Cain across the check with it, leaving a nasty bleeding gash.

Letting go of his brother for a moment, Cain roared in pain. "Son of a soosky! Now you're in for it!" he cried as he walloped Abel in the stomach. When Abel doubled over, Cain grabbed a rock and started to pound Abel with it on the back of his head.

A minute or two went by until Cain realized that his brother was no longer attempting to fight back. He dropped the rock and stared at his brother.

Abel did not move.

"Come on, you weakling! Get up and get what's coming to you."

Abel did not reply. It began to dawn on Cain that something might be wrong. He gently prodded his inanimate brother with his foot. "Abel?" Another prod. "Abel? Come on; you're beginning to scare me. All right, if that's the way you want to play it" Cain put one hand behind his brother's head, and supported Abel's legs with his other arm, lifting his brother's body. Still, Abel did not move. Cain thought he felt something warm and wet on the hand behind his brother's head. Pulling his hand away, he saw it was covered by a warm, red fluid

"What the---?"

Cain looked at the back of Abel's head and saw that there was a large gash at the point where the rock had hit Abel's head. The fluid seemed to be coming from the wound.

All was quiet except for the sound of Cain's breathing. "Oh, shit!" he exclaimed, as something dawned on him. "Wait until Dad finds out. Hell, wait until *Mom* finds out! I think I'm in big trouble."

Cain didn't know the half of it. Though Eve would indeed give him Hell over it, he had something bigger to worry about.

He had me!

Book III – Of Adam and Eve and Cain and Abel

And, I instantaneously knew what had happened, and my reaction was just as instantaneous. I've mentioned before that there is a tremendous difference between an abstract concept and the experience of a thing. How do you explain love to someone who has never felt it? How do you explain fear, or horror, or—anger! And for the first—and, unfortunately, not the last—time I was utterly pissed off. Even the heavenly hosts went quiet when they understood what had happened, for my anger flowed into them. We were all taken aback—not only at the act of murder—but also at our reaction to that murder. At first, it took us over, swept every other thing from us. What had Cain done? How could he do such a thing? One-minute Abel was a happy young man, then a profound change happened in the universal structure as if a time of innocent wonder had been lost forever. And what was this now that we were feeling—sadness, despair? We were rocked by these feelings never known before. And there was the urge to seek vengeance against what we saw as the source of these feelings. For the poet who wrote the story down was not too far wrong when he had me say, "Your brother's blood cries out to me from the ground."[37]

But, still, I am God. And while humanity is a part of me, my ways are not that of humanity.

---

[37] Genesis 4:10

Meanwhile, Cain was trying to cover up the evidence of what he had done. Taking advantage of his strength, he was covering Abel's body underneath some large rocks when I decided to speak to him directly.

"Cain, what is this that you've done?"

"Me? I didn't do nothing."

"Look, who do you think you're dealing with here? I wasn't born yesterday.[38] Don't make it any worse than it already is, young man. So, let's try again. Cain, do you understand what's happened to your brother?"

"I don't know. Am I responsible for my brother? He made me do it."

"Enough!" I shouted, cutting him off. "You were not given life just so you could take it from another. You were not put here to bring misery into the world. You weren't given a brain, and self-awareness in order to destroy. It is not your place to judge the worth of another's life. You should use your gifts to create, to benefit yourself and all others. Think what you and your brother could have done together. But, see what you've accomplished. Yes, the rival for your mother's affection is gone; the rival for the affection of Nemaha is gone. But your brother, your dearest friend, is lost to this world forever—you will no longer hear his voice. His song will never gladden your heart as it used to when you were just children. You will no longer share any secrets. When you run and leap and

---

[38] Of course, being God, I wasn't "born" at all.

Book III – Of Adam and Eve and Cain and Abel

laugh at the joy of being alive, you will remember that the one who shared that joy with you is gone — never to laugh, to play, to bring happiness to others again."

I waited for Cain to say something more. I knew that his anger at his brother was abating and being replaced by the realization of what he had done.

He looked at the mound covering his brother's body. "Oh, Abel, I'm so sorry." His remorse took him, and he wept.

Finally, he turned to me. "Are you going to punish me?"

"No, "I said more gently, my own anger abating, my sorrow growing. "It's not I who will punish you. You will do that all by yourself. I think, Cain that you are beginning to understand the enormity of what you did. And you can never forget it. You are under your own curse. When you work the ground, you will re-member how you and your brother used to work side by side to till the land, and then you will also remember how you attempted to hide your crime. How will your parents react? How will you be able to look at them, knowing that there is no way to make up for Abel's loss? And what will you see in their eyes, when you will always be a reminder to them of the murder of their other son? Eventually, you will drive yourself out, a restless wanderer on the earth. And the gash on your cheek that still bleeds from where your brother cut you — that will become the scar, the mark that will al-ways be the visible remembrance that you are the first murderer."

75

I'm God and You're Not

Cain wept. "My punishment is more than I can bear. How do I go on living with my brother's blood on my hands?"

But, I didn't give him a choice. He was not to compound the crime by also being the world's first suicide.

And that's the way it happened. The mark of Cain was the scar left from the wound Abel gave him. I did not need to mark him so that he wouldn't be killed himself by "whoever finds me" — as the Bible supposes he said to me. But, wait a second! Take away Adam, Eve, and his sisters, and at that point, after we had finished creation, there was no one else he could meet up in the entire world! There was no "whoever" to find him! So, what was the Bible talking about, then?

And, as I predicted, it became too much for Cain to face his parents each day—he packed up with one of his sisters (not Nemaha, for after Abel's murder she never spoke to Cain again), and headed east to the land of Nod, far away from his family. And, perhaps he took my words about creating and not destroying to heart, for as the Bible states correctly, Cain, the first murderer, there built the first city.[39]

And, like Cain, the celestial hosts can never forget what happened. Stupid, stupid, stupid; murder is always stupid! And in the end, murder, war, destruction is just so senseless. What I said to Cain, that "you were not given life in order to take it," applies to all

---

[39] Genesis 4:17

of you, humanity. And it is perhaps my greatest regret that even though it's been codified into the commandments that you pay lip service to — YOU SHALL NOT MURDER! — you still go on and on, even claiming "self-defense" as an excuse, destroying instead of building, instead of creating a better world for all. You don't know how much Eve — and Adam as well, for in truth he did love his son — wept for her beloved Abel. And you don't know how, to this day, how sad the heavens become each time we hear the mothers cry for the lives you snuff out. And how miserable it is for us, how the Heavens reel in horror and despair, when you say you do it in my name.

.

Book IV- Of Arks and Towers

One son had been murdered. The other was the murderer. Would there have been any blame to Adam and Eve if the horror of it stopped them from having any more children? If that had happened, there would be no story to tell, and thousands of years of hope and struggle, thousands of years of the human drama could very well have ended right there. And you, the recipient of my words, would not be here to hear them today. But, there is something in the human spirit, some life force, which, when confronted by the dark side of human nature, ultimately rejects despair. What inner fire is there that, despite the blows of fortune that seem part of the human condition, gives humanity the strength and determination to achieve the greatness of which it is capable? And this is where Adam and Eve gained my respect and a bit of admiration—for, despite their despair at their loss, despite the evidence to the contrary—they chose that Life itself was good and worth living. They chose to go on.

And so it was that Seth was born, whom Eve saw as comfort for the loss of Abel. And in due time, Adam and Eve had many other sons and daughters. And eventually there were grandchildren and great-grandchildren to brighten their hearts. As Genesis says it, Adam "begat" Seth who "begat" Enos who "begat" Kenan who "begat" Mahalalel who "begat" Jared who "begat" Enoch who "begat" Methuselah who "begat" Lamech who "begat" Noah, and so on and so forth.

By this time, we thought we had tuned Creation to the point at which we could let it evolve "naturally," and we took a more "hands-off" approach to you humans. We knew that if we constantly were in your face (so to speak) that we would be unintentionally influencing and changing your development. That would eventually defeat the whole purpose of creating an intelligent, self-aware, autonomous creature. [40] Our visits became less and less and more selective, and for most of your kind, the nature of "God" became a question — if "God" created mankind, who exactly was this "God" and what was "He" like? And what did "He" want from humanity anyway? As would happen throughout your history, people began to re-create me in terms of their own ideas. So, religions began to be born and "...men began to call on the name of the Lord."[41]

Did you ever wonder about that peculiar little bit about Enoch, that we find in Genesis 5:24: "Enoch walked with God; then he was no more, because God took him away."? The fact of the matter was something else.

Enoch had a thing about volcanoes and thought that God could be found there. It kinds of makes some sense, I suppose, since he knew nothing about science and about what causes a volcano to

---

[40] "Intelligent, self-aware, autonomous"—I am talking about *you* here, humanity—but sometimes I think I'm dealing with something else!
[41] Genesis 5:26

rumble and roar, to spew forth dark clouds up overhead and fire and lava — what could this be but the voice of God? And imagine a volcano three times the height of Mount Everest and twenty times wider than it is tall — which, is sort of like putting together a pile of about one hundred Hawaiian volcanoes. Just to give you the measurements of the thing, it was about fifteen miles high and three hundred forty miles across while today the largest volcano on Earth, Mauna Loa, is six miles high and seventy-five miles across. So, you might indeed call that sucker "God" yourself. Actually, back then it was known as "Bob," but is today called "Olympus Mons."[42]

And Enoch was convinced that this monster volcano was the home of God. So, telling his family that he was off to seek God, he made his way to this monster and climbed his way to its crater.

And then, the dumb fool jumped right in.

Obviously, he was never seen again. He went away all right — but I had nothing to do with it.

But, as I was saying, on the whole, we were pretty satisfied with the direction of things. Life was off to an auspicious start; man was discovering and inventing things for himself: cities, tents, agriculture, the domestication of animals, flutes, harps, tools of bronze and iron, and so on. Humanity was thriving, and it looked like things were going superbly on Mars.

[42] Yes, that is indeed the name of the largest volcano on the planet Mars!

Yes, I said *Mars*. Remember, I told you that our first attempt at life was on Mars. So, yes, that long-discounted theory that the Garden of Eden was on Mars is correct! But, you don't live on Mars, do you?[43]

I want to make it clear here that creation is bound by certain rules — and, in order to maintain the universe as it is, these rules can never be changed. And that allows you to have things like gravity, atoms, dimension, density, energy, mass, mathematics, and so on, as well as actual measurable laws of your reality like $E=MC^2$, and that for every action there is an equal and opposite reaction. Etc., etc. And you also get one of the fundamental rules of a dynamic, unfolding universe: Shit happens.

Your solar system is quite a busy place. Your sun bathes the planets in light, warmth, and solar flares. The planets move around the sun on their various orbits. Moons twirl around those planets. Comets come to visit. Asteroids move around in their own journey in and out and around the planets and the sun as well. And sometimes, things get in each other's way.

For example, quite some time before humanity finally came to Earth, there was a massive collision between it and a meteor. Good thing for you it *was* before your time — because this basically wiped out life on the planet. Yes, I know that your scientists believe that though species like the dinosaur were wiped out by the meteor,

---

[43] Yes, I know— "Men are from Mars, Woman are from Venus." You do realize that you are not supposed to take that literally, don't you?

other species must have survived, such as the mammals from which — according to evolution — humanity descended. Of course, those scientists know nothing about humanity's origin on Mars and of the events that I'm now discussing. Remember, that Earth was sort of our "control" system for what was happening as we developed life on Mars before the coming of human beings. Boy, were the angels pissed about that collision. As if it were my fault! Azrael, who had been the mastermind behind the control system, wouldn't speak to me for eons. But, he finally simmered down, but decided to keep an eye on things so that we would know well in advance if anything like this was due to happen again.

And one day...

"'Scuse me, Sir," Azrael said, using my least favorite form of address, "do you have a minute? I need to call an assembly together."

"Done!" I replied. The Heavenly Hosts were, as always, assembled in a blink of my thought, and we waited to hear what Azrael had to say.

"I asked you all here," he began hesitantly, "to advise you on a problem we're about to have with the Mars project. If I can call your attention to the planet Jupiter — "

"Jupiter?" exclaimed Raquel. "I thought you said, 'Mars.' You know, that's Mars with an 'M.'"

Azrael was used to Raquel's sarcastic side, and he didn't let it faze him one bit. "No, I mean Jupiter. And that's Jupiter with a 'J' and that rhymes with 'K' and that stands for 'Ka-Boom!'"

"Ka-Boom?" Raquel echoed. "What on earth—sorry, Mars—sorry, *Jupiter*! — are you talking about?"

"According to my calculations, Jupiter is about to experience a cosmic event."

"Azrael, Jupiter is part of the cosmos," Beelzebub pointed out. "Any event it experiences is a cosmic event."

"If you are all done with the interruptions?" Azrael waited for silence, which he soon got. "...Good! I'm trying to tell you that there's about to be an explosion on Jupiter. You know how we always argued about whether Jupiter was too hot, too big; whether Jupiter was more like a second sun than anything else? Well, it's about to eject some of itself out into space." He paused.

"And?" I interjected, motioning for him to go on.

"And it just happens that that part, that bit of matter, is just big enough to cause us some problems. Especially, since it's going to head straight for Mars. Ka-boom!"

And, realizing what that implied for life on Mars, with one voice, the Heavenly Hosts exclaimed "Oh, shit!"

"You got it," nodded Azrael. "We can kiss humanity goodbye! They're not going to be able to survive the changes in climate, the seismographic effects of the earthquakes, the tidal waves, the dust, the smoke, the fires, the ...."

"Okay, okay, "I said. "I think we have the picture. Thank you very much, Azrael." I frowned. "I think we all agree that we've come too far humankind's development to try to start the whole thing over again at this point?"

"Yep," said Luce. "God knows what would get loused up the next time!"

"So, any suggestions?"

After much discussion, we agreed that we had to get you off Mars and move you to Earth. Funny, that what had seemed to be a calamity for Earth when that old meteor had hit it off of Yucatan would later serve to save your ass. You might want to argue that it was a good thing that the dinosaurs had been wiped out because you wouldn't have stood a chance against those mothers! Frankly, if there were a match-up between Tyrannosaurus Rex with its six-inch long, sharp, serrated teeth and a human with a slingshot or a knife, I'd bet on good old T-Rex every time.

Now, we couldn't just wave our arms and POOF! you're on earth. The shock to your mental and physical systems would have been much too great. We would have had to invent psychoanalysis about four thousand six hundred years too early.

We decided that the best approach was to transport you across space from Mars to the Earth in a number of giant space-ships. Of course, we could just willy-nilly have spaceships appear on Mars for you...what would you have made of that? You were just beginning the Copper Age, and suddenly you would have been in the Space Age! No, no, that would have destroyed everything.

We did have some time—about two hundred of your earth years—to pull off the exodus. We would send down a number of the angels to intermingle with you and set up our cover story—that there was going to be a great Flood that would wipe out all life. These angels would "build" what you would think were big boats, or arks, of wood, but would actually be disguised spacecrafts. With a little coercion, slight-of-hand, and a big of "magic," which I'll get to momentarily, you'd be convinced you were on a boat above rising waters, and that when the waters receded, you would still be on the same planet. Of course, we'd have really piloted you to the Earth. What would work to our advantage was the fact that you had never referred to the planet you were on as Mars, you referred to it as the "dust beneath our feet." So, there would be no problem there.

So, down went Michael and assumed the name of Noah. Down went Raphael as Manu, Gabriel as Oklatibishi, Suruph as Fuhi, Lucifer as Utnapishtim, Azrael as Xisuthrus, Sarakiel as Prometheus, etc., etc. Once they had established themselves as part of their various communities, other angles then came down as their spouses, and children, so that the angels could make a façade of being human families, while secretly working together as small teams to pull off the move. We thought we had you fooled here. But, apparently, we weren't all that clever here, because there are some hints of what we had done in your writings. Just, for example, the Bible says, right before the Flood story, that "the Nephilim were on earth in those days—and also afterward—when the sons of God went to the daughters of men and had children by them."[44]

But, for the most part, things went along much as we planned. For example, after settling in, Michael was soon comfortable with his 'Noah' persona. So, let's refer to him as Noah for the rest of this part of the story.

Noah and his family started working on their craft. They'd go out day after day, and the neighbors could hear them hard at work. It did get quite a bit noisy, and one day, a delegation of the town, came forth to find out exactly what was going on.

They found Noah and his sons, Shem, Ham, and Japheth, down near the river, where they appeared to be building a huge structure. It was just about the tallest, and the widest, and the longest thing any of them had ever seen. If you have ever seen one of those humongous cruise ships that sail around the Caribbean, you have a small idea of the size of this thing.

"What the heck is that?" Afrinerah whispered.

"You got me, "Chad whispered back. "What do you think, Isamaiah?"

"I don't know! How in the name of Adam's Rib would I have a clue what Noah's doing?"

The whispering continued. "Well, go ask him."

---

[44] Genesis 6:4

"Why don't you ask him, Chad?"

"Me? Oh, no, you're much better with people than I am, Isamaiah. You're supposed to be in charge, anyway."

Isamaiah sighed. "It's always me, isn't it? The ordure pile would still be smelling up downtown if I hadn't raised enough of a stink about it. And who had to organize the last three berry picking parties, huh?"

"Well, you were at Japheth's birthday. Noah likes you."

"Okay, okay," Isamaiah finally agreed. Aloud, he said " Yo, Noah, my man!. What's happening?"

Noah smiled. "Sorry, Isamaiah. I don't have time for idle chitchat right now. I have too much work to do."

"That's an awfully big, uh—what do you call that thing?"

"Ark. It's called an ark."

"Okay." Isamaiah nodded, thoughtfully. "Kind of big, isn't it? I bet you could get your entire family in there, and never see each other for weeks. "

Everyone laughed, including Noah.

"Yep," Noah replied. "But it's meant to hold a lot more than just the Noah clan. I bet I could get everyone in the city into the ark and have room left over."

"Oh, come on," Chad yelled. "That's ridiculous."

Noah smiled. "Oh yeah, care to make a bet? Give me two weeks to finish up. I'll bet you I can get all of you, your families, your relatives, your friends, yes, the entire city — no, the entire countryside AND the city into this baby."

"You're nuts!" exclaimed Isamaiah.

"No, I'm serious. Look, I'll turn it into a picnic for all who show up. If you all fit, you come for an ark ride with me. If I'm wrong, you can all have a good laugh at my expense. Free eats, drink, all on me. So, how about it?"

The delegates discussed it and realized that they had nothing to lose.

"Okay, then," Isamaiah agreed on behalf of all. "Two weeks from today, then. Party time!"

Word was spread throughout the land, and exactly two weeks later, people started to assemble before the ark. The whole town and most of the country folk turned out for what they were sure was going to be one hell of a wingding.

Isamaiah and Chad stood at the front of the still-growing crowd, trying to maintain some order.

"Where's Noah?" Chad had to practically yell in Isamaiah's ear to be heard above the noise of the crowd. "Where's the food? We're going to have a riot soon if something isn't done."

"Hold them back, Chad. Let me see what I can find out," yelled Isamaiah as he walked toward the ark. Two poles, each with a small shiny box that seemed to have a red eye that faced the other, were raised in the ground before him. As he passed them, there was a loud sound that sounded like something electronic would sound like if you didn't know what electronics were — remember, this was a few thousand years ago, and Isamaiah and all of you would have had no concept of any such things. To him, it sounded like a trumpet blast, and he fell to the earth, bowing. The crowd immediately bowed down as well. Actually, it was the sound of a ramp being lowered from the doorway of the ark.

"Oh, Lord, I await your command." Isamaiah trembled, his eyes averted.

"Oh, get up, Isamaiah," Noah now called from the doorway. He used his angel voice, and the entire crowd could hear every word he said. That's one of the things I always told my boys when we were preparing for public speaking, keep your eye on the rear of the audience and project your voice to them. Of course, it doesn't hurt to use a microphone now and again; two thousand people are a rather large crowd. "All of you get up. Welcome, welcome, welcome. There's plenty of food and drink just waiting inside."

"Ah, Noah, there you are," Isamaiah smiled. "Well, just about everyone's here, I guess. You're not going to call off the bet, are you? You don't want to piss off a mob like this, you know."

"No, no, of course not. This crowd is nothing! There's plenty of room for all. I invite one and all for the time of your life. This way!"

He motioned Isamaiah into the ark. Isamaiah was followed by his family, but Chad and the others held back. A minute or so went by, and then Isamaiah stuck his head out of the doorway.

"It's wonderful," he cried. "You gotta see this thing. Come on, everyone."

And with that, the crowd, guided by Noah, Shem, Ham, Japheth, and their "wives" and "children," proceeded into the vastness of the ark.

Now, what no one knew (except for the angels, of course, and me) is that right at the entrance to the ark, we were pumping in hallucinogen-laced, odorless, colorless gas. Yep, we wanted you high and happy because we were pulling off the biggest flim-flam in history (recorded or otherwise). We also didn't want you to freak when the ships took off from Mars. [45]

By the time each of you reached the ark's central hall, you were feeling no pain. No indeed—in fact, you were all very happy campers. It was easy to get you into the various sleeping quarters and lounges and make you ready for the trip of a lifetime.

And no, I am definitely NOT going to give any clue as to what hallucinogen we used.   Let me tell you, this baby certainly

---

[45] G-force was not a major problem for us to overcome. You really can't conceive of the technology we used. It makes the Enterprise on Star Trek look like a Roman chariot.

beat the hell out of hashish or soma. In fact, it was created especially for the occasion and, since one of the elements in its formula is NOT known to your chemists, it happily cannot be reproduced on earth. And you can thank God for that, let me tell you. There are plenty of crazies in and out of your governments who would just love to get their dirty little hands on a drug that could be used like this one, you know?

And besides, you really can't find me in drugs, humanity. It's so much simpler than that. If you would just open yourself up for a second, I'm already there.

Once everyone was settled in, the doors were closed, and the fake wood exterior panels were retracted into the ark. If you were still outside, you would have now seen an actual spaceship — big, shiny, metallic; no windows, because we didn't want the passengers looking out and seeing that they were traveling through space instead of bopping about on the ocean. Of course, if you were indeed still outside, since you had no experience of flight, your brain, trying to fit the craft into its idea of reality, would be working overtime to convince you that you must have really tied one on the night before and that it might be a really good thing to swear off drinking that cheap wine Uncle Ephraim made in the backyard.

Noah's voice came over the loudspeaker system. "Hi, gang. This is your old pal, Noah, speaking. Welcome aboard the good ship Ark the 223rd. I'll be your captain on our little voyage, and everything will be done to keep you happy, healthy, and secure for the duration of our trip. I just took a look outside, and it appears we are about to face the mother of all storms. It is going to rain for—oh, something like forty days and forty nights" He laughed.

Of course, everyone thought he was joking but with the gas—hey, no problem-o!

"But there's nothing to worry about," Noah continued. "We've got plenty of food, drink, and entertainment. So, now it's party time, dudes."

Okay, it really didn't take forty days and forty nights—it actually took about sixteen days, just slightly less than two and one-half weeks. [46] And yes, we could have done it pretty much over-night express. But, we were dodging the Jupiter bullet, which was bound to screw up things celestially for a while, and we needed some time to get the earth just the way we wanted it before we transplanted you.

Everyone was exceptionally mellow. With all that laced gas we kept pumping out, they'd sure have to be.

"Hey, Noah," Chad laughed, "you throw one hell of a party. But, what about the animals?"

"Taken care of, Chad, my man! We have them down below, two by two, and they're coming with us."

Of course, we really didn't have the animals aboard the ark! What an idea! We all got a good laugh out of that one when it got written down. I mean, imagine if that were true. Can you imagine

---

[46] Everything gets exaggerated in the retelling, doesn't it?

the smell? Look, you can pretty well get humans to do just about anything, but a decently intelligent animal isn't going to buy that whole "let's take a ride in a big boat and get out of the rain" story no way, no how. Animals are a lot more resilient than you humans anyway. They'd have to be to put up with your shenanigans! We'd already pretty well restocked Earth with most of the animal kingdom well before you even left Mars.

Still, pity about those dinosaurs, though.

Also, in my defense, I should point out something in the traditional Noah story that really gets my goat. I can understand why you might think I'd want to wipe out all of humanity—but why would I want to destroy the animals, too? What kind of a God do you think I am, anyway? What harm had any of those animals done outside of doing what animals are meant to do? Personally, I'm a big animal lover. It seems kind of unfair—killing off all those innocent animals just because humanity was such a louse-up! And, as I so often point out, if I ever did or do want to destroy the whole lot of you; I don't need a flood to do it. It would be SHEBANG! and you're all instant toast—gone, forgotten, no forty days and forty nights bit, and probably most of the animals would be better off for it anyway. A lot less work, a lot less mess, nice, neat, simple—bye bye, humanity! Nice knowing you—wait a week and it's "who were those guys anyway?" Out of sight, out of mind.

The very idea…drowning all those poor innocent animals— takes a human being to think of something like that!

Now, in all modesty, I would have to tell you that George Lucas's Industrial Light and Magic can't hold a candle to the gang and me when it comes to special effects. We had set up the interior of the spacecrafts like a gigantic three hundred sixty-degree panoramic screen and surround sound spectacular. You looked out of fake windows and thought you were still looking outside at the usual Martian landscape. And just as the ship took off, we had a totally convincing light and sound show of a torrential rainstorm beginning. And between the artificial gravity and the gas-enhanced images, you never felt liftoff; you never had a clue that you were now rising from the planet to achieve escape velocity and beginning the voyage to Earth. It was easy to convince all of you that the noise and sensations you did feel were because "all the springs of the great deep burst forth, and the floodgates of the heavens were opened."[47] Our timing was quite good, and we were well on our way with a large margin of safety by the time the Jupiter bullet hit Mars.

Mars shook visibly in its orbit. The site of the impact was flattened, and other areas rose higher. Vast clouds of gas rose into the air and darkness filled the lands. And the precious oxygen, so necessary to life, began to dissipate into the void of space.

So, Mars was left, barren, bereft of life, a dead world that you turn your eyes towards even now and wonder "Was there ever life on Mars?"

---

[47] Genesis 7:11

Now, you know. Now, instead of squandering billions of dollars on flights to Mars, how about spending those billions to make life better on Earth instead? Where do you get off planning on conquering outer space when you can't even conquer poverty or hunger on your own planet?

Man! —Can you first fix the mess you made on your world before you start messing up the rest of my creation, huh?

Now we changed the gas and put all of you into suspended animation for the remainder of the journey. What? —did you think we were going to clean up after all of you?

The ships landed in different areas—some in Africa, some in Asia, some in the Americas, and so on. Before we let the passengers out, we lowered the fake wooden exterior panels so that when it was time to disembark, everyone knew that they were returning to a world that had been renewed and made whole by the rain.

Now, it was merely a coincidence that it had just finished raining near Noah's boat, and, as the people left that particular ark, a rainbow appeared in the sky. I'd like to take credit for that one, but nope, not that time.

You know, sometimes things just happen!

After a while, you were pretty well spread out on the Earth—which you now thought was the planet you had always been on—and human life progressed again. And because you were so spread out, as new words and concepts entered your vocabulary, the common language that all man spoke broke apart, first into dialects and eventually into entirely different languages.

What's that you ask? — "What about the Tower of Babel"? No, no, no. Think this one through. What do you think those ancient Babylonians had for building materials? Did you believe that ancient astronauts came down from the skies and used teleportation devices to build towers for them? Nope, it was basic human sweat that would build the glory that was Babylon, and the other wonders of the ancient world.

And where do you think the heaven that the story in Genesis 10 says they were trying to reach is located, a mile up? Remember the mountains? Were you paying attention when we talked about the Creation? Who the heck do you think built those? The two tallest mountains on the earth, Everest, and K2, are both better than five miles high! How high do you think *you* can build anyway? The tallest building in the world today is less than one-third of a mile tall! I'll repeat that. Less than one-third of a mile tall! So, let's see: Mankind: one-third of a mile, God and company: five miles. You're not even beginning to play in my league!

So, how tall do you think the Tower of Babel was? Two hundred and sixty-five feet!! There are apartment buildings in New York taller than that! I was going to get in a tether over something like that?

Book IV- Of Arks and Towers

Now, some would claim that it wasn't the tower's height that got me peeved, but that I got ticked off because you were rebelling against me, that I wanted to scatter you over the earth, and you didn't want to go. Look, it doesn't work that way! Sometimes it seems like you are *always* rebelling against me! Sheesh! Why is everything always my fault? A wall collapses—Don't blame the builder; it was God's will! Look, I don't go around thinking to myself "Let's see what I can do to shake up humanity today? I know! Let's collapse that wall so innocent people will be killed! Let's have a drought so people will starve of thirst! Let's have the crops fail so people will go hungry! That'll show them I mean business." I am not that kind of God— only humans willfully act in ways to hurt other humans!

And I hate to burst your bubble, but I also don't go around picking and choosing individuals to save from these calamities, either. I allways wonder when someone goes "It was a miracle that Bob Smith was the only survivor of the mid-air collision of two jumbo aircraft that resulted in the death of seven hundred sixty passengers and crew. God must have been looking out for him!" You mean, I didn't give a shit about the other seven hundred sixty people, just good old Pete (who happens to beat his wife and kids every day, and runs the utility company that's poisoning your water and air)? Man, if that were true, I should be committed to a ward for the criminally insane! You ever hear of luck? I may move in mysterious ways, but that's not one of them.

Unfortunately, you don't live in a perfect creation — there would be no point to that anyway   The Creation would be stagnant; no growth, no striving, no dreams, no hope, and no point. The living Creation has to have natural laws in order to exist — and if I were to change any of them, you, all life, the Universe itself, would all cease to exist. There's a price to be paid for existence — and it can be hard, very hard. I wish it could be otherwise, but that's the way it has to be. That's the paradox of existence. No, it does not justify the death of a single child — nothing can! And that is much to my sorrow.

But, can't you learn from experience? Can't you try to make things better? There's an earthquake in San Francisco — who told you to keep living in an earthquake zone? Having done it before many times, tidal waves wipe out homes along a coastline — Shmuck! Who told you to continue building your homes there! A tornado rips through Oklahoma — yes, it's tragic and terrible, but I never issued a commandment saying, "Thou shalt knowingly live in Tornado Alley"! Mt Etna erupts, and hundreds are killed from the lava and smoke — it's a volcano, that's what they do, and if you keep building a house on the side of one, eventually it might just go boom and blow your ass dead!

And then there's the way you allow human suffering to continue. People need water to survive — and you value water rates more than a human life. People are starving — and you let food rot in silos because that keeps the price up. Children are dying of diseases—but you can't give them medicine for free. After all, that might lower the price of your drug stocks., and we couldn't have that now, could we?[48] War kills people—who the hell told you it was okay to blow up women and children? I don't care what your so-called religions or political leaders tell you—I didn't tell you to go around invading each other! Don't blame *me* because you chose to follow murderers, liars, and thieves. Damn it—if you finally blow yourselves up in a nuclear holocaust, some idiot is going to say that was my will, too!

But that's okay, isn't it? Why should *you* be responsible for your actions? All you have to do is come into a house of worship and pay lip service to me. Why, sure you're forgiven! I love lip service! Yep, that's what worshipping me is all about, isn't it? Who cares what I might actually wish you would do?

Time and again, before their teachings were corrupted, your holy teachers—great souls like Buddha, Zarathustra, Moses, Jesus, Mohammed, etc., etc., etc.—gave you the answer. And time and time again, you seem to be unable to hear something so simple. "Love your neighbor as yourself."

You, humanity, are the greatest source of human suffering.

Oh, maybe the whole thing really is my fault. After all, I gave you life in the first place!

---

[48] Damn, I keep forgetting…I'm supposed to be a card-carrying right-wing free-trade Capitalist type, aren't I? Or am I in favor of absolute monarchists? Whose flag am I supposed to be flying in Heaven, anyway?

So, to get back to Babel, what possible difference do you think it would have made if you migrated to Nineveh or Thebes or Xanadu or the Riviera or Pittsburgh for that matter in say 3745 BCE or 3231 BCE! No skin off my nose! We gave you the planet to live on; you're perfectly free to decide where you want to live without me telling you where to go. Anyway, eventually if you all stayed on one spot of the earth, it would have just gotten too crowded for you and some of you would have moved on to other areas anyway. And if I did confound your language…what, eventually there wouldn't be translators? You mean there aren't international efforts involving people of different languages working together for the greater good (or bad) of humanity? I'd have to be a pretty short-sighted god if I would have thought screwing around with your language was going change anything long term.

And, as I told you, when we used the arks to get you to Earth, they landed in different places. So, you were already scattered.

I'll tell you the truth — the story was written because somebody was jealous! A young merchant from Jerusalem named Manasseh made a business trip to Babylon and wondered why the tribes of Israel didn't have anything to match up against the Tower. Since there was always a rivalry between the Jerusalemites and the Babylonians, he came up with the story as a way of putting the Babylonians down a peg. Just another case of tower envy, I suppose.

Besides, the damn thing collapsed in the very next earth-quake, anyway!

And the years went by.

Until the coming of Abraham.

Book V - Abraham

$\mathcal{A}$h, Abraham, Abraham, Abraham! How could you know that by becoming the "father of nations" you would be the father of so much strife? That the beauty of your desire to know me would lead down the ages to so much horror and ugliness? That even your resting place in the Cave of Machpelah would not escape from the madness of bloodlust? "Father of nations," even thousands of years after you first touched my Divinity, those "nations" deny each other their birthright—instead of embracing as true brothers—and seek to destroy each other.

And yet, your spark still burns like a fiery beacon in the darkness. And it reminds me of what I love in all your human striving.

When you speak of the great holy teachers of your faiths, you say that I, God, choose whom I will. But you have that backward. In truth, it is they who choose me. And that makes all the difference. It's not that I see a fellow named Farad and suddenly say, "Hi, Farad. It's me, God. How's it going?" No, it's Farad's quest to find something outside his day-to-day existence, something more than the vain pursuit for land, power, money, success, what have you, something wherein he finds my voice. It's when he says "hello" to me with his open heart that our conversations start.

Book V - Abraham

Come: right now, there's a young man from New York standing on the walls of the Old City of Jerusalem. His heart feels torn, troubled by the hate that radiates from so many who call this the Holy Land. Walking on the ancient wall, somewhere between the Golden Gate and St. Stephen's Gate, he stops and gazes up to the top of Mount of Olives. And as he does so, a small voice somewhere between his head and his heart is saying to him "They *all* got it wrong. There is another way." And so he begins his own journey to the heart of the Divine.

Whether the first such journey began with Abraham or with someone else is entirely beside the point. What is important is that it did not end with him.

Let me remind you again: Because, as I've related, Life ultimately springs from me, there is something of my Divine Essence in each of you. And, though it often seems as if you forget it is there, that Essence is deep within you. Time after time, there arises in the human heart the feeling that humankind is something more than just the dust of the earth, and great souls are born that seek to know the meaning of the depth that is in that glimpse of Spirit. They are not satisfied with the answers handed down to them by those who came before; they feel the longing inside themselves to seek their ways to what feels right and true in their spirit, to come to grips with what is best in their own human potential. They are reborn from their old ways. And they come to me so that we may

103

both learn together what it means to be man and what it means to be God.

And I meet them all; I cannot be contained by one path. Just for the record—I don't have a favorite religion. I know that disappoints a great many of you, but, as I said earlier, I'm not Jewish, Christian, Moslem, Hindu, Zoroastrian, Baha'ist, Taoist, Buddhist, this-that-or-the-other-ist. Sure, there are general ethical principles I'd wish humanity would finally learn to follow, but they are part of so many paths to me. I'm not particularly concerned that you even believe in me! Some of the ones whose hearts are closest to me are atheists! If you truly seek what is best in you, you find me despite yourself.

When the heavens despair of our creation, it is that holy striving that constantly awakens my love for you.

Dear Abraham, a surprising man—a man in love with his God.[49] But, even he did not get everything right. We are talking about a man who at least twice tried to foster off his wife, Sarai, as his sister so that she would enter into a richer, more powerful personage's harem. And somehow when the truth came out, that personage, rather than getting pissed off, rewarded Abraham with sheep, cattle, servants, and money to cover the offense—once it was to the Pharaoh of Egypt, and once to the king of Gerar.

---

[49] That's me, by the way, just in case you've forgotten

The Bible explains that he did this sort of thing because he was afraid that because Sarai was supposedly so beautiful, he would be killed for her. Now, I know you have a saying that "beauty is in the eyes of the beholder," but if Abraham was already over 75 years old—how old do you think Sarai was?

Besides, if Abraham had been killed, well that would have been the end of the entire story: no Isaac, no Jacob, no Joseph, no Moses, no Mount Sinai, no Ten Commandments, no King David, no Holy City of Jerusalem, no Judaism, no Christianity, no Islam— none of it! So, maybe his faith wasn't exactly perfect, but that's okay—it's the struggle to find that faith that counts, anyway.

And then there's that little matter of having a child with his wife's servant. Not exactly something to hold your head up high over, but you have to remember that Abraham was a man of his time. Though it's not something I approve of—just in case any of you get any ideas—let's not judge the man by the standards of the 21st Century.[50]

But, I'm getting ahead of myself. Over the many years since we brought you to earth, mankind evolved its idea of supreme beings. A lot of it had to do with fertility, natural phenomena such as storms, since, obviously, someone or something had to be responsible for lightning, water, the sun, and such. We let things develop

---

[50] Whatever they turn out to be—that's if this century finally ever has any standards at all!

for quite some time, as the human race invented a myriad of gods and goddesses, building and carving idols to worship as manifestations of the forces of nature.

And in a workshop in Harran, a young man of seventy-five years,[51] known as Abram worked alongside his father Terah, and his nephew Lot, carving idols.

It was years since they had left their native city of Ur. Originally, they were planning on going to Canaan, but having reached Harran, decided to settle there and go into the idol-making business. It wasn't a bad living, but Abram was always a bit of a dreamer, a thinker, a person who did not just take what others said on faith, but sought to make sense out of his world through reason, to find out what seemed right and true for himself — the sort of man who, given the right set of circumstances, becomes dangerous to the status quo. The sort of man who, sometimes, is the birth of progress.

I think the problem started because Abram just wasn't all that handy. His nephew, Lot was a master carver; he could carve your likeness before you could whistle a chorus of the Chaldean drinking song — and it basically goes like this: "Drink! Drink! Drink!" Abram was slower, more deliberate in his work, but he just

---

[51] About this age thing. You must remember that the time scale was different back then (a remnant of the Martian times), and when you consider that the Bible says that Abraham's father, Terah, lived to be 205, and fathered Abraham at the age of 70, then 75 is indeed "young"!

didn't have the touch.

"Abram, be careful. That's a five-shekel piece of cedar you're ruining there. And El Rem-a-Dai has three eyes, not four!" yelled Terah, as he passed Abram and Lot hard at work on an order for a dozen idols for the Haran Treasury Chamber.

"Sorry, father," sighed Abram. He started to attack the piece of wood with his knife even harder

"Hey, take it easy, Unc," Lot laughed. "El Rem-a-Dai is supposed to have a good twenty-four inches with which to impress Asheena-Veega. The way you're going at it, Asheena-Veega will be impregnating *him*!"

Abram laughed. "Maybe I'm working too hard, Lot. I don't know. There just has to be more to life than sitting around carving these statues. It's the same thing day after day. 'Give me three Trun-da-nuhs and a dozen of those little Nivibs—you know how the children like to cuddle those Nivibs in their cribs at night.' 'Oh, what? You're having a two for one special! Great, I always wanted a nice big status of Ad-Bal'droi by the front steps—but could you make him look a bit more like my mother, that will fix the old battle-ax!'"

He sighed. "I don't know, Lot. How can we take this all seriously? These are gods we carved ourselves. I can cut them to bits with a knife, or an ax. How can an idol made by man be a god?

Does that mean the gods don't exist? That they are figments of our imagination? Or are we looking for God in the wrong place, the wrong—."

Smack! Terah had snuck up behind him and gave him a thwack on the back of his head, which set Abram reeling.

"Watch what you say, boy! Do you want to bring the priests down on our heads? Look, these gods give us a nice little living, so don't complain. As long as the customer is paying, if he wants to think a fig is a god, I'll sell it to him"

His anger abated, Terah sat down beside Abram and hugged him. "Ah," he sighed, "alright, alright, my son. Maybe I am working you too hard. We've been quite busy the past few months ever since the drought began. Well, we've got two more idols to get out, and then, why don't you take a week off, and chill out, eh?"

And that Saturday, Abram took up his walking stick and headed out to the desert to be alone to do some thinking.

And after a day's journey, he settled in for the night, and Abram lay himself down to rest. He was about to have a vision of the infinite that would echo throughout history.

Abram starts to dream.

Somewhere a voice calls, softly: "Abram!"

Just the sound of snoring.

Again: "Abram!" A bit louder, more insistently.

Abram rolls over a bit, mumbles something to himself, and settles back into his sleep.

A moment's pause. Then a loud sigh. And now loudly: "Damn it, would you wake up already when I'm talking to you? Abram!!"

In his dream, Abram sleepily looks up, his eyes still closed. "Huh? Wha? Who's that? "

"It's me!"

"Me? Me, who?"

"Me! The one you've been seeking. You know, the Lord."

"'The Lord' who?"

"Oh, cut that out. You know perfectly well "the Lord' who'! The Lord, God the Creator, God Almighty, the one true Lord God without form or substance, and so forth, and like that, and so on. I am...the Great Wazoo!"

Look, what did you expect? This was Abram's interpretation of his inner experience. This was the beginning of his conscious response to the meaning of God. It isn't all that easy getting perfection when you're working with raw clay—know what I mean? We're still very early in the whole man/god relationship, and both you and I still had a lot to learn about what that actually meant.

"I don't understand, "Abram whispered. "Is this a dream?"

"Sure, it is. But sometimes we find the truth in our dreams, you know. Look, it's simple. It's like you said—how could anything made by man be God? Abram, you can't find me in the eyes of the idols you are carving—by the way, Lot was right, Sha-na-na has four arms, not three. Abram, the time has come for you to leave your father's house and make your own journey in the world. You will wander through lands where you will be the stranger. You will confront and challenge everything you think about God. And in the end—."

"I shall be made great and the father of many nations?"

"Er—well, one thing at a time, eh? Gather your wife, your nephew, and all you own. If you keep going around Haran questioning what they think about the gods, some self-righteous nut is going to be calling for a stoning or a burning. Funny how people take this religious stuff so personally. Anyway, get yourself going!"

Abram speedily made his way back to Harran where he found an angry crowd gathering around Terah's workshop. When they saw Abram, they began to call out.

"Stone the blasphemer. Kill the unbeliever."

Abram was able to force his way into the living quarters where he found Sarai and Lot huddled together. Terah came into the room, dragging a large bag behind him.

"What's going on?" asked Abram, breathlessly.

"It started up just about half an hour ago. People started to gather around, calling for your head. I knew it. First, it was laughing at idols, then it was 'Hey, if lightning can destroy an idol, then there's something greater than the idol.' That wasn't bad enough. No, you had to start with that 'maybe there's just one God' thing. I told you something terrible would happen."

"What's with the clothes and the pots, and aren't those my tools you have wrapped up there? What are you doing with those?"

"Abram," Sarai said. "Because of all the work Terah has done for the town, he was able to get the elders to agree that if you and I left and promised never to return upon pain of death, we could go freely. Terah and Lot have packed up our belongings, gathered up our servants, and everything is waiting out the back."

Abram started for the tent entrance "Look, let me talk to the crowd—."

Terah and Lot grabbed Abram. "No, you don't!" Terah cried. "You want to give them more reason to stone you? No more time for talk. Go! Now!"

And after Sarai, Abram, and Lot said their goodbyes to the old idol maker, they made a hasty departure from the back gate of Harran.

There was something about Abram that intrigued me. And as he and his company slowly made their way to Canaan, I decided that this might be an opportunity. Could Abram be the agent whereby God and man could meet? So, I would take to coming down to sit with Abram by his tent while the others slept, and we really started to get mutually acquainted.

Oh, he was a bit of a scalawag at times, but…look, did you ever meet someone and taken an instant liking to them? It's as though something clicks between the two of you, and you find that you're on the same wavelength, there's some understanding, some camaraderie that allows you to be able to just be in the other's presence and feel great. You don't need a lot of words to under-stand each other, and even when you may differ now and then, there's an underlying love that only grows stronger with time. No distance can truly separate the two of you—you always carry some part of the other in you no matter how far apart you may roam. And when you're together, it's like coming home. Two buddies that can share happiness and sorrow and yet can always find a smile for each other. Well, that's sort of Abram and me. I just loved the guy! Still do.

The guy had guts. And he wasn't nobody's fool.[52] Give him credit. He thought things out for himself; he didn't just blindly ac-cept what others told him. Heck, he even had the guts to argue with me over a few things…and that's something even I have to respect! He accepted what seemed true and real to him—he relied on his

_____

[52] Yeah, double negative there. I'm God and I don't have to follow grammar rules.

112

common sense and intelligence in approaching me. And so he came to know me as much as any man could.

And, I suppose, you could say that Abram was my friend. [53]

The Bible says that when Abram stopped at Shechem, I appeared to him and said, "I will give this land to your offspring." And to this day, Jews and Arabs are still fighting over exactly who gets the land. Can I point out that it says "offspring" and not "first-born" or "second-born" or "third-cousin-on-mother's-side"? The children of Abram, through Ishmael and Isaac, would eventually become the Arabs and the Jews of today. Which only goes to show that there's always some sort of fight even in the best of families.

Of course, I remember the actual conversation Abram and I had about this. We were sitting down, sharing a cup of wine, and watching the sun set over Mt. Ebal as night descended on the city of Shechem.

"My God—"Abram began.

"Yes?" I answered.

"Oh, sorry…I didn't mean You literally." Abram continued, sheepishly. "But I was just thinking what a lovely spot this is. A man could do quite well settling here."

---

[53] Now you might wonder how the angels took this. But, since the Heavenly Hosts are perfect, and love is infinite, we are incapable of feeling jealousy. Yes, I know all about that "I, the LORD your God, am a jealous God" bit…well, we'll get to that in its proper place.

I smiled. "Why, bless you, Abram. Ready to settle in and raise that family, eh?"

"Oh, not just yet, Lord. Don't tell Sarai, but I just made a down payment on the very land we're sitting on. It seemed wise given the current interest rates! One thing Terah always said was 'Sheep come and go. But land is yours forever.' And there are some other places I'd like to check out, and maybe help Lot find a nice place of his own when he's ready. I hear Bethel is also quite lovely…and Sarai keeps bugging me about maybe taking a vacation in Egypt."

I still don't understand how you humans think you can buy and sell something that I made for all of you. When's the last time you heard of someone getting zapped by me because he ignored a "Private Property: Keep Out" sign. Besides, if I created the seas and the land, then I'm the real owner. And I sort of granted the earth to *all* humankind, no charge, either. Man, I'd make one hell of a lousy capitalist! The planet hasn't been sold to some fool that wants to cover it with steel and glass monstrosities and put his name on everything! I sure as hell didn't sign any deed over to Sparky so he could defoliate it, strip-mine it, pollute the waters, and put poisons into the ground so that your kid gets a major dose of mercury along with the vitamins in those vegetables you have such a hard time getting little Bobby to eat in the first place! You know, you really better watch it—I might decide to take the whole thing back one of these days.

"Well, in any case, you have something to leave to the children," I mused to Abram. "But, I will say this. Keep going like you are: treat your neighbors like you would treat yourself, deal with charity and kindness towards strangers, and try to find the good in others, and all will say they are blessed because of you. And your children and their children's children shall inherit the land from you in peace."

That was the conversation. Just please—when someone asks why peace is so elusive, don't answer, "Only God knows." It seems to me that something that would do the greatest good for all of you should be something you would want. Don't just pray to me to bring "peace to earth"—do something to bring it about. Sadly, it sometimes seems that the only way to do it would be to wipe the lot of you out and start all over again—and I'm not inclined to that solution.

Why is peace so elusive? Only You know!

I'm not going to go over every incident in the Bible, nor even each one in the life of Abraham. But, if only because you can't get over it, let's deal with Sodom and Gomorrah. It's rather a long tale, so hang in there.

To begin: The Dead Sea is the lowest point on earth, about one thousand three hundred and twenty feet below sea level. It's approximately forty-seven miles long, and about ten miles wide at its broadest point. It is also the saltiest and most mineral-laden body of water in the world. Why is it called the Dead Sea? Well, it's so salty—about six times saltier than the ocean—that, with the exception of a few microbes, no organic life can exist in it. There is no seaweed. There are no plants. Fish, accidentally making their way into it from the Jordan River, immediately perish in it, and their bodies become covered with a layer of salt crystals. Because of the density of the minerals, even if you've never been anywhere near the water before, you will float in the Dead Sea—just don't try it if you have any cuts because they will sting something god-awful. And just about everywhere you look, you see white salt. On the southwestern shore of the sea is the salt mountain range of *Mount Sodom.* And there your tour guide will happily point out a curious rock salt formation and tell you that this is Lot's wife, and this is the spot where, the Bible story goes, she was turned into salt after disobeying the warning not to look back on the destruction of the two cities. And there she still stands after all this time.

But four thousand years ago or so, the climate was wetter. On the north shore, a factory did an excellent business in olive oil, and there were thriving towns. The towns of Sodom and Gomorrah were built right along the shore in order to allow the locals to gather the blocks of asphalt that would float to the surface of the sea, which would be a lucrative source of trade with Egypt, where asphalt was used to embalm their dead. In fact, the Egyptian word "moumiah" — "mummy" to most of you—means asphalt.

I remember Sodom and Gomorrah quite well. Just to keep things simple, let's concentrate on Sodom, and you can assume that everything I mention also applies to Gomorrah as well. I suppose you want to know what really was going on with the 'outcry' against Sodom and Gomorra.[54] Exactly what was so terrible that the whole shebang had to be destroyed?

Well now, children, pull the blanket up tight around you, and I'll tell you a little story...

Once upon a time, there was a kingdom called Shinar. And Shinar was a grand and mighty kingdom, full of gold and lapis lazuli. Its cities were tall and proud, and likewise, its people were tall and proud and wanted for nothing. But to its rulers came tales of the wealth to be had along the Valley of Siddim, and they said to themselves:

"Let us send colonists to this valley, that we may seize the asphalt and other riches to be had in that land and make it our own. And build new settlements, new cities, that our empire may expand and grow even greater."

And so it was done. And braving the Zuzites in Ham, conquering the Ammorites of Hazazon Taamar, subduing the challenge of the Rephaites in Ashteroth Karnaim, eventually, the Shinarites were able to dominate the valley. And they saw the

---

[54] Genesis 18 and 19

wealth of the minerals to be gathered there, and so they built their cities by the shores of the Salt Sea.

At first, these colonists were a happy lot. There were the occasional wars in the area, in part due to Egypt's attempt to get control of the Valley by aligning itself with the Horites, but Shinar and the colonists were able to subdue their rivals, and cause Egypt to give up more and more of the land surrounding the Salt Sea to the Shinarite colonists. But, as time went on, these colonists saw that the mother country of Shinar seemed to require more and more from them. Perhaps this was because of the high cost of the Egypt and Horite Wars, as Shinar claimed, but the colonists thought to themselves that they were becoming more and more repressed by the motherland.

One thing after another: a tax on sewage removal, a tax on papyrus, a tax on olive oil, the king of Shinar still kept soldiers stationed among the colonist just in case any Horite got uppity — and, since someone had to pay for their upkeep, and it sure was not going to be the taxpayers of Shinar itself, no sir-ree Moloch!, the soldiers felt perfectly justified in living off the locals. And the colonists didn't have much say in the matter, either since the king and his counselors in Shinar largely dictated the laws of the land.

And then there was the famous Siddim Wine Party. Well, it was famous in its time, but now largely forgotten since no one ever wrote the story down.

It seems the Grand Vizier in charge of the Royal Monies convinced the king that it would be a grand thing to impose a tax on wine shipped to the colonists. For, I have to tell you, those colonists really loved their wine, and drank it like it was water — and yes, by the way, there was a water tax, too. Sure, they were pretty inured to most hardships, but taxing wine! — Now, *this* really was too much. So, a group, calling themselves the Sons of the Daughters of the Fathers of the Holy Gecko called for a boycott of the wine brought into the area by the East Harappa Wine Company (or the EHWC for short), which had the monopoly on the wine trade from Shinar. The colonists began to smuggle in wine from the Hittites. [55] And the boycott was so effective that the EHWC saw the amount of wine it sold fall from nine hundred thousand gallons to two hundred thirty-seven thousand just three years later.

"This won't do," said the head of the EHWC. "Our warehouses are filled with wine. If we can't sell it to the colonists, we'll soon have warehouses filled with vinegar. If this keeps up, we'll go bankrupt."

No, this wouldn't do, thought the Grand Vizier, s secret partner in the EHWC himself, and he whispered in the king's ear. And so, they decided to allow the EHWC to bypass the wine merchants of the Valley and undercut the price of the smuggled Hittite wine.

---

[55] No relation to the Horites. And yes, there sure were a lot of –ites out there (Horites, Azorites, Perrizites, Jesubites, Yurites, Norites, Yugotnorites, etc.)

So, a caravan carrying nine thousand barrels of wine soon stood at the way station in the town of Siddim. And the governor of Siddim, who took his orders from the king and valued his head, insisted that the wine be unloaded.

That night, a man named Elum Adamas called the locals to action. Disguising themselves as Horites, they snuck into the way station and broke open the barrels of wine and poured it all in to the Salt Sea. [56]

Now, the king and the Grand Vizier were royally pissed. The king decreed that all trade to and from Siddim would be forbidden until the wine was paid for, that there could be no meeting without the governor's consent, and that the king's soldiers must be quartered wherever the king desired — including the homes of the colonists themselves.

But, wouldn't you know it? Like most attempts at tyranny, this exploded in the king's face, and the other towns in the Valley, including Sodom as well as Gomorrah, rallied behind Siddim, for they realized that either they were all in this together, or eventually the king and his Vizier would take them out, one by one.

And soon the entire Valley was involved in revolution against great odds — for how could the colonists ever hope to defeat the great power of Shinar. The colonists had appointed, Ga'h-wist-non, to lead their forces against the Shinarites, but he seemed to

---

[56] It's not true that the combination of this wine mixed with all that salt is the origin of your modern bottled cooking wine.

spend most of his time checking out the sleeping areas of the local caravanserais and having only very little success against the Shinarite army. And the situation at times seemed hopeless — until the colonists realized that their real hope lay in getting another great power on their side against Shinar.

So, diplomats were sent to the glorious kingdom in Thebes, the capital city of the royal court of Egypt, to seek succor from the great Pharaoh.

And the Pharaoh and his advisors sat with the diplomats from Siddim and realized that this was a golden opportunity to sock it to the Shinarites as payback for their defeat in the Egyptian and Horite Wars twenty years earlier. And they nodded to themselves, and the diplomats nodded to themselves as well, as they all recalled that ancient saying "the enemy of my enemy is my friend."[57]

And soon, Egypt was sending its mighty chariots into the Valley to block the Shinarites at every turn. Finally, after much hardship and many battles, Ga'h-wistnon and his armies together with the Egyptians managed to surround the Shinarite general, Wasslisnoc'r, and the war was over.

The twin cities of Sodom and Gomorrah, now finding themselves free of Shinar, looked at each other and smiled. They were free to pursue their own destinies. But, realizing that their new

---

[57] Of course, most people don't remember the rest of it, which goes "until he pisses me off."

found freedom was precarious, they got together with Siddim and other cities in the area and became united as the kingdom of Sodom-Gomorrah so that they could — well, just to quote from their founding papers — "bring justice to the land, give the blessings of peace to our people, yet to stand united in all we whole sacred as a people, to work together for the common good, and bless ourselves and our children with liberty." [58] And to see that this would be true, certain laws were made the rule of the land.

I think it might interest you to know what some of those laws were.

First, and I really like this one, the rulers could not dictate the religious beliefs of the people, nor could they prevent anyone from worshipping me as they saw fit. There would be no stoning of blasphemers, no beheading of infidels, and no burning of heretics or unbelievers. Yes, a truly enlightened idea — that a person's relationship with me was between that person and me alone, and no one else's business.

Then there was the truly revolutionary idea that people had the right to say whatever they wanted, to be able to disagree with the actions of their leaders, without some king offing his head. And that a difference of opinion, and peacefully protesting against what one believes to be wrong is not an act of treason, but sometimes may be the act of the highest morality and the greatest love of country.

---

[58] Preamble to the Constitution of the United Kingdom of Sodom-Gomorrah.

People had a right to privacy, and to be secure in their own homes.

The government could not arbitrarily deprive a person of life, liberty, rights, property without a public trial by impartial juries, and the defendant would know what he was being charged with, was allowed to be confronted with the witnesses against him and would be provided with counsel to aid in his defense. No, the government could not just decide to take someone away and either kill them or lock them in jail without what the rules called "due process."

Oh, there was much more, too. And you've got to be wondering: okay, that all sounds fine and dandy. So, why were Sodom and Gomorrah finally destroyed?

Hang in there. We're getting to it.

Ga'h-wistnon was appointed the first ruler of the new kingdom of Sodom-Gomorrah. And things seemed to go pretty well for a while. Except for a few "minor" details...

Like slavery. You would think someone might have pointed out that there was some sort of hypocrisy in claiming that "all men are created free" when slavery was legal. It kind of ruins the effect, if you know what I mean. Though there were people in the area of Sodom who realized this, the truth was that the area surrounding of Gomorrah depended on its slave to work out in the asphalt fields. And eventually, eighty-seven years after they had united as one, the kingdom split apart. Sodom and Gomorrah went to war against each other over this and other issues — a terrible war of brother against brother, thousands lost in battle after battle in the carnage that enveloped the kingdom for over five years — and in the end, slavery was outlawed, too.

But, at the same time, the reunited Sodom and Gomorrah — now collectively called "the Kingdom of Sodom" or just "Sodom" for short — looked over the land around them, the land where the Shosonites and the Lakotites and the Apachites and others hunted and gathered and fished, and learnt that there were vast tracks of asphalt along their shorelines, and in their hills could be found gold and silver. And greed entered the hearts of the Sodomites.

The Sodomites became very shrewd. They would find a member of a tribe who would agree to sell the land to them, even if that person had no authority over that tribe, and then the Sodomites would say they had a "sacred and unbreakable" treaty with the tribe. And they would send their armies to force the tribe off the land, and bring them to other areas, not so rich nor so good, telling the tribe that this new area was theirs forever. And later, when a Sodomite found that there was gold or silver or precious jewels in this new land given to the tribe, they would say that there was no treaty, or that the tribe had violated it somehow, or that the Sodomites and the tribe could not live together in peace and that for the good of the tribe it had to be moved to yet another and still smaller place. And any resistance was met by all the powers of the Sodomite government. The woman and the children of the tribes would be massacred while the men of the tribe were off hunting for food. And survivors would be forced to march hundreds of miles with little provision into the desert areas, their tears leaving trails to mark their passage. Until finally, the Lakotites and the Apachites and the Shoshonites and the Shaianites and the Hopites and so many others were rounded up and gathered into little enclaves far from the lands of their ancestors and their gods, and these proud and brave people were left betrayed and robbed of their land and riches and their heritage and reduced to a shadow people. To bring justice to the land.

And the Sodomites saw that this was good. But good is not what I saw.

Years passed. And Sodom became great among the nations. It was a relatively young nation as nations went then, and yet you might find it incredible that this one country somehow managed to get involved in some sort of war every twenty years. In order to secure the blessings of peace.

And still, the Sodomites saw that this was good. But good is not what I saw.

Ah, what a land. What a people!. [59]

Lucifer, Michael and I were totally fascinated by this hypocrisy. And we wondered what we would find if we went down to

---

[59] Of course, such happenings could never occur in your modern, enlightened, moral, God-fearing nations.

Sodom for a little "vacation." We decided we would visit the two largest cities of the kingdom, the great city of Sodom itself, and then Gomorrah. On the way, we stopped by Abraham's tent to say hello and told him of our plans.

"My God, are you nuts! Why on earth would you want to go there?"

Michael laughed. "Aw, come on, Abe. Doesn't it appeal to you in the slightest? I hear that's where all the action is nowadays around here."

"No thank you!" Abraham said. "My meshuganah nephew, Lot, lives out there and the stories he tells me! And don't call me Abe, thank you very much. Why I bet you can't find—oh, let's say—fifty honest men there."

Lucifer laughed. "Yeah, I've heard it's one great place to get ripped off. You know, I'll up you bet. I bet we can't find even forty."

Abraham looked at Lucifer. "Well, we're all gentlemen so we can call this a gentlemen's bet, but what about thirty?"

"Done!" cried Michael.

"Okay Michael, I'll up it. Let's say twenty!" Lucifer cried.

"Okay, twenty." Michael agreed.

Abraham looked at Michael and Lucifer and then turned to me. Lifting his glass of wine, he said, "Very well. Lord, if Michael and Lucifer can find ten honest men there, I'll eat my hat!"

I laughed. "You're on."

Then Abraham looked at me, wondering. "You won't do anything rash, will you Lord?"

I smiled at him. "That's not how I work, Abraham. If it keeps going the way it seems to be, Sodom will do a very good job of destroying itself without any help from me. But, just to keep you from worrying, I'll just send Michael and Lucifer and stay behind myself."

"Thank you, Lord. Oh, and Michael and Lucifer, say hello to Lot for me."

So, Michael and Lucifer went down to Sodom. A day or two went by, and then they came back up to Heaven and told the Heavenly Hosts all about Sodom and Gomorrah.

"We first stopped off to visit Lot," Michael explained. "Nice guy—even offered to put us up for the night. It was really kind of tight there; he only had a two-bedroom modified-Aram Naharaim tent—for which the poor man kept apologizing. To tell you the truth, it looked like a handyman's special, if you know what I mean. Do you know the price of a decent hut in Sodom is going for over 500 shekels while the average tradesman makes only 30 shekels a year? How in goodness sakes do people afford that? Anyway, his two daughters shared one bedroom—but they went to visit friends that evening, so we were comfortable enough. Actually, the poor guy's been dying to move out of Sodom but just can't afford it on what they're paying him. Since Abraham had given him a stake to get him started when Lot first moved out from Abraham's household, Lot just felt that he couldn't just ask Abraham to lend him some more. So, I hope you don't mind, but Lucifer and I gave him a loan—which we'll conveniently forget about, of course—and, when we left, he was packing up himself and his family to get out of Sodom. He told us he was going to take a look at some town called Zoar."

"But, I don't understand, why would anyone want to leave Sodom, Lord," Sophia wondered "Don't we constantly hear the people of Sodom pay homage to you in their way?"

"Yes, yes," I agreed, annoyed. "You know how it goes— 'Oh Great God of _____,[60] pour forth your blessings on our land, and guide and protect us your holy agents upon the Earth, who bring your will and your majesty and power to the heathens of the world. For there is no God greater than you, our God, and in the name of your divine love, in the name of Peace itself, we'll knock the living crap out of anyone who thinks differently.' And they express their deep devotion to me by spending a whole hour or two a week in their temples, saying 'Oh we are but poor sinners and unworthy to stand clean before you, oh God.'"

"But," protested Lucifer, "it's in some of those temples that the holiest and noblest strivings of humanity get expressed—peace, charity, love of neighbor."

---

[60] Fill in the blank with the name of the god of your choice.

"'Peace, charity, love of neighbor,'" I echoed. "'Love your neighbor as you would yourself.' They're all for that. But, tell me then, any of you, why on earth do they then go out and spend the rest of the week doing the exact opposite?"

The Heavenly Hosts were silent.

I sighed. "Well, what do we tell Abraham? Remember when the people of Sodom agreed that they should create social agencies to help feed the hungry, that their rulers should use some of their riches to make sure that the poor and infirmed had shelter and access to their holy medicine men, that the workers who gave their service to gathering up the asphalt and carting it to Egypt should not be left helpless when they were too old to continue to work? I thought Sodom was actually on the way to really practicing what they preached. What happened to that?"

Lucifer sighed. "I don't know how to tell you. It seems as time went on, and the asphalt merchants got richer and richer, they were able to appoint leaders who they could control. And, it seems to me that they must think that your proper name, Lord, is 'Mammon.' Because they've decided that Sodom can't afford, should not afford this sort of expense. It's like they think that the greatest good comes from taking the money that would be spent on helping the poor and old and weak, and giving it to the people who they seem to think need it even more—the ones who already have all the money! Why, we listened to a meeting of their governing council, and we just couldn't believe what they were saying. It's too expensive to feed a starving child because that might mean that an asphalt merchant can't quite afford that new gold statue of himself that he just has to have. When is enough, enough? Maybe they really think that's fair—I heard someone argue that if you give the poor money, they would just foolishly waste it on food for themselves and their families—and then they might think they were entitled to a handout instead of working for a living."

"Well," I asked, "can they find jobs?"

"The asphalt merchants keep cutting jobs so that they can keep more money for themselves. Do you know that the average asphalt merchant in Sodom makes over 400 times as much as one of their workers? That means these merchants can make more in a day than their workers earn in a year."

"When *is* enough, enough?" I mused.

"And Lord," Michael added, "the counselors who are beholding to the merchants go around saying that the very idea of someone seeking a handout from the government is anti-Sodomite! At the same time, the merchants are able to get the counselors to agree to give them more and more breaks on the taxes they pay to the government."

"Hold it," I said. "Isn't that a handout of sorts?"

"And you know, Lord," Michael continued, "it seems that the rulers of Sodom think it's too expensive to care for the sick if that means that they can't afford bigger and bigger armies. There's a war on, you know?"

"When isn't there a war going on!" I exclaimed.

Michael and Lucifer told us that Sodom had a long history of going into neighboring towns and secretly providing arms to groups that would help overthrow the current leader of that town if Sodom perceived that that leader might be acting in ways that might hinder the Sodom merchants from gathering even more wealth. There had been a long period of clandestine moves like this...helping to train squads of rebels who would invade the neighboring town, rape, and pillage, and set up puppet states that would be friendly to Sodom. And Sodom was able to turn a blind eye to just about anything if it served its purpose. Just to take one example: they had helped Repha Lavi become King of Ir and allowed his internal legion to torture and kill the people of Ir until finally, they rose up while Lavi was visiting Sodom and overthrew the kingdom.

Lucifer told us of another case of Sodomite duplicity. The forerunners of the current leader of Sodom had heavily armed the leader of Saidyeh, Amandis Sedhus, himself controlling a good portion of the available asphalt of the Dead Sea. In fact, there were merchants in Sodom who, with the tacit approval of the Sodom rulers, sold Amandis poisons that were banned in Sodom, terrible poisons that Amandis turned on his own people when they disagreed with him. He and his armies, using these weapons and poisons, killed thousands of them. And again, Sodom just winked and kept quiet about it, because they saw Amadis as an ally against the now hostile land of Ir. [61]

"And the people of Sodom can't understand why there might be a moral problem with this?" I asked.

"Lord," Luce said softly, "you know, it's Sodom—the holy warrior of God, and the only force for good in the world."

And the people of Sodom, not paying attention to what their rulers did in their name, did not see that they were making enemies all around them.

So, the Sodomites were absolutely surprised when Amandis used those self-same weapons against another Cir Awat, an ally of Sodom. It was only then that, Sodom, under Geshegubor I—who had been the old king's next-in-line when the government allowed the weapons to be sold in the first place, fought Amandis to a standstill, but allowed him to keep his sovereignty, forcing him to destroy all his weapons and effectively neutralizing him. And the Sodomites were proud, not knowing the history of the thing.

Eventually, Geshegubor I's rule ended. And while the Sodomites worried about the private sexual appetite of his successor, their enemies' thoughts darkened, and horrible plots made.

So, it stood for eight long years.

---

[61] Of course, you today all only treat each other with the greatest respect and dignity, and if anyone would dare to do the same as these ancient Sodomites did, they would disappear from the public eye immediately, back into a deserved oblivion.

Book V - Abraham

And on the eleventh day of the ninth month in the first year of the usurper, Geshegubor II, while the people of Sodom were just beginning their day, they were attacked with no warning by cowards using the anger against Sodom as justification for the murder of innocents. And the leader of those cowards — who's name I refuse to utter; let it be blotted out from history for all time! — is forever cursed for saying that this act would be pleasing to me, and would be their way to heaven. But, I hear the cries of the widows, of the fatherless, of the motherless — and it isn't Heaven that awaits those who kill in my name. On either side!

As you would expect, Geshegubor II rallied his people, and war was fought to destroy the cowards who attacked Sodom. But, hardly had that war ended — without capturing or killing the leader of the cowards — when Geshegubor II, who seemed consumed with hate for Amandis, lied to his own people, in order to justify an attack on Saidyeh and finish off Amandis where his father had failed to do so. Geshegubor II and his counselors said that Amandis was allied with the ones who had attacked Sodom — although they knew that this was not true — and still had many spears and weapons of boiling oils and vast quantities of poison, and that he was about to attack Sodom with his weapons of destruction. There was no time to waste. And so, the armies of the Sodomites marched out, and invaded Saidyeh, and against the advice of most of their allies — and found that there were indeed no such weapons, and for the first time in their history, had started a war unprovoked and without reason.

And while this was happening, the biggest supporters of Geshegubor II ensured that they would control the rebuilding of Saidyeh and lined their pockets with more wealth as the sons and daughters of their countrymen fought and died there.

And I asked Lucifer and Michael to tell us what was happening in Sodom while this was going on.

"Lord, "Michael began. "Since we last talked, there have been two kings since Geshegubor II, and the state of Sodom has deteriorated so badly that perhaps it is impossible to restore it.

"What have the fools been doing?" I asked.

"Well, while all the nonsense was going on in Saidyeh, the asphalt merchants decided that they could force their workers to do more and more work for less and less money," Michael explained. "They cast aside many thousands of their loyal workers even as the merchants arranged to increase their own wealth and reward. And the remaining workers were frightened, for those without work often had to go through all they have until they despair of being able to give their children even bread."

"The leaders said that the workers must be patient and that by giving more wealth to the asphalt merchants, eventually, these merchants would hire the workers back. Of course, they lied! And it looks to me that Sodom is becoming divided between the haves and the have-nots."

"Didn't anyone speak up?"

"My Lord, "Lucifer began, "there certainly were those who disagreed, who felt that this was all wrong and that there could be a better way. But they were shouted down, called 'traitor' or 'scum.' And Geshegubor II used the cry of '9/11' to justify anything he did. But underneath, it's like the good of Sodom is nothing more than the good of the wealthy. When the bottom fell out on some insane thing called partial asphalt derivatives — whatever the hell that was, none of us could figure it out — and all of Sodom was suffering, do you have any idea what they did?"

"I would hope that they would help the poor and suffering and punish those who brought the ruin on the land."

Luce laughed ruefully. "No such luck. The leaders decided that it was more important to make sure that those who financed the whole debacle were kept solvent — and so they arranged the funds in the Sodom treasury would be used to bail them out. But, the ones hurt most by the scandal---they got nothing."

I frowned. "You mean, no one was punished?"

"Oh, maybe a few heads were cut off, and some merchants went under. There were even attempts, under the next ruler, Bara'Om, to make new laws to prevent this from happening again, and slowly it looked like Sodom was beginning to recover, but there was so much animosity towards Bara'Om from the elders of the old ruling class that they stopped any good he tried to do. And factions in Sodom got further and further apart, so where once there was civilized disagreements and a sense of compromise for the good of the nation, people could only shout at each other, totally convinced that their side is correct and have you, Lord, on their side. And the other side consists of the forces of evil and must be destroyed. No compromise, only hate and threats as if a civil war would break out any moment."

"And let me tell you about the current ruler of Sodom," added Michael, "Lord Duntramp—obviously no relationship to you, Lord---the son of a wealthy owner of the largest house of prostitution in Sodom. Following in his father's example, Duntramp used his father's money to purchase property all around Sodom and putting the Duntramp name in big gaudy gold letters on all of it. But he was playing a long con, always pretending to be richer than he was, buying gambling houses and watching them fail to leave his associates ruined while he sold out just in time. Why, he got so caught up in debt, that his bankers had no choice but to keep lending him money—because if he failed, they would never get their prior investments back, and they would go down with him. "

"What a wonderful role model," I said, sarcastically. "How in my name did this jackass become ruler of Sodom?"

"Public relations and bullshit. He would go around, bragging to the town criers that his buildings were the greatest, that he was incredibly wealthy because he knew better than anyone how to arrange matters so that he would always win. Why, he was the smartest, the handsomest, the cleverest, the shrewdest, the most sexually attractive male of the age. Of course, none of this was true—but, as you well know, if you repeat a lie long enough, you'll always find naïve people who will believe it.

"Eventually, when the reign of his predecessor Bara'Om was coming to an end, Duntramp was ecstatic. He had always hated Bara'Om—even going to the extent of suggesting that he was not a born native of Sodom and hence an illegal ruler. He had proof, he said. But that proof never came, because, once again, Duntramp was full of shit.

"And he thought to himself, 'Being ruler isn't a big deal. But I could use that position to make myself really rich—it's an easy con. If Bara'Om could do it, it should be easy for me. This could be the ultimate con of my career!'

"So, he started going around, claiming to have the only answer to everything, as he screamed out new lies every day, calling facts fake, his ramblings reality, up is down, night is day, love is hate, hate is love, and anyone who disagrees with him is the harbinger of all that is fake and evil. Most people thought that Sodom was too advanced, too sophisticated to fall for this—but there were enough people who felt left behind by the changes in Sodom over the years, that Duntramp was able to sway to support him. And in the end, his faction succeeded. Then, the real problems started as he and his ministers sought, like so many rulers before them,[62] to make certain people scapegoats for all the

---

[62] God here again: And so many after them to this very day.

problems they themselves and their predecessors under the Geshegubors caused — to the point where some citizens of Sodom were screaming to force these "others" out of Sodom and build walls to keep them out.

And, would you believe it, not satisfied with having ninety-five percent of all the wealth of Sodom he and the ruling class arranged to steal even more by giving themselves a great break in taxes while giving a temporary pittance to everyone else — putting the country on the road in the impossible situation of potential bankruptcy."

"What?" I cried. 'Don't the people know any better than to reward the very ones who are out to hurt them?"

"He has his town criers twist and lie about events so that many of them worship him as if he were you, God, himself! And 'love your neighbor as you would yourself' has become 'Screw the other guy — as long as I got mine!'" Luce concluded, sadly.

"And it is almost funny when it's not frightening, Lord, "Michael added, "how Duntramp and his supporters talk about you, how you are on his side against the forces of evil. Maybe they need to take a good look in the mirror."

"Well, they better be careful," I mused. "They just might cut themselves when that mirror cracks from the hypocrisy! Oh right, the guy breaks every moral thing I stand for, and I'm supposed to wave his flag? Take my name in vain, will he? Enough of that putz! What exactly is going on with those people? Why aren't they up in arms about this stuff?"

"And get this, Lord." Michael went on. "Duntramp's followers believe that he was divinely selected by you to lead Sodom, that he is leading the nation towards a great moral and spiritual awakening. Oh, he pays lip service to you—invokes your name when he's speaking to the public and has his advisory meetings begin with a token prayer after which he precedes to find new ways to do the opposite of your will. But his followers go on believing in him---even when facts are to the contrary. The guy's been known for making gross remarks about women that would even make Lucifer blush. He repeatedly cheated on his wives—he's up to wife number three-or is it four now—who can keep track? He's constantly having affairs with other women during his marriages. Nice guy, right? "

"What?" I said. "That's nuts! Why, you would think that the Sodomites would be outraged. Why, if you think about it, it mocks their whole belief system about marriage. So, what did they do about it? "

"His followers just don't seem to give a damn—because he is leading the way to, as he often says in his slogan, 'Make Sodom Superior Again.'"

"Yet, the same time, they argue whether two people of the same sex, who have lived together for twenty years or more, loving each other, caring for each other, committed to each other, have the same ability to get married. I don't get it!"

I looked at Michael. "*That's* what these people are screaming about? So you are telling me that, according to the Sodomites, a committed relationship of that kind threatens their institution of marriage and should be punished, but a joke like that Duntramp should be rewarded and considered a person to look up to and be proud of?. I'm confused."

"That's not all," said Lucifer. "Here's one for you. Some of the temple singers make up songs that have lyrics saying that all women were only good for rape and that anyone who gets in the temple singers' way is going to be shot, or stabbed, or stoned, or some other such."

"What?" I said. "I'm sure the people find this shocking and wouldn't stand for this sort of thing. Certainly, no children hear this crap, do they, Luce?"

"Sorry Lord, but it's constantly explained that this is all make-believe, just entertainment, and so it's okay. And— "

I groaned. "Don't tell me, let me guess. Those temple singers are rich and living like kings."

"Yep. And you can hear their music just about everywhere. Oh, and they have this sport where the point seems to be how many ways can someone bash another's brains in. And they go to the arena and watch this. I heard them screaming "Kill the bastard!" while one guy was hitting another in the balls with a wooden bat."

I couldn't believe it. "What kind of sick minds do these people have? The next thing you know, they'll show someone being beaten to a pulp and then crucified and sell tickets to it!"

"So, check this out. They bring their children to see this stuff and the kids scream for blood right along with them. And, it doesn't seem to bother them. But, breastfeed a child in public or expose a female breast and the crowd goes nuts."

"I guess it's okay to let their kids watch blood and violence and murder, but not okay to let them see a part of their own anatomy," Michael mused. "Some one's got their values ass-backward."

"Yes, indeed," I agreed. "Especially since what that kingdom is doing while invoking my name might bother me a whole lot more than what part of someone's anatomy is being exposed in the town square. Let's get this straight: they're in the middle of a war; they may destroy their civilization—such as it is—at any moment; their leaders take them down paths that lead further and further from me. Poverty, hunger, injustice, disease, that doesn't faze them at all—but who is sleeping with who, someone's breast exposed in their face, which person can beat the other's brains out—*that's* the sort of shit they're worried about?"

Now, on the whole, I was normally rather slow to anger, but by now I was getting pissed. "Damn these people, what's with them? Do I have to go down there and kick some ass?"

Well, in the end, I didn't kick butt, and I didn't break a promise to Abraham either — although we never did get around to really settling the bet.

It was indeed a good thing Michael and Lucifer helped get Lot out of town that day. Because there was retribution for Sodom and Gomorrah, I know it says that "..the Lord rained down burning sulfur on Sodom and Gomorrah from the Lord out of the heavens. Then he overthrew those cities and the entire plain, including all those living in the cities and also the vegetation in the land."[63] But it wasn't my show.

It was just before dawn on the 29th of June 3123 BCE. A Sumerian astrologer looks up in the sky and sees a sight that fills him with horror. He sees what looks like a "white stone bowl" sweeping along the sky: an asteroid more than half a mile across coming in low, heading to the area of what is now called the Austrian Alps. The asteroid clips an ancient mountain called Gaskell above where the modern town of Längenfeld lies, about seven miles from Köfels in the Tyrol. As it travels down the valley, it becomes a fireball, around five kilometers in diameter, supersonic shock waves leaving a trail of destruction. It hit Köfels with a cataclysmic explosion, equivalent to more than one thousand tons of TNT, pulverizing the rock. Should you come to Köfels, today, you can see evidence of an ancient landslide three miles wide and a quarter of a mile thick.

---

[63] Genesis 19:24

Two-thirds of the asteroid's debris was hurled back along its route and created a flash that reached temperatures as high as four hundred degrees Centigrade (seven hundred fifty-two degrees Fahrenheit), killing anyone in its path. The mushroom cloud bent over the Mediterranean Sea and re-entered the atmosphere over the Palestine region, raining "brimstone and fire"[64] on Sodom.

So, it is true that when Abraham looked down toward where Sodom and Gomorrah had stood, "he saw dense smoke rising from the land, like smoke from a furnace."[65]

Abraham sent his swiftest man to find out what had happened. And this is just one of the reasons I loved Abraham so. When he found out that Sodom and Gomorrah had been destroyed, he said to his servant "Those poor people. We have to find out if anyone has survived—they'll need food, clothing, shelter, medicine men."

"But, master, "the servant responded, "they were corrupt. They did much evil. Sodom only got what it deserved."

Abraham looked at his servant. "They are still children of God—no matter how often they might have forgotten that. We all forget that we're creations of God at times. And all God's creatures suffer, and struggle, and hurt. And if I, who am also a child of God, have no compassion for them in their need, then I am unworthy of God."

---

[64] Genesis 19:24
[65] Genesis 19:28

I was listening when he said that and smiled in my heart. And that's the sort of thing that keeps even me humble. Sometimes I forget that I have as much to learn from you, as you do from me.

Because Abraham was widely respected as a man of justice and goodness, the surrounding nations responded immediately to his call for a humanitarian relief effort to rescue the survivors of the destruction. Those few were even taken into the homes of those who they had regarded as enemies or lesser men and helped to make whole.

Compassion for the human condition.

So, Sodom and Gomorrah passed from human history and into the realm of legend.

This brings us to Ishmael and Isaac. Things get quite messy here. I mean, you have the whole argument about which son Abram, now called Abraham,[66] was going to sacrifice, supposedly by my command. The Bible, and therefore Christians and Jews, say that the son to be sacrificed was Isaac (coincidentally, from whom the Israelites descended). The Qur'an doesn't say which one, but Moslems generally believe that it was Ishmael (coincidentally, from whom the Arabs descended.). Neither is exactly unbiased here. But first, you'd have to remember that Abram/Abraham lived some four thousand years ago. The stories about him

---

[66] Abram (which means "Noble Father") was so delighted at the birth of Sarai's son Isaac—having thought that Sarai was too old to ever have a child—that he changed his name to Abraham, meaning 'Father of a Multitude."

144

were not written down until at least eight hundred to one thousand years later in the case of the Bible, nor until about two thousand, six hundred years later in the case of the Qur'an. Have you ever played that old children's game of "telephone"? You know, one kid starts with a message, and whispers it to the next kid, who whispers it to the next kid, and on and on. And the fun is in noticing how the original message gets distorted in passing it down so that in the end, it's something entirely different. For example, say we start with something like "The Peace of the Lord be unto you, God shall bless all the children of Abraham," at the end we might wind up with something like "It is God's will that you kill the unbelievers."

So, it's just possible that there's more to the story than you know.

Anyway, Ishmael and Isaac. Ishmael was the son of Hagar, that servant of Sarai that I mentioned earlier. Isaac was the son of Sarai. Two brothers, right? Well...not exactly. What is not written down is that Abraham had yet *another* son, named Hochme, by his cook, Zazu. That's right...*three* brothers. And Hochme was the eldest.

And you're probably wondering why you've never heard of Hochme. Well...hang on a minute.

Abraham truly loved his kids, really, as much as any father ever loved his children. He had waited many years before his first child was born: a child whose laughter brought joy and happiness to Abraham's soul. Seeing his son's unconditional trust and love in

145

him, Abraham was transported, and in his son's smiling face, the man learned more about my true nature than he ever would or could by any other means. So, the story of the test of Abraham, as it is told in the twenty-second chapter of Genesis, is tremendously profound. For, as it says, even as my angel stays Abraham's hand from his son's throat, Genesis quotes him as saying:

Now I know that you fear God, because you have not withheld from me your son, your only son.[67]

I would ask any of you fathers or mothers, looking into the face of your child: *Could you find it in your heart to do the same? Would you willingly sacrifice your child's life to me if it were what I asked?*

No, of course, I don't want human sacrifice to me. I am not going to ask that of you. This whole test thing — it's so human! Like an insecure lover: "You say you love me, but how do I really know it. If you really loved me, you'd jump into a volcano for me!" No, no, no…. love is not demanding; love merely is there for you to accept.

"Now I know that you *fear* God." Am I Love? Or Am I Fear? And which is it that I want: for you to *fear* me, or to *love* me? Which is it you want from your God?

Abraham was learning to know me in his heart, soul, and mind in ways that you humans had not done before. Unfortunately, Abraham lived in a world where human sacrifice was accepted. It was a hard world — that's not to be denied. Sickness,

---

[67] Genesis 22:12

famine, disease, catastrophes of nature—these seemed to be the apparent work of a god (or gods) who required human appeasement.

I did not ask for such a test. I am NOT that kind of god. I was long sickened by the blood of the innocents cascading from your temples, the cries of the children, the despairing parents too frightened of their priests and the imagined anger of their gods to cry out as their children were thrown on the fire. And there were always some (and there are, unfortunately so many today) who saw no wrong in this—that the giver of life required appeasement by the taking of life, that to die for God was greater than to live for God.

A drought had come to the land, bringing sickness with it. The flocks of sheep were being decimated by disease, humans were dying, and the holy men had no cure for what was happening. But, they knew the traditions of the ancestors. And throughout the land, the cry went up that the heavens thirsted too—not for water, but for human blood.

Abraham knew these traditions and beliefs of his ancestors and had not entirely freed himself of them himself. And the traditions held that the gods demanded a sacrifice to appease their wrath, or to ensure their favor—and the sacrifice required was the firstborn.

So, out of these traditions of his ancestors, and a misplaced sense of his God's desires, Abraham, with tears in his eyes and a heart that was rent, took his son, who loved and trusted him, to the top of Mount Moriah where he had built the altar for the sacrifice.

"Father," asked Hochme "where is the animal we are going to sacrifice to the Lord?"

Abraham looked tenderly at him. "My son, the Lord will provide his own sacrifice. Do you love me?"

"Always, father."

"As I love you. Do you trust me?"

Hochme, innocent child, could only stare with trust at his father—his beloved father who surely would never do him any harm. And Abraham tenderly lifted up his child and tied him to the altar.

And he hesitated.

Hochme watched his father, tears in his eyes, raise the sacrificial knife.

Then Abraham lowered it and uttered a prayer.

And I looked down and saw what was about to happen. I motioned to Sophia, and we materialized on Mt. Moriah, even as Abraham raised the knife once more to Hochme's throat

"No, "cried Abraham, throwing the knife aside. "This is not just. What kind of God would ask such a thing? How could I even worship a God like that? This is not the God I know."

"Would a God like that even be worthy of your worship, Abraham?" I asked as Sophia picked up the knife and cut the cords that bound Hochme. "Do I want the blood of innocents spilled on my altars? Look into your heart, Abraham and tell me what I want?"

And Abraham's heart was full when he discovered the answer.

And the Bible says that Abraham "...returned to his servants, and they set off together for Beersheba." Abraham and his servants. What about his son? Why is no mention made of him? Because Sophia and Abraham worked out a deception with Hochme, to protect him from anyone who might seek his life now since the "sacred" blood sacrifice had been interrupted. Sophia would take charge of Hochme and keep him safe until Abraham found an excuse to free Zazu. After, having sworn her to utter secrecy about what had happened, she was reunited with her son. And, though Abraham was often in communication with his son, Hochme passed out of our story, and out of the memory of those who later passed the story on. But, just so you know, he eventually made his way back into Mesopotamia and settled down in Haran with Terah's family, married, and became quite a success on his own.

Abraham was left with two sons, Ishmael and Isaac. And sometime after Sarai died, he married a woman named Keturah who bore him six sons. And he also had more sons by his concubines. Unfortunately for Abraham, his family just couldn't get along with each other, and all went their separate ways and founded their own dynasties in the east. So Abraham did become the father of many. But when he died, only Isaac and Ishmael stood together to bury him in the cave of Machpelah where he had buried his beloved wife Sarai years ago. And then Isaac and Ishmael went their separate ways. So sad.

And today their descendants are at each other's throat, even fighting over the right to pray at Abraham's grave.

Book VI - Jacob

*A*s you may recall from your Bible stories, Isaac grew to manhood and married Rebekah who gave birth to the fraternal twins, Esau and Jacob. And Isaac prospered.

In a way, the rest of Genesis has more to do with the family history of Abraham than it does with me. Genesis tells a story that Jacob, the younger brother, egged on by his mother Rebekah, fooled the aged Isaac into giving Jacob the blessing he had meant for the elder son, Esau. Esau was roundly pissed at Jacob and bided his time, thinking that he would wait until Isaac died and then kill Jacob. Rebekah arranged to have Jacob seek refuge with her brother Laban who lived in Haran.

Jacob stopped for the night to sleep and dreamt. I take no responsibility for the dream, but Jacob had a vision in which he saw a ladder resting on earth with the top in heaven, and he saw angels ascending and descending on it. Now, consider the fact that—oops, I do hope this doesn't come as a shock considering all we discussed about Creation a while ago—the earth is not exactly next door to heaven. Look up tonight if you can see the stars. The nearest star to your solar system (not counting the Sun) is about 4.3 light years away. And a light year is nearly 5.8 trillion miles, [68] making the distance to that one star over 24.8 trillion miles. Now, I would hate

---

[68] That's 5,800,000,000,000 miles, folks!

to tell you just how far the distance in your space/time continuum is between earth and the heavenly abode because your minds couldn't contemplate it in the first place. [69] Look, for a rocket ship to escape the earth's gravitation and get into space, it has to be going at over twenty-five thousand miles per hour or around seven miles *per second*. How fast do you think those angels Jacob supposedly saw would have to be traveling to ever reach heaven if they started on Earth? Certainly, so fast that Jacob wouldn't be able to see it!

But whatever vision Jacob saw, he felt my presence in that spot.[70] This was probably his first religious experience of me and began his metamorphosis from a self-centered boy into a man worthy of his ancestors. He remembered the stories he had heard from Isaac about the God of Abraham, and he became thoughtful. For the first time, he prayed to me and made me his God.

Eventually, he arrived at his uncle's, met his cousin Rachel and fell in love with her loveliness and gentleness. And he agreed to work for Laban for seven years if he could have Rachel for his wife. Laban tricked him, for he had another and older daughter named Leah, and when the marriage was celebrated, it wasn't Rachel that Jacob found in the marriage bed, but Leah. But such was his love for Rachel that he agreed that if Laban gave him Rachel

---

[69] Now, that's something I'd like to see: one of your computers tries to calculate that number—blows the calculation of PI right out of the water
[70] Actually, I was taking a bit of a personal interest in him since he was Abraham's grandson, after all!

after the seven-day bridal week with Leah, he would work for him for an additional seven years.

Yes, Laban was a louse! And yes, we're talking polygamy: you know, why is it that all these figures in the Bible did okay with more than one wife, and you twenty-first century people go absolutely bat-shit about anything other than one man, one woman relationships. I didn't damn anyone for it. It didn't threaten the foundation of society. Look, I'm not that interested in what you do in the privacy of your homes between two consenting adults — actually, the whole things rather bores me. I don't care!

But, to get back to Jacob and Rachel.... Fourteen years. Okay, call me an incurable romantic, but that really gets me. A man is willing to toil for fourteen years just to be able to have the woman he loves. That's really beautiful. It's really the first great love story of the Old Testament. Love — so fleeting, so hard to find, so ennobling of your human soul — I think that second to Life itself, it's the greatest blessing I gave you. And the one that brings you closest to me.

Jacob did not love Leah, no fault of her own. But she did bear Jacob the first of his children: Reuben, Simeon, Levi, and Judah. But Rachel stayed barren, and jealous of her sister, gave Jacob her maidservant, Bilhah, as her surrogate. And Bilhah gave birth to Dan and then Naphtali. If anyone is keeping score, we're up to six at this point.

What did you think Leah did? Did she think to herself, "Well, all well and good that Rachel had to give Jacob her maidservant as a wife—Dan and Naphtali aren't really her sons, but Reuben, Simeon, Levi, and Judah are my own flesh?" Did this make her feel she was one up on Rachel? Nope—now Leah gives Jacob *her* handmaiden, Zilpah, and he has two kids with her: Gad and Asher. And now we're up to eight!

You have got to wonder. Jacob's out working the fields for Laban, he comes home, and ZIP, BANG! Man, this is one prolific fella! And they didn't have Viagra then, either.

You think we'd be done by now. Nope, because Rachel finds out that Reuben has been out gathering mandrakes and, after an argument with Leah, she agrees that in exchange for Reuben's mandrakes, Leah can sleep with Jacob. What's with the mandrakes you ask? Well, Rachel, dear, sweet Rachel, still wanted desperately to be a mother, to be able to hold a child of her own and her beloved Jacob in her arms. And the mandrake (also called "love apples," by the way) was thought to be an aphrodisiac. Now, I think I'll let you use your imagination here a bit, so I won't even mention the fact that the root of the mandrake looks something like a human phallus.

Meanwhile, Leah informs Jacob that she's essentially bought him for the night! And, yep, you guessed it. Leah now has yet another son: Issachar, and yet another, Zebulun. And we're up to ten sons! We do have a break because next, Leah gives birth to a daughter, Dinah.

But, now, it's back to Rachel. And Jacob the stud does it again. Or maybe it was the mandrake. For dear Rachel now finally gives birth to her firstborn, a son named Joseph. We're going to learn more about him later, by the way.

So, for now, the count is eleven sons, one daughter. That's Leah: six sons, one daughter. Leah's maidservant Zilpah: two sons. Rachel's maidservant, Bilhah: two sons. And finally, Rachel: one son.

And Rachel already gave Jacob a hint that she wasn't done yet, because the name Joseph means, "May he add" — and it wasn't arithmetic she had in mind, either.

And now Jacob calls for a timeout! It's been so many years since he had fled the land of Canaan and Esau's wrath. So many years of serving Laban, who readily admits to Jacob that he himself had prospered only because of Jacob's good work. Ah, good, old Laban — who probably lives on in the hearts of a lot of your big corporations' Chief Executive Officers. Yes, good old Laban — first he cheated Jacob out of an additional seven years of service by pulling the swticheroo of giving him Leah instead of Rachel, and now, Laban tries to cheat Jacob yet again! They work out an agreement whereby Jacob will take all the spotted sheep, the dark-colored lambs and the spotted or speckled goats from Laban's stock and take them as his final wages. But, since Laban doesn't like anyone messing around with his stock options, he removes all the animals that Jacob would have gotten and puts them in the care of his sons. Then he goes on a business trip with them, so Jacob looks to be left with nothing.

Jacob is an honest man. He doesn't steal the rest of the sheep left behind, but using a little animal husbandry, mates the remaining herds in such a way that bit by bit the offspring become speckled, streaked, or spotted. And after a few years, he had his own strong flock meeting the terms of Laban's agreement and left his father-in-law with the weaker remains. Call it the model of an excellent corporate takeover.

Laban, caught unaware by this maneuver of Jacob's, is not exactly happy about things- since now his stock options are worth a whole lot less than before. Jacob gathers up his family and his flocks and flees before Laban. But he and Laban do have one final confrontation in the hills of Gilead.

"Hey, Jacob, buddy, son-in-law," says Laban. "What's this? You've gone off like a thief in the night. You should have told me you were ready to go—we could have had a going-away party. You know, I really could do you some serious harm here, but your God warned me not to harm you. So here we are."

Jacob looked at Laban, looked at his own forces, and laughed. "Bullshit! Let's stop this right now. Here, before all my relatives and my servants, and before your relatives and servants, let me put it to you. I've taken care of your sheep for twenty years.

When the wild animals tore a sheep, you took it out of my wages. If a sheep got stolen day or night, you took it out of my wagers. In the heat of summer, in the cold of winter, day and night I slaved for you. You never even brought me the wood for a fire—that came out of my wages too if I didn't cut it myself. Not once when one of your daughters gave birth did you say to me, 'Jacob, take some time off. Be with your family.' I got sick. You didn't pay me. Remember: I worked fourteen years for your two daughters, six years for your flocks, and you changed my wages ten times. Heck, if you had your way, I would have left with nothing, you greedy son-of-a-bitch! Now, how would you like it if my relatives and I let the word get around exactly how you honor your deals arrangements, Laban, old buddy, old father-in-law of mine? How long do you think it'll be until you're up to your armpits in dung—and it won't be from your flocks, either!"

Laban thought this over. "Okay. You win, Jacob, what do you want?"

Jacob drew a line in the sand. "You stay on your side of this line, and I'll stay on my side. I'll take care of your daughters, and your grandchildren, and keep and honor them, and you stay on your side of this line, and we leave each other alone, and we agree that what's done is done and leave it at that."

Laban nodded. "Deal."

And the next morning, after Laban and his people had left, it was with a great deal of trepidation that Jacob continued on his way home to deal with Esau. Nervously, Jacob sent messengers to Esau, who lived in Edom, to tell him of his coming, and that he was returning with wealth from his labors for Laban.

The messengers returned and told Jacob that Esau was coming to meet him and bringing along four hundred men.

And now Jacob was really afraid. So, he divided up his camp into two groups, thinking that if Esau were to attack one of the camps, the other could make its escape in the meantime.

He looked deep into his heart and was uneasy. He remembered the dream he had had when he first set out and fell to his knees and prayed that I would save him from his brother's anger.

The prayer lifted his spirits a bit, and he thought some more about how he could influence Esau. "I've got one thing I can try," he thought to himself. "A bribe!" He took a part of his herd and put the animals in the care of his servants, instructing them to stay ahead of the main part of Jacob's camp and to tell Esau that this was a gift to him from his brother. In this way, maybe he could pacify Esau.

The night came. And as happens with many, the darkness brought back all his doubts and fears. His bravado in front of Laban was once thing — there was nothing with which he could bluff Esau. It would be an easy matter for Esau to overwhelm him and kill not only him but his entire family as well. He went off a way by himself and stared up into the star-filled canopy above him. How small he felt. How insignificant. And to think that in the morning, he might lose everything. Who could guide him through and help him see a way?

"Who are you that you would dare to think that God would hear your voice?" he heard a voice whisper in the darkness. And he recognized it as his own voice.

"I'm unworthy of it," he answered himself. And he suddenly felt totally alone, totally abandoned. He felt himself shrinking into the darkness and his despair. Jacob felt weak that he could not face what the morning would bring. Should he turn tail and flee, abandon his family and all he loved and had worked for these long years, and give up?

His thoughts turned to his family. The many children he was blessed with from the eldest Reuben already a robust, vigorous man down to little Joseph, his favorite. Joseph—whose smiling, loving face, the chuckle of whose laughter as Jacob swung him high in his arms, the light in his eyes as Rachel sang to him—would lighten his father's heart. And it was in those moments that Jacob would feel the presence of some mysterious power higher and greater than himself, as if in those soft blue eyes of the child he could almost see me there. He thought of Rachel, his beloved—her gentleness and sweetness, the knowledge that her love for him was something he could never lose, and a source of his own strength. He knew he was blessed. Even Leah—who loved him despite the fact that he could not return those feelings—he had come to appreciate her fortitude and wisdom. Another rock on which to stand.

So many loved him, and cared for him—and, looking deeper inside, he knew that there was something in the core of his being that, despite his fear and anguish, wanted to say "Yes" to life, to love, and to all the blessings he had received.

And he thought about the long years slaving for Laban and how he had prospered. Even when he had been discouraged, somehow things had worked out, as if someone had been looking out for his best interests despite himself. And he felt grateful and his soul filled with tears. Now he knew I was present and that he was not abandoned, not forgotten. And that in that deepness of his soul, he could find the strength, the courage, and the trust to go on.

Finally, he fell asleep. And in his dream, the wrestling with his despair and with his God manifested itself. He was wrestling with a stranger, holding on with all his might, not strong enough to overpower the stranger, yet not overwhelmed by him either.

And so it often is with those who love me best and the ones I love the most—they wrestle with their doubt and their belief, and finally find their way to what I truly am.

I blessed Jacob, and the legend arose of his night of struggle. Jacob—whose name meant, "He grabs" (for when he and Esau had been born, Jacob had come out holding Esau's heel)—would now be known as Israel ("He struggles with God"). And you, humankind, it seems, would always struggle with me, what I am, and what your own humanity means.

Morning came. Esau approached at the head of his 400 men, and Jacob came forth to meet him and his fate. And Esau, he of the hunt, he of the quick impulse and the burning anger, had also grown in the long time since he had last seen his brother. Esau ran to his brother, held him in his arms, and kissed him. Jacob looked at his brother and cried. Esau looked at Jacob and cried as well.

And the brothers were together as one and the long years forgotten. And there was peace between them.

Book VII - Joseph

ou might find it interesting to speculate what would have happened if everyone had stayed put. Perhaps these Biblical ancestors of the Israelites would have faded into the forgotten realms of history, without leaving the legacy of their way of looking at "the Lord of Hosts" — a.k.a. yours truly. Perhaps there would have been no Ten Commandments, no Torah, no nation of Israel, no glory of King David and his city of Jerusalem — no Judaism, and hence no Christianity, and no Islam. And perhaps we wouldn't even be having this discussion right now.

But as it turned out, the descendants of Abraham made their way into Egypt — and that became the source of their troubles and yet the source of their triumph. And it all begins with Jacob's beloved son, Joseph, or as he was called by the Egyptians: "Zaphnath-paaneah" (which meant something like "Discoverer of Hidden Things" — and what those things were you'll understand in due course).

If you read the Bible story of Joseph, you might notice that there really isn't a lot of me in this one. Not that this reflects poorly on Joseph — he sort of took me as a given and did the best he could under some very trying circumstances. I'm not going to go into the whole story of Joseph — it took Thomas Mann about fifteen hundred pages to tell the tale in his four-part *Joseph and His Brothers*, and if we continue this at *that rate*, you won't finish reading this one before Armageddon.[71]

Of course, you can always do the "Joseph and the Technicolor Dreamcoat" version if you wish instead—though I think poor Jacob, Joseph and all his brethren would be turning in their graves over that one, considering that the patriarchs' idea of a musical was joining together and clapping hands while someone blew into a shofar.

It's perfectly true that Jacob loved Joseph above his other eleven sons. I'm not condoning it—it did set the kids up for some rather nasty sibling rivalry—but I do understand it. To Jacob, Joseph was the constant reminder of his beloved Rachel, Joseph's mother—he had the same wavy brown hair and baby blue eyes that his mother had. When Joseph looked at you, even when he was a baby, you would catch a glimpse of the hidden depths behind his eyes—the sense that there was always something private and quite profound going on inside of him. Even I admit Joseph was one handsome child—always laughing and smiling. That kid had some kind of infectious chuckle—you would watch him, and you just had to smile. Just a real endearing boy!

You may ask about Benjamin, who after all, was Joseph's younger brother, and the baby of the family. Sorry to say but, Jacob unintentionally held it against little Benjamin that Rachel had died

---

[71] Figuratively speaking, of course. I don't even mean to imply that Armageddon is in the plan. Though if you do succeed in blowing yourselves to Kingdom Come, don't blame me, humanity!

in giving him birth—not to say that Jacob didn't love Benjamin, but he paled next to Joseph. And, the other brothers, being of different mothers than Joseph and Benjamin, just could not compete in Jacob's eyes.

Joseph did not help matters by being a real smart-ass sometimes. You just don't go around rubbing your sibling's faces in the "Pop likes me best" department. You remember those so-called dreams that the Bible mentions? First, there was the one about his brother's sheaves of grain bowing down to his, and then the one about the sun, and the moon, and the eleven stars bowing down to him—I mean, not the smartest move telling your family those kind of things.... especially as Joseph made them up. If you have a large family, well, you know how sibling rivalry gets sometimes. And then there was the tattling. Okay, so his brothers liked to party a bit when they were out tending the flocks. A seventeen-year-old just does not look all that good snitching to Daddy about everything his elder brothers did. It was bound to piss them off.

Just not a good move. The real problem was that Joseph was just full of himself—he thought he was God's gift to the world, so to speak.

He wasn't, of course.

The traditional story, as told in Genesis, has it that Joseph's brothers got so jealous of him that when Jacob sent him to check up on them, they saw him coming and plotted to kill him. It would seem that one of the brothers, Reuben, had a conscience because he convinced the others to merely (!) bind up Joseph and put him in a pit while they considered what to do with him. Actually, he was going to wait for a chance to free Joseph, but you really have to wonder what would have happened when Joseph returned home to Jacob and told him what happened. That would have been interesting! Would Jacob have disowned his other sons, and would we now be talking about the Joe-ish people instead of the Jewish people[72] since the name "Jew" comes from Judah?

It's so trite to say that "history is told by the victors,"[73] but don't you wonder why Joseph (who is not really mentioned anywhere in Egyptian history) comes across as such a major player in the Bible story? Well, who do you think wrote the whole thing down—it was the descendants of Joseph and his sons, of course! Do you think that the descendants of Judah would write such nasty things about their forefather?[74] So, of course, Joseph comes out looking good, and the other brothers come out on the short end of the stick.

Just to begin to set the record straight: Joseph was not captured by his brothers, and he was not sold to traders who took

---

[72] Yeah, I know that's an awful pun. Even with me, they can't always be winners.

[73] I prefer "history is distorted by the victors." Just an example—Americans are very quick to remind the French about how the US saved them in World War II and accuse them of ingratitude when France doesn't blindly support US positions. It's quite convenient that the Americans forget that if the French hadn't interceded on their side during the Revolutionary War there would most likely not even be a United States. The English would have finally whipped Washington! So, who're the ingrates?

[74] Unless there was some unresolved dysfunctional family stuff going on here!

him to Egypt as a slave! And if you read between the lines of a story inserted right into the middle of the Joseph tale, you might intimate what the truth of the matter was. I'm referring to the curious story of Judah and Tamar, which interrupts the adventures of Joseph with a nasty tale of how Judah supposedly had sex with his own daughter-in-law. Ever wonder why this story is even inserted here? I'll give you a clue: it wasn't Judah!

It was Joseph who had encountered the woman the Bible calls Tamar and later denied the whole thing until Tamar proved him wrong pretty much as the tale is told about Judah, though even in the case of Judah the Bible tries to clean up the story a bit.

First of all, the real name of the woman in question was Tzefirah. She actually was Joseph's first-cousin through Judah. Joseph became entranced by her and invited her to dinner. She was initially reluctant but, flattered by the attention and admittedly somewhat attracted to her cousin, eventually agreed. Well, you know how it goes— a bit too much wine and one thing led to another and after a night of passion, [75] Joseph felt pretty damn pleased with himself. This is, until about three months later, when Tzefirah realized she was pregnant with Joseph's child, and when the camel dung hit the tent wall (as the original saying has it), Jacob and his other sons were appalled, to say the least. To try to hush the whole scandal up, Judah suggested that Joseph get out of town on the next caravan to Egypt.

---

[75] More Joseph's than Tzefirah's.

And so, Joseph took to the road.

But if you think this humbled him, no way. Of course, he had to come up with some way to make a living, so Joseph set himself up as an interpreter of dreams. This was quite the thing at the time in old Egypt—since the temple priests were clueless about it and Sigmund Freud would not be born for about five thousand years or so. They would do their best to interpret what Ptah or Bastet or Osiris were telling someone in a dream, but since these archangels of mine didn't have anything to do with sending dreams to people in the first place, I'm sure you can understand how this might not have really worked out.

Joseph had two advantages: First, he was pretty darn smart, and second, he was pretty darn lucky. Actually, he was usually right about two-thirds of the time, which is darn good. It's certainly a lot better than your economists predicting job growth, or your stock analysts predicting where the Dow is going to wind up next week, and it completely slaughters your local weatherperson (oops, sorry, meteorologist).[76] He also had those good innocent exotic boy-from-the-boondocks looks that turned the women on, but because the Egyptian males saw him as a hick from the sticks they didn't feel threatened by him. So, Joseph soon developed quite a reputation and quite a following.

---

[76] And isn't it great that in those jobs you can be wrong more than you are right—and keep the job! What would happen to your job if you were wrong more often that you are right, eh? Guess you could always be the "head of the free world," eh?

Then, along came Potiphar. Potiphar was suffering from a recurring nightmare---and I don't mean Sex and the City reruns. Though it did have to do with sex.

Every night, he would dream that he was rolled up in a huge piece of papyrus — large enough to completely cover him from head to toe. There was a dark cave in front of him, and he was trying desperately to get into that cave, who's opening seemed just a little too small to let him inside. He repeatedly pushed himself into the opening, which seemed to expand a bit more each time. It was warm, and there was s viscous fluid oozing out of it around it, that encased him as he kept thrusting himself in and out of it. Then, suddenly an explosion and he saw himself as what looked like a strange snake, with a large head and a very skinny body, swimming through a dark underwater cave where a single white ball was suspended in the center. As he reached the ball, the top of his head would start to smoke, flare up for a second, and then settle down into a deep reddish glow. Finally, he would find himself, transformed back into his real form, traveling head first slowly into a yawning black pit with a faint light-filled opening far in the distance. As he entered this hole, he would feel warmth and stickiness enveloping him as he pushed his way towards the light. Then, he'd wake up in terror.

He'd visited the temple priest — they had no explanation. He went to the local apothecary — there was no potion he could give him to stop him from dreaming this dream, night after night. He went to the mages—but the idea of rolling around in Nile mud and then letting it dry all over him into a black cake in the hot Egyptian sun just didn't seem to appeal to him. There seemed to be no one who could help him.

Finally, someone pointed him in Joseph's direction. He told his dream to Joseph. Joseph smiled and then explained the dream's significance.[77]

That evening, for the first time in weeks, Potiphar slept peacefully through the night, much to his relief and delight. The next morning, he sought Joseph out once more. Thanking him most profusely, Potiphar invited Joseph to be an overnight guest in his home to celebrate his freedom from the dream which had enslaved him. I suppose that Potiphar was a little nervous that this dream or another like it would come back, and he wanted Joseph around for a while for a quick fix. Joseph gratefully accepted and appeared that night at Potiphar's home for the great feast.

Egyptian royalty was known for its great abundance of exotic foods, and Joseph enjoyed many unique delicacies that had not been available to him when he had been living with Jacob and his brothers. But, there was one delicacy that especially caught his eye.

All through the meal a young Egyptian beauty served him food, poured him wine, and fussed over him. And why not? After

---

[77] And since we're not here to feed your prurient interest—I'm NOT going to tell you what Joseph said. You can figure that out for yourselves. You've already become much too much a society of voyeurs. Please, get a life already!

all, Joseph's good looks as an adolescent had manifested themselves in a remarkably attractive and virile-looking young man of twenty-five. Potiphar, in his delight at his salvation, never noticed the looks that passed between the young beauty and the young man.

She smiled at Joseph. He smiled back.

"Perhaps our honored guest would like some tea to end his meal?" she said, somewhat seductively.

"Excellent, my dear," Potiphar said. "None for me though, you know it doesn't agree with me."

The young woman bowed, excused herself and went off. In a few minutes, she was back with two cups of streaming white tea.

"A special brew of my own, from the leaves of the lotus. I have always found it refreshing and invigorating to my spirit. I hope you like it."

Joseph raised his cup in salute to the young woman, and they slowly drank their tea while the entertainment continued.

Perhaps a half-hour went by. Joseph found himself more and more intrigued by this young woman. She batted her deep violet eyes at him. He looked at her with desire. Still, Potiphar remained oblivious to what was happening before his eyes.

And that night, after all had retired, would it be entirely shocking if Joseph, hearing the delighted laughter of a young woman approaching his bed, welcomed her in? After all, he was young. He was virile. He was horny.

And would it be totally surprising if, after a night of passion, Joseph awoke to find his host standing over him, and learned that the beautiful Egyptian girl with whom he had shared such delights was in reality the wife of his host?

I will turn the veil over the beating Joseph received, the walling of Potiphar's wife who pleaded her innocence to her husband, claiming that Joseph had forced her into his bed, and the stupidity of an elderly man who thought that money and power were enough to keep such a trophy. Potiphar was about to strike the boy's head off when he began to realize that being the butt of such a scandal would not be the best thing for him in front of the Pharaoh and the court. So, Joseph was quickly hushed up and hustled off to jail, where the cuckolded husband hoped the young man would be forgotten and left to rot.

But, that was not how it was to be. For after Potiphar was caught cooking the Royal Treasury books and was cheerily executed by Pharaoh's orders in a manner so painful that I prefer to spare you the details, [78] something or someone intervened in Joseph's life. You can call it "Fate," or "Destiny," or "Luck," or me, or perhaps we could call it "Melvin." The last one is roughly the English equivalent of the Egyptian name of the Pharaoh's butler

Because, as the Bible tells us, [79] both the Pharaoh's baker and butler had been thrown into prison beside him for various offenses

---

[78] Though it probably would have gotten its own chapter in the Bible!
[79] Yes, occasionally the Bible gets some of the story correct.

171

to the royal personage. Both of them had dreams, and Joseph correctly interpreted them, telling the two which one of them would be restored to Pharaoh's favor, and which one would soon be losing his head. And so, it came to pass.

Here the Bible would tell you that Pharaoh had a dream about seven fat cows being followed up and then swallowed by seven lean cows, and the baker remembered Joseph in prison and got him out to interpret the Pharaoh's dream. To tell the truth, the dream was about something fat being swallowed by something small—but it wasn't exactly cows that were the problem, if you get my drift. If you don't get my drift…well, if you consider that the Pharaoh's Biblical dream has to do with fertility… No, still don't get it, do you?

Okay, let's be blunt. It seems that the father of the nation couldn't father. His dream was about a certain part of his anatomy. Seven nice fat, big, potent ones being swallowed by seven skinny, small flaccid ones.

So, it wasn't really that the wise men and the priests couldn't interpret Pharaoh's dream—it was rather obvious to them what the connection was. It was just that, valuing the part of their anatomy above their torsos more than they valued the part of the anatomy troubling their ruler, it occurred to them that it might be a bit dangerous to speak about it to the Pharaoh. And even if they did, the only treatment they knew about was to rub the hearts of baby crocodiles on the royal shaft—and you might imagine just how well that would work. [80]

So, when everyone copped out on this hot item, they were quite willing to listen to Bob when he suggested that they bring in an "expert" like Joseph.

Besides, he was expendable.

Joseph was taken from the prison. While they cleaned him up—after all, a year in a prison cell isn't the best thing for bodily hygiene—and got him an acceptable outfit, the high priest explained the situation to Joseph.

Joseph nodded thoughtfully. And he recalled some of the lessons his mother Rachel had taught him about herbs and flowers. He remembered the tea that Potiphar's wife had made for him out of lotus leaves, and the effect it had had on him.

And, with a touch of the doctor and the touch of the charlatan, the touch of the psychiatrist and the touch of the showman, he soon had Pharaoh up and around.[81]   And he soon had Pharaoh eating out of his hand.[82]

Which is really how Joseph became the governor of all Egypt, subject to Pharaoh himself.

---

[80] And if you can't imagine, the answer is "not at all."
[81] Literally!
[82] Not literally!

Meanwhile, back in Canaan, old Jacob missed his son. Figuring that more than enough time had elapsed since the Tamar incident, Jacob sent Benjamin to Egypt to tell Joseph it was time to come home.

Once in Egypt, the poor boy was astonished by the magnificence of the great kingdom—unlike anything he knew back home. And once he made himself known to Joseph, it took very little on Joseph's part to convince him that "we got a good thing going here, let's not mess it up."

To be truthful, Joseph didn't miss his brothers all that much, but seeing Benjamin reminded him of his father—and he was overcome with the desire to see Jacob once more.

Writing a long note to Jacob, he sent Benjamin as his emissary back to Jacob. Perhaps Jacob and his other ten sons would have met Benjamin's stories of what Egypt was like with some disbelief, and they would have scoffed at his tale of how Joseph had risen in power and affluence—but his escort of chariots and precious gifts kind of tilted the scales in his favor. Especially the part of Joseph's note that said, "More where this came from!"

And soon Jacob and his sons made their way to Joseph in Egypt.

Just one little problem—and it wasn't a matter of religion. You can call it class snobbery, but the Egyptians just weren't too keen about shepherds. They weren't up on the latest royal gossip; they just weren't that into fashion; they went months—maybe years — without shaving…and then, there was this funky smell that seemed always to follow them around. Why, you certainly wouldn't want your daughter to get involved with one! — or your son, for that matter.

Jacob and his family settled in an area known as Goshen, about a good day's journey away from the upper-class district of the land of Rameses. And they would pretty well dwell there for the next four hundred years or so until the time of Moses.

What tends to puzzle scholars nowadays about the whole Joseph story is that there is absolutely NO Egyptian record that he ever existed — neither under the name of Joseph nor under Zaphnath-paaneah. You would have expected that he would have been mentioned in some hieroglyphic stele or on someone's tomb down in the Valley of the Kings, or that there would have been at least one statue dedicated to the man, or perhaps some mention of him chiseled into some pillar in Egypt. Nope — nothing, nada. Why? What happened?

Well, you could make a case that, considering what happened all those years later when Moses burst on the scene, the Egyptians might not exactly want to commemorate his ancestor, nor would they want anyone to know that they had a Jewish governor at some point of time.

But, that's not it.

Those of you familiar with the Biblical story of Joseph might be wondering what about the famine that Joseph was supposed to have predicted and guided Egypt through to his great glory. The Bible says that because, thanks to his interpretations of the Pharaoh's dreams, Joseph knew that a famine was coming, he gathered up all the food in Egypt during the preceding seven years of plenty and stored it all against the seven years of famine. Well, the truth of it is that he didn't do any of it because of predictions of a famine — that just serves as a convenient justification for some of the things Joseph did while governor.[83]

Joseph gathered up the food from his subjects as a form of tax because he suffered from one of those peculiar diseases that often hit your leaders — its call "spending beyond your means." First, he was content to make the food business a government monopoly under his control. All the farmers had to sell their grain and other food goods to his agents at a price set by Joseph. Then all of Egypt had to buy food from him at a price set by — you guessed it! — Joseph again! Naturally, he was making a mint! And it wasn't that he would just sell it back to the Egyptians at inflated prices; no, he'd sell it to anyone as long as they met his price. Does this make Joseph the first capitalist?

Of course, this slowly drove more and more Egyptians into poverty. That was okay with Joseph — he was too tender-hearted to let them starve — if they couldn't pay with gold, they could pay him with their cattle; if they had no cattle, they could pay him with their land and with themselves. Yep, in a strange foreshadowing of the

---

[83] Remember, who did I say wrote the whole story down in the first place?

fate of the Hebrews in Egypt, Joseph made the Egyptians slaves to Pharaoh and hence to himself as well. You can read all about this in the Bible.[84]

Some nice guy, that Joseph, eh?

Any wonder that the country was on the point of revolution? Only the priests were safe from Joseph, and they were themselves alarmed at what was going on. And the priests began to whisper into Pharaoh's ear that maybe—just maybe—he should consider that Joseph was overstaying his welcome.

At first, Pharaoh paid them no mind. Joseph was still his golden boy. Hadn't Joseph cured his "delicate condition"? Wasn't Pharaoh wealthy beyond wealth with Joseph's "reforms"? Pharaoh knew a good thing when he saw it.

And Joseph wasn't worried. He also had the market on mandrake root.

But, as often happens to those who believe their own hype, Joseph made a fatal mistake. Because while he was gathering up the people from the countryside and moving them around to suit his fancy, things got worse. If all the food and the profit were under his control, if all the people were slaves, then the only inducement for them to grow the crops on which the whole edifice depended was fear of punishment. So, they only grew the bare minimum they needed to satisfy Joseph's collectors—and Joseph didn't notice at first that day by day he was collecting less and less.

---

[84] Genesis, Chapter 47:13-26

And it was then that famine, unpredicted by Joseph, fell upon an unprepared Egypt. Starvation reared in the face of the slaves of Egypt and suddenly Pharaoh saw the problem in enslaving so many of his people: there were a lot more of them then there were guards to control them. And while the Bible says that the world came to Egypt for help with the famine, the truth is that Egypt, mighty Egypt, was faced with the possibility of having to beg for its food.

And that could not be allowed. Someone had to be responsible; someone had to be sacrificed to appease the masses. And that someone was Joseph.

He was stripped of his offices, his wealth, his prestige, and banished to live out his days in Goshen with his brothers. Pharaoh ordered the food stores opened to the people and realizing that a nice, sharp knife in the back could easily kill even a god such as himself, began the emancipation of the Egyptians. He gave them seed for their fields to grow food. But he wasn't entirely a fool about it—for he ruled that one-fifth of the produce would be his part—and after being slaves and possibly starving to death, paying a twenty percent tax didn't seem all that bad a deal to the populous.

So, the name of Zaphnath-paaneah was blotted out from the land of Egypt. And the years slowly turned until 400 years passed by, and a child was born who would change the Hebrew people forever.

Book VII - Joseph

Book VIII – Of Moses and the Exodus

Four hundred years and thirty years they stayed in Goshen. While to me, four hundred years or so isn't even an idle thought—on the human scale, a lot changes in four hundred years. Just for perspective: In four hundred years, humanity has gone from threatening Galileo with heresy for saying the earth circles around the sun to traveling to the moon and Mars.[85] In four hundred years, England, Spain, and France went from finding colonies and becoming world powers to losing their colonial possessions. Within four hundred years, America went from the founding of the little settlement of Jamestown, Virginia to becoming the superpower of the world—from the Revolutionary War through the War of 1812 through the Civil War through the Spanish-American War through World War I through World War II through Korea through Vietnam through Iraq through Afghanistan and back to Iraq again (and, mind you, that's just the highlights!).

Not to forget that in four hundred years you've gone from flintlocks to the hydrogen bomb—way to go, humanity!

And of course, let's not forget the vast progress you've made in religious tolerance! I'm glad that you've all finally come to realize that I don't give a damn what door you approach me

---

[85] That's not to say that there aren't some who still think it's flat and the center of the Universe.

though, that there is NO one religion that has a monopoly on my truth, that what's in your heart and what kind of person you are may matter a great deal more to me, and that you've finally stopped killing each other in my name...

Who do I think I'm kidding?

...Oh well, a God can dream, can't he?

Four hundred and thirty years. In Egypt, Pharaohs came, and Pharaohs went. And, as the Bible states in the opening lines of Exodus, there came a time when "a new king ascended the throne of Egypt, one that did not know about Joseph."[86] The Bible pretty well ignores everything that happened in those four hundred years before Moses. But we won't.

The Egyptians — as well as most of the ancient world at this time — worshipped many gods. I suppose that's partly my own fault — the angels were spending a lot of time on Earth intermingling with the population, and — as I already mentioned with Bastet, Ptah and Osiris, for example--the populous soon thought of them as gods in their own right. There were gods for everything — gods of the water, gods of rain, gods of sun, gods of the moon, gods of the harvest, gods of the hunt, gods of birth, gods of death, gods of the afterlife, gods of volcanoes, gods of music, gods of war, gods of peace, gods of hair loss, gods of sex, gods of money, gods of fire,

---

[86] Exodus, 1, 8

gods of cold, gods of bowel movements,—gods for just about everything you could think of. Why did I tolerate it?

Hey, no skin off of my nose—God is God. I 'm really not the kind of megalomaniac so many of you seem to think I am.[87] As long as no one was getting hurt by worshipping or not worshipping a particular god, what do I care? Live and let live works for me.

Actually, having all these gods seemed too chaotic for some of your ancestors. At first, they attempted to have some order by imposing a God (with a capital "G") to be head god over the other gods—which just coincidentally served to justify absolute rule by Pharaohs or kings or emperors, etc. And this worked out fine for many—particularly the Pharaohs, kings, and emperors.

But there were those who concluded that having one and only one god was more than enough. And, about thirty-three thousand three hundred and eighty years ago, one such a fellow just happened to be a Pharaoh of Egypt called Amenhotep IV. He took his name from the god Amon, who was known as "the Hidden One." But Amenhotep IV wasn't content with the traditional view of the gods of Egypt

He concluded that there was indeed one god ruling over all. So far so good. But, he just happened to think that this one god just happened to be the sun—whom the Egyptians called "Aton." The sun, eh? Just think—if he had only listened to his mommy

---

[87] Yeah, I know "You shall have no other Gods before me"—but we haven't gotten to the Ten Commandments just yet, have we? Patience.

when she warned him against staring at the sun all day! Anyway, in keeping with his beliefs, he changed his name to Akhenaton, which meant "Glory of Aton," and moved the capital from beautiful Thebes to a new city he was in the process of building, to be called Akhenaton ("the Horizon of Aton").

And like any good religious leader who feels he has the absolute truth, he started a war of persecution against the priests of all the other gods of Egypt. Aten or nothing!

It was soon to be nothing! The Egyptians weren't all too happy with all this, and Akhenaton died under some "mysterious circumstances,"[88] and things reverted to normal in merry old Egypt. And the priests tried to blot out all traces of the hated Aton and the name Akhenaton from the Egyptian records.

Of course, they didn't entirely succeed. Because the idea of one god and one religion would percolate as an undercurrent in Egypt. Until along came Moses.

Need I say that the Bible gives special importance to Moses. After all, the first five books of the Old Testament are collectively referred to as the Five Books of Moses.[89] And no, Moses did not write any of them—how on earth could he tell you that he was "...a

---

[88] "Mysterious circumstances," indeed. A nice way for the persecuted priests, seizing power again, to get around saying that he'd been assassinated---by those very priests!

[89] Also called the "Torah," which is Hebrew for 'Teaching," in Judaism, or the "Penta-teuch" which means "five books

hundred and twenty years old when he died, his sight undimmed, his vigor unimpaired"[90] or "there has never yet risen in Israel a prophet like Moses..."[91] while he was still alive to write it?. Did he dictate it to a psychic after his death? Of the first five books, the story of Moses takes up the all but the first one of them — and we've gone through over one hundred and eighty pages here before we even got to this point. [92] But, don't worry; I think I can tell you all about Moses within a single chapter. So, deep breath, humanity, and let's begin.

The sun beats down hard in the wilderness and has no mercy on the wanderer. Tired, and thirsty, he thinks back to what brought him to this pass.

"Stupid sheep!"

Moses took a swig from the water bag that his wife had prepared for him for the day's work. Funny tasting water. "I hope Zipporah isn't playing one of her practical jokes again." he thought. He took another couple of sips.

What a bring-down, Moses thought. Once upon a time, he'd been a prince in Egypt, now here he was a lowly shepherd about to get into trouble with his father-in-law because he kept daydreaming and losing the little bastards, — oops, darlings. If it hadn't been for him and his temper, he'd still be enjoying the good life in

---

[90] Deuteronomy 34:7
[91] Deuteronomy 34:10
[92] The second book of the Bible, known as "Exodus".

Thebes, but no! He'd been warned a number of times, "Moses! Watch your temper," "Moses! Stop with the kvetching already," "Moses! Why don't you go pick on somebody your own size," and of course, there was "That Moses! Pssh! Just because he's a prince, he thinks he's a Prince. One of these days he's going to go too far, and then...ooh boy!"

Finally, there was that day when everything changed.

He'd gone down to visit the Jewish slaves yet again. Moses had always been fascinated by them, though he could not tell you why. There were all these stories that the Egyptians told about them...how they were so different from the Egyptians, they didn't worship the same gods that the Egyptians did, their customs were different—why, they even tended sheep. How disgusting! No good Egyptian would ever let her daughter go anywhere near one of those...those sheep lovers!!!! Good thing Pharaoh had turned them into slaves, made them build new monuments and new cities after that Akhenaton nonsense with Thebes...yep, things were much better now.

Well, that was Moses...always fascinated with the forbidden. Just could not seem to mind his own business. Look where it got him. There he was out watching the Hebrew slaves at work in the hot sun when an old man stumbled at his feet under the weight of a load of bricks. The Egyptian overseer thought this was hysterical, but while he was having a good laugh, Moses went to the old man, sat him in the shade, and began to give him a drink of water from his own water bag.

"We'll have none of this!" said the overseer. "If he can't meet his quota, no water for him." He grabbed the water bag from the old man, threw it on the ground and laughed as the precious water fell on the hot ground and evaporated. He pulled out his whip and began to beat the old man. "Get back to work and earn your keep."

"Why, you son of a dog!" cried Moses. Before he even knew what he was doing, he had wrestled the whip from the overseer and was using it against him. "See how you like it!"

"No sir, don't," cried the old man, pulling on Moses' arm. "Don't get in trouble because of me."

A couple of Hebrew slaves saw what was happening and tried to pull Moses away from the overseer, but....

Too late! Moses had beaten the overseer to death.

"Run, young master," said the old man. "The Pharaoh's justice is death to any who kill his work masters."

And before he could realize, the hot-tempered young Moses was off, and heading out into the Egyptian desert bound for...

"Damn sheep, where are you?"

... that flight across the desert, hot, dry, no GPS in those days to get you to the next oasis.

But after a three-day journey, he reached the site of the last known spring, only to find it dry and barren of life in the increasing heat of the summer desert sun.

Have you ever been to the desert? Those dry lands of Sinai, or Judea for example. Ever felt how the sun beats down on you with such a dry heat that you don't even sweat? The water evaporates out of you without you even being aware of it. Suddenly without any sort of warning, without even the sensation of being thirsty, the desert starts to take you over. You begin to sway with dizziness, and it's an observant friend who forces you to drink from his water bottle. You're dehydrating without even knowing it. You don't even feel thirsty, but the water revitalizes you. It's such an easy thing.

But, you were lucky. Someone was with you, knew what was happening, and was able to save the situation before it went too far.

And food! Bit of a miracle that you'd survive at all on what you could find for food. The locusts were okay if a bit crunchy, but those dung beetles really tasted like crap!

Of course, we are not talking about your sanitized, homogenized, pasteurized, transistorized, accessorized, semi-lobotomized modern world here. And if I were you, I would not be too smug about how you would have survived in any of the societies of that ancestral time— "Survivor" TV shows, my ass! Out there alone under such influences, a person already seeking for that which is greater than himself might equally hear the voice of "God" or "Satan" calling him. So perhaps it is not such a surprise that it is the dessert that gave forth so many visionaries, so many prophets, and so many "beloved of God."

Or perhaps the message has always already inside you, and only awaits the turning of the proper key to reveal itself.

So, alone, burning by day, freezing by night, Moses was subject to all kinds of bizarre thoughts and hallucinations. Once he thought that he saw some sort of a blue box appear out of nowhere with a horrible grinding sound, a bright light coming from the top. Two people (no, it must have been angels!) came out, wearing the strangest costumes he'd ever seen. The one who appeared to be the leader pointed at Moses. Then the two ran back inside, and with that same awful noise, the box disappeared as suddenly as it has appeared. Or there were those times, as he came closer the more mountainous regions to the southwest, there would be a sudden whoosh and fire would appear out of the ground like a sudden flame, distant rumbles of thunder that shook the ground, yet no rain would come. He'd just about begun to think he'd entered the land of the dead when he stumbled into the oasis of Midian.

He sat down by the cool of a tree and drank some water. Refreshed, he watched as seven young women approached the well to gather water for their flocks. However, a couple of shepherds stood in their way.

"Hey, Baby....," said one of them, making crude kissing noises.

Another one leaned over a rock, almost exposing himself to the young girls.

"C'mon, Zipporah," he oozed at the one that Moses thought was the prettiest. Twisting about to block her as she tried to get away, the shepherd grabbed her by the arm. "You know you want it!"

That was too much for Moses. He got up, and grabbed the second shepherd by the arm, forcing him to let go of the trembling Zipporah. He twisted the shepherd's arm back, and then suddenly let go, sending the idiot sprawling into the dust around the well.

"Hey, do the hell do you think you're messing with!" roared the first shepherd. He charged at Moses, who grabbed him with both arms around the chest, then lifted him up into the air, and held him there.

"Who the hell do you think *you're* messing with!" Moses replied. The second shepherd took a good look at the stranger who had dared challenge them, realized that the foreigner had an advantage in height and strength, and quickly learned what would eventually become the old proverb "The wise win renown, but disgrace is the portion of fools." [93] And "A scoundrel and a knave is one who goes around with crooked talk, a wink of the eye, a nudge

---

[93] Proverbs 3:35

with the foot, a gesture with the fingers. His mind is set on subversion; all the time he plots mischief and sows strife. That is why disaster comes upon him suddenly; in an instant, he is broken beyond all remedy."[94] And again "When a stupid man talks, contention follows; his words provoke blows."[95]

Seeing that his opponent had had enough, Moses gave him a kick in the rear and sent him on his way.

He turned to the women. He liked what he saw. "I trust you are all okay." He looked at Zipporah, and his heart skipped a beat. "Not bad," he thought. "Not bad at all." He gave her his most winning smile.

Zipporah looked back at the noble stranger. Her heart skipped a beat. "Not bad," she thought. "Not bad at all." Aloud she said, "Kind sir, thank you for saving my sisters and me from that gang of fools. Please accept the hospitality of my father's tent. I know he will want to meet you and reward you for your kindness."

Since he had no other plans or place to go, and that those seven sisters seemed mighty attractive and that after all he could do much worse, Moses gladly accepted.

And what would have been a small overnight became a long-term stay. Eventually, Moses married Zipporah, and in the course of time, they had a boy named Gershom and then another

---

[94] Proverbs 6:12-15
[95] Proverbs 18:6

named Eliezer. And Moses became generally resigned to his life, tending the sheep of his father-in-law, Jethro the priest of Midian, during the day and coming home to Zipporah and Gershom. Of course, sometimes he couldn't help himself, he'd think back on the good life in Egypt, and Zipporah knew that those were the times to best to mix him a batch of her special tea and leave him alone until he calmed down.

Days blended into days, months in months, and year to years, and life went on its way.

But life has a way of throwing a left curve just when you think you've already caught the ball. Don't blame me!

"Oh, come on, sheepy, sheepy. Nice sheepy, sheepy. I've got some nice fresh grass for you," Moses called. One of the real hassles of being a shepherd was that when a sheep went missing, you had to go search for it. And here he had fallen asleep, and the whole flock had scattered.

Moses followed their tracks and saw that they followed the path up Mt. Horeb.

"Great," he thought. "Like I'm in the mood for a hike." But it was his duty. Taking a deep drink from his water bag, he started to climb the mountain.

"Here I am. Could have been a leader of men in Egypt, now I'm just a leader of sheep! Where are you, you little...."

He thought he heard the bleating of his sheep and got excited. "There you are, you little...." Not paying attention, he slipped, and fell down, banging his head against the rocky slope, and knocking himself unconscious for about ten minutes.

When he came to......

The missing sheep was licking his face. "Gotcha!" said Moses, grabbing the sheep. Then, feeling woozy, he sat down to get his bearings. He was high up the mountain, but he could feel a deep heat from beneath where he was sitting. The air itself smelt of gas. Then, he saw it.

The bush. To his eyes, it looked like flames were coming from the middle of the bush, and yet it was not being consumed. The way Moses would tell it, he heard a voice coming from the bush saying "Moses! Moses!"

Now, I hate to bust your bubble here, but let me explain what was really going on. That liquid that Moses was swigging wasn't exactly water. Zipporah had filled his bag with a brew made from 2 plants: the acacia tree and the harmal bush. Not exactly the Biblical equivalent of Gatorade. Actually, he was swilling a liquid concoction of N,N-Dimethyltryptamine (DMT), which for those of you who don't know, is a psychedelic! You could say Moses was tripping, and the DMT was making him hallucinate, making it seem that time was stopping. To you, what would have been a second, was now to Moses an hour.

So, Moses watched a bush burn. It only took a minute or two in real time, but in the altered state Moses was in, to him the bush was still aflame like a still photograph.

Anyway, with some hesitation, Moses came closer to the bush, and replied: "I guess that's me!"

And the bush said, "I am the God of your father, the God of Abraham, the God of Isaac, and the God of Jacob."

And Moses said, "You're a bush!"

"Oy, "the bush sighed. "Don't be a smartass! I'm talking to you *through* this bush."

"Oh," Moses nodded. "O-kay. So, what can I do for you, err-God you say?"

"When your ancestor Jacob went to Egypt with his people, he thought it was only going to be a short visit. But, his son, Joseph, convinced him to stay, and things were pretty good for them for a while. But years passed by, the Pharaohs forgot about Jacob and Joseph and saw their descendants as troublemakers and low-lives, and eventually made them slaves. But I haven't forgotten, Moses. I want you to go back to Egypt and tell the Pharaoh to let the Israelites return to the land of Abraham."

"Whoa! You want me to do *what?*"

The bush flared up, and thunder sounded all around Moses.

"I want you to go to Egypt and bring back the descendants of Jacob."

"Why me?"

"Why not you? You're Egyptian; you were royalty, the people who were after you for the overseer's murder are dead. You hate being a shepherd, and don't tell me you don't think you were meant for greater stuff. Moses, you pull this off and books will be written about you, you'll be remembered throughout the ages; people will name their kids after you; there'll be ..."

Moses smiled. His ego, never all that small, was being massaged in a very nice way—drugs aside. Yeah, why not him? If he had stayed in Egypt, who knows? He might have wound up Pharaoh himself by now! Lousy breaks. He was tired of the dirt, tired of the bleating of sheep, and the boredom of it all... Taking on the Pharaoh himself, now with God on his side? Wow! That would be a hard one to top.

"You got it, Lord."

"Okay, now get packing!"

The flames surrounding the bush rose higher, finally consuming it as the ground seemed to shake in the wake of a tremendous crash of thunder. Moses was overwhelmed and fell to the ground, unconscious.

When he woke, all was quiet, except for the gently bleating of a long-missing sheep.

Moses leaped to his feet, and he and the sheep made their way down Mt. Horeb and then back to the herd.

And in the early evening, an excited Moses rushed into his tent and told Zipporah the good news. Oddly, she did not seem all that pleased.

"You're going to Egypt?" she asked, incredulously

"Yep."

"You say, God spoke to you out of a flaming bush, and told you to free the Israelites there?"

"That's about the size of it."

She looked at him for a moment. "So, tell me, Mr. Wonderful, while you're doing this, what am I doing? What's your son doing?"

"Well, you, Gershom, and Eliezer will be here, waiting for me, of course. I'll bring you all back some nice presents from Thebes."

"Uh-huh," she nodded, and then repeated what Moses had said in a very soft whisper. "You're going to Egypt, and the boys and I get to stay here until you return?"

Quickly she threw a pot at him and reached for a knife. "In a pig's eye, we will. I'm not going to have my husband doing who knows what with who knows what in the big city while I'm stuck in a backwater little sty of a place with two little kids. Over my dead body."

Moses backed away, keeping his eye on the knife. It was just sharp enough and big enough to put a serious dent in any future plans he might have to obey the old command "be fruitful and multiply" — if you get my drift.

"Now wait a minute! Let's talk about this."

Zipporah made a lunge for him, fortunately missing his privates by a few inches.

He grabbed her arm and forced the knife from her hand. "Okay, okay. Have it your way. You and the boys want to go trekking across the desert with me to Egypt, fine. You win."

Years later, when Moses was crossing the Sinai Peninsula with the freed Israelites, the tribesmen would rib him about this. But that wouldn't have looked good to Moses' reputation as a true leader. And so, this fight between Zipporah and Moses kind of got changed in the story of Exodus. It says that "At a lodging place on the way the LORD met him and sought to put him to death. Then Zipporah took a flint and cut off her son's foreskin and touched Moses feet with it and said, 'Surely you are a bridegroom of blood to me!' So, he let him alone. It was then that she said, 'A bridegroom of blood,' because of the circumcision."[96]

Now you tell me, because here's the thing. If I had just sent Moses to save over six hundred thousand men,[97] plus women and children — why would I jeopardize the whole thing over one lousy foreskin?

---

[96] Exodus 4:24-26
[97] Sorry—but Exodus only mentions the number of men, so don't hang any misogynic stuff on me

See, that's what I really get pissed off about. Somehow, someway, I always get blamed for everything. It's too hot---oh, God must be angry. It's too cold—God must be pissed.

Then on top of it, you come up with the dumbest reasons *why* I'm supposed to be angry. There's an earthquake—God wants us to kill the _____.[98] A flood—well, God is mad because we're not sacrificing virgins on the altar.

And please, don't even mention the plagues![99]

Everything is my fault, isn't it?

So, Moses, with his family riding his best donkey made their way to Egypt. He met his brother Aaron by Mt. Sinai, and the small party made their way to Goshen where the Jewish slaves resided.

Now, I'm pretty sure most of you have seen Cecil D. DeMille's *The Ten Commandments* at least once in your life, so you're familiar with the official story of what happened in Egypt—well, at least interpreted by Hollywood—how Moses and Aaron asked Pharaoh to let the Jews go free, and how ten plagues came to Egypt due to his refusal, after which the Pharaoh let them go only to pursue them to the Red Sea and so on....[100]

Well....

---

[98] Fill in the blank with the innocents of your choice!

[99] Okay, I guess we have to, since they'll be coming up in a couple of pages.

[100] Not to mention that great dialogue, like Nefertiti to Moses: "Oh Moses, Moses, you stubborn, splendid, adorable fool!"

As I just said, the first thing Moses did once he arrived in Egypt was to travel to the Hebrew area of Goshen and make himself known to the community. He was a bit surprised at their reaction to his tale of a burning bush, and of God's call for them to return to the land of their forefathers.

"Yeah, right," said one doubter. "You and what army?"

"So, let me understand this," said another. "God speaks to you out of a burning bush and tells you to come here and tell Pharaoh to let the people go. Ha!" he laughed and whispered to his friends, "I think this guy Moses had one too many swigs of the old grape juice, if you know what I mean."

Others just shook their head and sighed, "Ay, meshugunah!" in the language of the times.

"No, no, wait, wait." Moses insisted. "You'll see."

Bit by bit, Moses's story spread through the Jewish community, and eventually to the Egyptian guards, to the priests of the Egyptian temples, and ultimately to Pharaoh himself who, thinking this would be good for a laugh, ordered Moses to be brought before him.

So, Moses traveled from Goshen, which was inland and close to the desert, to the capital city of Pi-Rameses on the Nile Delta.[101]

---

[101] Remember that the Israelites were shepherds when they arrived in Egypt and thus were considered an abomination to the Egyptians. Therefore, their dwelling place was kept far away from the natives—foreshadowing the Ghettos in what, thousands of years later, would become the long, sad history of the Jewish people in the Diaspora.

"So, Moses," said Pharaoh, "what's this story I hear about you leading the slaves out of my kingdom?"

"The one true God has sent me to tell you that they have suffered long enough under your lash, and that you are to let them return to their homeland."

Pharaoh roared with laughter. "The one true God? Ha, you're one of those Akhenaton nuts, one of those sun god worshippers. Why, I thought we got rid of you all years ago."

"The one true God is greater than the Sun. The one true God is the creator of everything, master of all, and is not to be trifled with. Let the people go!"

"'Let the people go'? Or what? He's going to give me a hangnail?"

"Wait, and you'll see."

Pharaoh laughed even harder. "Moses, I like you. This is the best laugh I've had in weeks. Sad but the palace priests aren't exactly the most fun bunch of guys. I had thought of having you killed, but no, no. Let's see how this plays out, eh? Tell your god that I am not going to let anyone go free, and that he's got some balls telling me what to do. Tell him just for that the slaves can now gather their own straw to make the bricks to build my cities. And they better produce at least the same number of bricks each day as before. They'll just have to do more with less. Tell that to your God and let him do his worse. I'll be waiting. Now, you may go."

And here's where Moses got extremely lucky, and the Egyptians got extremely unlucky.

Egypt had enjoyed many years of prosperity. It relied on the yearly flooding of the Nile to water the land so that the crops would flourish. For a number of years, there had been plenty of rain, and the country had prospered. But now the wet period was now just a memory. The climate had changed, and the country was now in a dry period. The temperatures were rising, and Mother Nile, the source of life in the Egyptian valley, had become a slow, muddy waterway.

This was a perfect environment for a particular alga, which scientists would later call the Burgundy Blood algae, to flourish. And as the algae died, the Nile was stained red by their remains.

And behold, the first plague: the Nile turned to Blood.

Moses, seeing this as a sign, went back to the Pharaoh.

"Now, mighty Pharaoh, will you let the people go?"

Pharaoh looked at him. "Are you nuts? This is just temporary. The imperial records show that something like this has happened before, though I admit not as bad as this time. But, give it a while, and things will be back to normal. No way am I going to release the slaves. Now, get out."

Seven days went by, and the Nile had resumed its normal color. Egypt breathed easier, but only for a moment—for the algae had caused the tadpoles that lived in the Nile to develop faster, and now the grown frogs invaded the land. Frogs everywhere, frogs in the bakery, frogs in the kitchen, frogs in the bed, frogs in your hair, frogs in your sandals, frogs when you were eating, frogs when you were defecating, frogs when you were procreating…. Frogs. frogs. frogs.

Again, Moses came before Pharaoh.

"Now what?" asked Pharaoh.

"Egypt is plagued with frogs, "replied Moses. "Now will you let the people go?"

Pharaoh glared at him. "When you have frogs, have frog legs for dinner! Get out of here."

Soon the frogs died. And without the frogs, there was no natural predator to keep the swarms of flies, mosquitos, and other little nasties under control. And the rotting corpses of the fish from the Nile and those of the frogs attracted even more of these pests to the areas around the Nile.

So, the third plague: gnats. Gnats everywhere, gnats in the bakery, gnats in the kitchen, gnats in the bed, gnats in your hair, gnats in your sandals, gnats when you were eating, gnats when you were defecating, gnats when you were procreating…. Gnats, gnats, gnats.

And as the gnats eventually died, came the fourth plague of flies and mosquitos, and the other nasties that would have been held in check by the frogs. Nasties everywhere: nasties in the bakery, nasties in the kitchen, nasties in the bed, nasties in your hair…you should get the idea by now.

Moses requested another audience with the Pharaoh, but he sent back a message saying that he was too busy swatting away the vermin, and to leave him alone if he didn't want to get swatted, too.

Next, the fifth plague: where the livestock that was in the field, the horses, the donkeys, the camels, the herds, and the flocks became sick and died from the various diseases, such as African horse sickness and Bluetongue, being spread by the insects.[102]

And the insects spread Malaria and other diseases to the Egyptians, and hence, the sixth plague: boils and epidemics.

Now, surely the Egyptians were having a rough time of it. But, so far, as you see, this series of plagues are natural consequences of each other. And now it seemed as if there was a lull for a while, that the plagues were ending, and things were getting back to normal, when....

April of that year continued the unseasonably warm weather that triggered the previous plagues. The fifth of April dawned hot and humid as the Egyptians began their day. The sky was full of dark, ominous clouds as the wind slowly started to blow. A soft rain began to fall, growing in intensity bit by bit. The wind gained strength and force; gusts began to sweep the Egyptians to and fro. And as the warm, moist sea air moving over the northern Delta collided with the cool, dry inland air, the skies opened like the Wrath of God.[103] Torrents of rain fell, lightning

---

[102] I really want to point out that I had nothing to do with this. I'm not the kind of a God that goes around killing innocent animals. More about that later.
[103] © 5778 BCE, God. All Rights Reserved.

flashed, and thunder crashed all around the Egyptians now seeking shelter from the storm. The weather shifted, and now hail fell. Heavy, big, destructive balls smashed down on people, what remained of the livestock, and especially the crops, ruining them just as harvest was nearing.

Moses again tried to convince Pharaoh that I was pissed at him, and again Pharaoh refused to consider the message.

And the winds from the storms blew through the land, east and then west from the desert, and bringing a guest from those desert areas: the desert locust. The so-called eighth plague, as the Bible says:

They will cover the face of the land so that it cannot be seen. They will eat up the last remnant left you by the hail. They will devour every tree that grows in your countryside. Your houses and your courtiers' houses, every house in Egypt, will be full of them; your fathers never saw the like, nor their fathers before them; such a thing has not happened from their time until now.[104]

So, the Egyptians were really getting a hard time of things. But still, the ancient records of the Egyptians showed that such had occurred before in their history, and so Moses' words fell on deaf ears yet again.

---

[104] Exodus 10: 5-6

Eventually, the winds shifted yet again, and the locusts were blown back to the desert. But this was not the end of the troubles that would plague them.[105]

The violent storms subsided, and it was quiet. But just as the Egyptians began to think that perhaps their troubles were over....

Just a short question for the audience. Do you believe in coincidences? Ever have one of those days when everything just seems to be against you? Well....

A brief break in the scene. We must leave the Nile Delta and travel some four hundred miles across the Mediterranean to the islands just north of Crete. In particular, the island of Santorini, otherwise known to the ancients as Thera.

If you are a modern tourist visiting the Greek islands, you might want to visit Santorini. It is about one hundred twenty-four miles from Greece's mainland, and a popular tourist spot full of natural beauty and legendary history. For example, it's been thought by some that Santorini is the place where the civilization of Atlantis once existed. However, Plato (that kidder!) still refuses to let on whether he made up the story or not.[106]

Many people consider this island to be one of the most beautiful places in the world. Panoramic views, breathtaking sunsets

---

[105] Yes, it's a terrible pun, but I couldn't resist.

[106] Yes, of course *I* know, but Plato asks me not to give it away. He and Socrates like to get together over a jug of wine and still debate philosophy with other luminaries like Nietzsche (boy, was he surprised when he found out I wasn't dead!), and Kant, and Heidegger, Camus, etc.

over the Aegean Sea, white-washed houses and churches that appear from the distance to be an illusion of snow, perched densely on the on top of its massive cliffs. But such beauty comes at a price. The villages that rest so peacefully there sit on a volcanic caldera which bears witness to one of the greatest volcanic explosions of all time, the second largest in all of your human history.

Exploding with a force greater than seventy thousand times the energy in the first atomic bomb that destroyed Hiroshima in your World War II, the volcanic plumb shot more than thirty miles high. Tsunami waves as tall as one hundred and fifty miles rushed across the Sea, devastating the islands in their way, killing tens of thousands. Volcanic ash and pumice fell across the Mediterranean Ocean, blanketing the skies in fire and then darkness, reaching places like Crete, Turkey…

And Egypt.

So, the ninth plague: Darkness so heavy it could be felt! A darkness lasting days that even spooked old Pharaoh. Yet Goshen, far enough from the royal cities of the Egyptians, had escaped the calamity and there was light in all of the Hebrews homes.

Once again, the Pharaoh ordered Moses to be brought to him.

"I want this stopped now!" he snapped at Moses. "What do you wish?"

"Let all the Children of Jacob be free to leave this land."

Pharaoh sighed. "Alright"

Moses smiled. "Wonderful. Give me a day to tell the people, and give them time to gather up their flocks and—"

"Their *what?*"

"Their sheep, their goats. We need them for our sacrifices to our God."

Pharaoh was pissed. "You worthless son of a slave! I am willing to let all your people go, deprive my subjects of their human property, and you want to take more? Those flocks belong to my people, not to yours. Who are you to bargain with me?"

Pharaoh threw down his scepter. "Moses, get out of my sight. We have no agreement. But you'll be the sacrifice to *my* God if you ever dare show your face to me again."

Moses sighed. Over and over he had come to Pharaoh pleading for the release of the slaves. He was weary and tired. "Whose death will it take, mighty Pharaoh, for you to finally let the people go?"

"Go, Moses, now! Only death awaits you here."

Moses returned to Goshen, sad and disheartened.

The Bible says that I kept hardening Pharaoh's heart after each plague so that I could better reveal my glory:

But I shall make him stubborn, and though I show sign after sign and portent after portent in the land of Egypt, Pharaoh will not listen to you. Then I shall assert my power in Egypt, and with mighty acts of judgement I shall bring my people, the Israelites, out of Egypt in their tribal hosts. When I exert my power against Egypt and bring the Israelites out of there, then the Egyptians shall know that I am the Lord.[107]

So, if I was responsible for the last and most terrible plague, then I am a mass murderer.

Wouldn't you wonder: what kind of a God needs to prove himself to a human being? Am I that insecure a deity? I hope not. I would hate to have to submit myself to psychoanalysis sessions...can you imagine me, God, on the couch? And Lord, which psychologist would I use: Freud (who despite everything got it wrong about Moses – sorry, Sigmund, but Moses was not killed by the Jews), Jung (let's get it straight, if there is a collective unconscious where do you think it comes from? And what would be my archetype if it isn't God: great mother, father, child, devil, god, wise old man, wise old woman, the trickster, the hero?), Adler (and please don't tell me God has an inferiority complex!)?

Anyway, what real difference should it make to me as the Supreme Being if the Egyptians knew that I am God or not? It's not like they got a vote.

So, we come to the final and most horrible of the plagues. If you watch that old Cecil B. DeMille film, it does look rather scary when this green hand comes down from the heavens and starts to

---

[107] Exodus 7:3-5

move over Egypt, slowly and methodically killing the firstborn. It's certainly enough to cause nightmares in young children. But, that's the Bible through the eyes of Hollywood, and they never get it correct.

The final plague that would change everything was not the hand of God, but the workings of the littlest of creatures, a fungus.

After the fifth, sixth, seventh, and eight plagues, food had now become scarce. The normal harvest, you may recall, had been ruined, so what grain remained was harvested and stored, even though it was still wet and covered in locust droppings. The grain was placed in the storage pits which were covered in sand, adding heat and humidity, and allowing the bacteria to grow and mold to be produced on the top of the grain. The spores' mycotoxins were capable of causing hemorrhaging of the lungs.

Why were only the firstborn affected? Representing the future of Egypt, they were "important," and then as now, "important" people get the first, and supposedly the best, of everything. And they also got extra helpings, sadly guaranteeing that the firstborn would get a lethal dose of the mycotoxins.

The Israelite slaves, living in Goshen away from the humid water area, had different methods of storing and preparing their food that did not involve the gathering of the infected grain in a way that it would be concentrated into lethal doses. They were eating meat, and bread which did not contain the toxins.

And so, the nights in Egypt were full of mourning. Parents watched helplessly as their beloved children, their hopes and dreams for the future, died mysteriously. And no one could seem to do anything, but they did wonder why the slaves seemed unaffected. No earthly power seemed able to stop the deaths of the firstborn, and no Egyptian family was safe.

Not even Pharaoh's.

It was the middle of the night when a disheveled Moses was flung down before the Pharaoh for what would be their last face-to-face meeting.

At first, Pharaoh said not a word. He seemed to stare into the distance, not even aware that Moses was before him. Then from somewhere deep inside of him came a cry. Not the cry of a warrior. Not the cry of the master of all he surveyed. Not a cry of victory, but a deep cry from the soul. A cry of a loss that could never be replaced. A cry of such despair that no one could hear it and not be moved to terrible sorrow. It was not the cry of a Pharaoh as he motioned to his servants to reveal the body of his heir lying before him; this was the cry of a father who had just lost his beloved son.

And it was only then that he acknowledged Moses' presence. "You exact a most terrible price, you and your God. It is too much, Moses, too much. Now, I tell you, take your people, their flocks, their belongings, and curse my lands no longer. You have bought your freedom through death. Be gone before the next setting of the sun, for I will not look on the face of you or any Hebrew in my lands again."

And for a moment, Moses saw, not an enemy, but a grieving father, just another human helpless before forces greater than his understanding or his control.

Moses bowed to the grieving Pharaoh, he himself humbled. Daring not to say a word, he turned and returned to Goshen.

Preparations had already been undertaken in his absence, rushed though they were on orders of the Pharaoh. The long-suffering descendants of Abraham, Isaac, and Jacob (who was otherwise known as Israel) were gathered with flocks, weapons, gold, jewelry...some just thrown at them by the Egyptians eager to get them out of their sight. Still, they were rushed because it is true that there was such chaos, such fear that they might yet be murdered before they got out of Goshen, that the Hebrews had no time to add yeast to the bread they were making, and thus took the unleavened bread with them.

Moses led the people from Goshen to Sukkoth, and then Etham so that he could give them a rest before the long trek through the desert that awaited them. A meeting of the tribes was called, and Moses stood before some six hundred thousand of them, most of them terrified at heading further into the unknown. He looked into the distance where smoke was still coming forth from the explosion of the Santorini caldera, and said:

"Quiet! Quiet! Can I get a little quiet here for a few minutes, people?"

As the crowd grew still, he continued, "Okay, good then. We'll never get anywhere if you all keep talking at once. The Lord, through his signs and miracles, has delivered us from the hands of the Egyptians, and He's not done yet. The smoke in the sky before you points our way, the Lord Himself points the way to our prom- ised land. Forward, you sons and daughters of Judah; onward you sons and daughters of Reuben; courage you sons and daughters of Dan; …."

Yes, he named each of the tribes making up the descendants of the 12 children of Jacob, but I'll spare you the rest of it --- I'm sure you get the idea.

Pointing his staff towards the pillar of smoke, Moses led his people into the desert. The smoke led them as a pillar by day, while by night they could see the fire of the eruption as a pillar lighting their way in the darkness.

Moses soon realized that leading the people further into the desert with limited or no food or water was not necessarily the smartest approach. Luckily, the winds shifted the perceived direc- tion of the pillars just enough to cause the wanderers to change their route accordingly, until they wound up camped by the Sea of Reeds, also known as the Lake of Tanis.

Long lost now due to thousands of years of geographic changes, this lagoon was located in the Nile Delta at the general vicinity of what is now Port Said. Moses and his followers camped there and waited for a sign.

Meanwhile, word got back to a Pharaoh now turning from grief to anger. "Dumb Hebrews," he said to his generals, "all they are doing is going around and around the same area while the desert acts like a great barrier to their final escape. They're trapped like sheep before the slaughterer." He laughed, with such evil intent that it chilled the hearts of those who heard it. "I was mad to release them from our service. Now, we shall bring the slaves back to us, or they shall be slaughtered to a man. Our children's deaths shall be avenged."

Pharaoh assembled his forces, all the chariots of Egypt and his armies, and approached the Israelite camp.

The thunder of horses' hoofs! The dust raised by chariot wheels! The sound of war trumpets resounding in the air. And the Israelites saw and heard and trembled.

"Moses, damn it," some cried. "We didn't have enough graves in Egypt that you had to drag us out here to die in the desert! We told you to leave us alone, but oh no! Mister Big Shot Moses had to go stick his nose into everything and causing trouble. Yeah, things were rough. But at least we had one square meal every other day, and steady employment. Thanks a lot! Now what do we do?"

Night was falling. Death seemed ready to meet them all in the morning. But, in their fear and complaints, none noticed that the wind was rising, getting stronger and stronger. After a few hours, it became a steady east wind of about sixty-five miles per hour, pushing the water west to the far end of Lake Tanis, as well as south, up the Nile river.

And there, to the amazement of Moses and the ex-slaves, they beheld an area of wide mud flats where the river entered the lake, and there before them was a land bridge high and dry, beckoning them to cross over.

Moses saw his opportunity. "It is the hand of God come to battle for you.[108] Move out and don't be afraid."

Easy for *him* to say! Still, it came down to two choices: trusting the mercy of the Egyptians or hoping the bridge would hold so they could get out of there. That didn't take much thought. Panicked, frightened, awe-struck, Moses's followers crossed over the bridge.

The winds pushed the pillar of cloud from in front of them until it was behind them, coming between the camp of the Egyptians and the camp of the Israelites. This cloud remained there even in the darkness, illuminating the night so that Egyptians could not come near their foe.

---

[108] Why is it every time something happens that the people of the time can't explain by their scientific knowledge, they have to go blame me! Always fighting battles about something or other! Give me a break, huh?

Four hours that wind held. And it was just enough, just enough for the Israelites to make it across, safe and dry, and not a man lost.

Then the winds shifted again. The cloud also lifted and now in the Pharaoh's camp, they watched the crossing in amazement. Pharaoh rallied his forces, saying "Forward! After them or I'll make slaves out of you. Do you want to come back to our people to their praise, or to their derision when they hear you were too frightened to pursue Moses and his filth?"

With Pharaoh in the lead, the mighty army of Egypt followed their prey into the parted waters. But the wheels of the chariots were unsteady in the mud, wobbling, making the pursuit slow and difficult, until the Egyptians were largely stuck. And with the dying wind, the waters began to return to their rightful place. And now it was the Egyptians turn to flee, to run in panic, leaving their chariots and horses.

But there was nowhere to run to.

And the chariots, and the horses, and the armies were all destroyed, drowned by the same waters that had allowed the Israelites to escape the wrath of the Great Pharaoh.

A great silence fell over the land.

There would be still more mourning in the land of Egypt.

"I'm hungry!"
"I'm thirsty!"

"I'm tired!"

"It's too hot!"

"It's too cold!"

"It's too humid."

"It's too dry!"

"Are we there yet? When are we gonna get there?"

Three months of nag, nag, nag. Poor Moses wondered why he ever took this job—bunch of ingrates, ask them to do one little thing for themselves, and it was Moses this, and Moses that. Did anyone ever ask him how he was doing? How his sandals were holding up? Maybe he wouldn't mind someone offering *him* a cool drink for a change.

Thank God,[109] that as a result of his fleeing Egypt all those years ago, he had a good idea of where to find water and the most likely places where to find food. Those flocks of quail had kept them going until they found spots where there were tamarisk twigs upon which tiny insects secreted the mouthwatering "honeydew," the "manna" which would dry in the hot sun and could be pounded into bread.

But the constant mumbling and demands on him were really getting to him. Now, as they camped before the volcanic Mount Sinai, he called Aaron, Joshua, and the elders together and said, "I'm going for a climb! I'll be back when I get back."

---

[109] Not literally, of course

Aaron looked up at the mountain before him which was billowing smoke and fire from the far top amidst the rumbling of thunder.

"Are you crazy?" he asked.

"No, but if I have to stay here with all of you and not have a break, I will be!"

So, Moses began his solitary climb up the mountain. Soon those below lost sight of him as he ascended into the smoky clouds obscuring the top two-thirds of the volcano.

Even with the rumbling of the volcano, he felt more at peace than he had at any time since they had left Goshen. It was a much-needed break.

But all too soon, his mind began to wander back to the camp that depended on his leadership.

"What am I going to do about them? How do I stop all the complaining and arguments? I'm not going to make it if this keeps up."

Then a brilliant idea came to mind. What if the Israelis had some rules to follow, some commandments that would guide them? He could write them down.... but why should they just listen to him?

The mountain trembled and roared from on high. "Man, that sounds like one pissed-off God up there." That was it! The commandments would be from God himself.

Moses looked around and found a sturdy tablet of stone where he could write the rules down. He thought for a while, and began:

"I am the Lord, your God. Through my miracles, you have been brought out of the house of Egypt.

"You shall not bitch."

But, then, as often happens to writers, he drew a blank. Nothing would come to him. He sat there, trying to think of more commandments, but his mind would wander back to the days in Egypt when he was young and to his days in Midian before the call to return there to set the slaves free. Much simpler times, with little or no responsibilities….

"Maybe a good nap would help," he thought. "I'll wake up refreshed, and perhaps the answer will come in my dreams."

He crawled into a nice shady cave and fell asleep.

Meanwhile, I'd been a bit preoccupied with some goings on near Betelgeuse, and then there was some nonsense going on in a galaxy, far, far away…but that's a different story and has nothing to do with Earth or the human race. Anyway, by now those problems were largely solved, so Michael and Lucifer asked for a quick meeting with me.

"What's up, guys?"

Lucifer smiled. "Look, Lord, we know how busy you get, and how much Remiel and Saraqael appreciated the extra help. But

Michael and I think it's time you thought about your old buddy Abraham and gave a check on what was going on with his descendants. It's been quite a while."

I sighed. "Yes. Busy, busy, busy. But you are right—I shouldn't neglect my old friend. So, tell me, what is going on?"

Michael, who took a special interest in the Hebrews, filled me in on the events that had occurred over the last few hundred years while I was preoccupied. I quickly decided that maybe it was time for a little personal intervention here, just a touch...otherwise, the Hebrews might be hanging around this one mountain for decades!

Michael, Lucifer, and I came down to Mr. Sinai, which is where we soon learned of Lucifer's sensitivity to smoke and ash,[110] and we entered the cave.

Moses, gently sleeping, with such an innocent, care-free look...seemed a shame to wake him, but....

"Moses," I whispered. He may have heard me a bit but turned over on his side and started to snore.

"Moses!" I called a little louder.

No response.

I sighed. "I really, really hate having to do this but..."

The mountain shook, and a roar came from its volcanic heart. Moses sat up, now partly awake.

"What? Who?"

---

[110] Yes, even an angel can develop asthma

"Moses, wake up. It's me! The one you are seeking."

"Huh?" He shook himself, looking around.

"It's God! Now, come on. We need to talk."

"How do I know it's really you?"

"Oh, for the love of me!" I cried. I clapped my hands, and suddenly, the four of us were high above the mountain, sitting on a large white cloud looking down over the desert and the Hebrews gathered at the foot of Sinai.

I clapped my hands again, and we were back by the cave.

"Okay, I'm convinced," Moses said, now wide awake.

"Boy, can't have a simple conversation anymore. Everything has to be by signs and wonders. Pain in my ass!"

"Sorry, Lord."

"Okay, okay. You're only human. So, I understand from my angels, that you are trying to write laws for your people to live by."

"Yes. But I'm stumped."

Lucifer asked. "Haven't you written anything?"

"Well, there is this." Moses timidly held out the tablet on which he had written his commandment.

Lucifer and Michael just could not help it. Both burst out laughing.

"Knock it off you two! It could just be so simple, Moses. If all of humanity just learns to follow the rule I will write for you, their lives will be happy They will all feel blessed, no one will suffer, there will be plenty for all, and I shall be dwelling in your hearts and souls, and you all will truly be as much my children as the angels in Heaven."

I waved my hand at the tablet, and Moses' writing disappeared. I looked at him and smiled. I pointed my right index finger at the tablet, and as I wrote it, each letter was like a little fire, burning itself into the stone.

"Read it, Moses."

This is what he read:

"Love each other! - signed God."

Moses looked at us. "Is that all? "

I smiled, and my two companions nodded. "All and everything," I said. "Now go!" I commanded as we vanished before him.

Moses picked up the tablet and almost ran down the mountain. Finally, he emerged among the waiting crowd.

"Hey look," someone shouted. "Moses is back!"

"What do you have there, Moses?"

Moses and stood on a large rock looking down on the crowd, and raised his hands. "I bring back the word of God."

He held up the tablet and showed it to the crowd.

Murmurs came from the crowd.

"Come on, Moses. That's pretty far away for us. Tell it what it says," said one.

"I bet it says something about sex. It's always about sex."

"Nah, it's got to be something about keeping your hands on your own stuff. Bunch of freeloaders in this group, if you ask me!"

Moses motioned for silence. Then, in a loud, clear voice, he read what I had written:

"'Love each other! - signed God.'"

Absolute silence reigned for about a minute. Then came the protests.

"See, I told you it would be about sex!"

"'Love each other'? That's it?"

"You've been gone forty days, and all we get is one lousy command? What kind of lousy God is that?"

"Scaring the bejesus out of us with thunder and lightning and He says, 'Love each other'! What a copout!"

Moses got angry. Nag, nag, nag, bitch, bitch, bitch, moan, moan, moan. These people could never be satisfied no matter what you did for them.

"Enough!" Moses shouted. In a fit of anger, he threw the tablet down, and it shattered into pieces before the crowd.

Moses surveyed the Hebrews in anger. "Now, see what you made me do! I have to go back up that stinking mountain, try to convince God to talk to me again, and come up with more commandments and write the damn thing again. Nice going there. You really want to piss Him off, don't you?"

Moses turned his back on the crowd and began to climb the mountain once again.

We were waiting.

"Well, he said, "that went over like a brick-making party back in Egypt!"

"Okay," I said. "Guess we have to do it the hard way. Luce, can we have a couple of tablets here?"

"I'm sorry," Moses said.

"Oh, it's not your fault. I just thought the better of human nature. But it seems humanity isn't ready to let go of an authoritarian figure and work it out yet. So, Moses, take a tablet and the chisel and start writing. I'll dictate.

"I. I am the Lord, your God. I am the one and only God. Believe in me or not, it does not matter. You are stuck with me. Hi!

"II. Believe what you want to believe. But you shall not be an asshole about it. Leave each other alone about it. Mind your own damn business.

"III. None of you is any better in my eyes than the any other of you. So, do not worship your fellow man or woman. Do not make celebrities out of each other, nor bow down to rulers unworthy to rule. Remember, you are all made the same, and no one's excrement smells any better than anyone else's.

"IV. Relax every now and then. Take at least a day or two each week to stop and marvel at everything around you. All work and no play will make you crazy. And you shall not keep those who labor for you from enjoying the time off either.

"V. You will not make a slave of your fellow human.

"VI. Do not steal. There is plenty for everyone. Share it.

"VII. Do not deprive your fellow of food, water, or shelter, nor dignity. Who do you think you are?"

"VIII. Do not murder. Do not make war on each other.

"IX. Do not tell lies about your fellows. Do not pretend that the brown shit you attempt to feed them is sugar.

"X. Be kind to each other."

Moses nodded. "Sounds good to me, Lord."

"Let's hope they get it this time, Moses. Because after this, you are on your own with these commandment things."

Once more Moses came down from Sinai, this time carrying two tablets containing the Commandments Release 2.0.

And this time, when he read them to the crowd assembled before him, the general response was:

"Well, it's a start!"

Now, with the basics of the "laws" settled, Moses gave the signal, and the Israelites continued their long march to the Promised Land.

But it was not more than a week later when representatives from the twelve tribes asked Moses for a meeting.

"What is it?"

Nachum of the tribe of Judah spoke first. "Well, after thinking it all over, we'd like to amend the commandments."

Moses said nothing for a few seconds. Then, doing a slow burn, he said "Are you trying to tell me that you want to change the word of God?! What kind of yutz came up with that idea?"

"Here us out, Moses. For example, we need a rule about mixing different types of garments together. It's so gauche. Some people just do not have an eye for fashion."

Moses was astounded. "Are you out of your mind? What possible difference does it make?"

But, emboldened by Nachum, the complaints, the trivial and petty differences came rolling down on Moses's head.

Baruck was the first to make Moses mad really. "And I don't want to associate with that couple Zechariah and Jacob. You know those homosexuals in the twentieth tent in my tribe? Always making eyes at each other, kissing in public...."

"What on earth is wrong with that?" asked Moses. "God made men and women equally. It's hard enough to find love in this world, and who elected you to judge them. What, you think you're perfect? Mind your own damn business. Worry about your own life and butt out of everyone else's."

Even Moses's brother, Aaron, and his sons started complaining. "We need to determine the ritual laws and how to worship our God. For example, where and how do we sacrifice to Him. Who can touch the holy vestiges of office? "

"Not you, too, Aaron, 'Moses cried. "For God's sake, if people want to pray, let them just say what prayer is in their heart. You want rituals? Did God ask for rituals? Worry more about how you treat each other than about some goddamn ritual!"

On and on. And Moses was just getting more and more pissed off. There they were going again, complaints, complaints, and more complaints. Never a *thank you Moses for the great job you've been doing.* Or *Gee, Moses, thanks for getting us water and food in the dessert* — no it was always *what have you done for us, lately.* First, they'd complain that there wasn't enough food, then they'd complain because they got bored eating the same food every day. Or they complained that this journey was taking too long, or that Moses was pushing them too hard. Now, this bullshit! Ten simple rules and everyone seemed to want to put their two cents in or add to it, make life more complicated, impose limitations on their fellows that I had never conceived of nor wanted.

Moses lost it. "That's it!" he said. "I've had it! I've tried and tried, but you stiff-neck people just want to complain about everything. You're never happy, no matter what I do, Well, that's it! You can go find your promised land by yourself; you're on your own now, gang. I'm out of here."

And Moses picked up his staff, and, to the astonishment of all, walked off. No entreaty stayed him; no promise made him hesitate.

Some, seeking power over the multitude, were not exactly all that sad to see him go.[111]

But many there were who wondered, "What do we do now?"

Moses disappeared into the desert, found his peace, and finally died and was buried where no one knows but me.

And frankly, the poor guy had suffered enough. So, I intend to keep it that way.

In the camp Moses left behind, the murmurs continued. For at the moment, no one had an answer.

Oh shit! What do we do now?

---

[111] And, as I will get into, this gave them the perfect opportunity to rewrite my Ten Laws into the Commandments you know today, and to create, change, and add new laws (Leviticus, Deuteronomy) as they wished.

Book IX – Of Joshua, Judges, and the Coming of the Kings

"Oh shit! What do we do now?" a collective cry went up from the Israelites, as they realized how totally screwed they were without Moses.

No one had any idea of what direction their Promised Land laid in. They couldn't go back to Egypt because odds were that way was certain death.

Unity is a hard thing to maintain under the very best of circumstances, but here, now that Moses was gone, who was going to take his place and be able to lead them on?

In short, they were royally fucked.

As the Hebrews were forced to wander in hostile territories, not sure where the next waterhole would be found, scavenging for food and frankly getting pretty damn sick of that manna stuff, that sense of oneness soon broke down. While each still considered themselves Children of Israel, their loyalty to their own tribe became more paramount to many. In the jockeying for power over all the tribes, however, there arose two opposing parties, which for the sake of keeping everything straight, we will call respectively the MannaGivers and the GoldenIdolers. It gets quite complicated, and there are contradictions left and right as to what they believed. In fact, it became so insane that to this day we up in Heaven can't quite figure it out. But, let me try my best.

227

Essentially, the MannaGivers interpreted the idea of "Do to others as you wish they would do to you" and the Commandments as meaning that they should try to do what is best for the community as a whole—that as they were all created equal, they were equally loved by me. To them, this meant that no one should needlessly suffer when there was actually plenty for all. The poor should be fed, the weak should be helped, and the innocent protected. It was a duty to treat everyone as if indeed they were brothers and sisters. These MannaGivers were so sure that they knew my desires that they were sure they knew best what everyone else should do. These were the people who would come up with such future laws as "When you reap the harvest in your field and overlook a sheaf, do not go back to pick it up; it is to be left to for the alien, the fatherless, and the widow,"[112] or "When an alien resides with you in your land, you must not oppress him. He is to be treated as a native born among you. Love him as yourself…,"[113] or "Rise in the presence of grey hairs, give honor to the aged."[114]

The GoldenIdolers took the point of view that what one got out of life, gold, position, status, was because of my favor. They felt that you got what you deserved in life—and if you had a reversal of fortune, got sick, old and weak—well, that was the workings of God and not their affair. There was nothing wrong with desiring and keeping wealth—that was God rewarding you. On the other

---

[112] Deuteronomy 24:19
[113] Leviticus 19:33
[114] Leviticus 19:32

hand, they held that if there was a plague, a flood, fire — any such "natural" event — it was a sign of my disfavor and was a divine punishment. Everyone was in their rightful place — and no human agency should try to change it. And they were so sure that they knew my desires that they were willing to stone anyone who disagreed. Those were the people who would come up with such future laws as "If a man has intercourse with a man as with a woman, both commit abomination. They must be put to death,"[115] or "When brothers live together and one of them dies without leaving a son, his widow is not to marry outside of the family. Her husband's brother is to have intercourse with her; he should take her in marriage and do his duty by her as her husband's brother,"[116] or "When two men are fighting and the wife of one of them intervenes to drag her husband clear of his opponent, if she puts out her hand and catches hold of the man by the genitals, you must cut off her hand and show her no mercy."[117]

At first, the two sides could agree to disagree and argue their side with rational and respectful discourse. For instance:

Question from the audience:

"So many people got sick from eating those pigs. We need to do something to make sure it doesn't happen again. But, what?"

GoldenIdolers:

---

[115] Leviticus 20:13
[116] Deuteronomy 25:5
[117] Deuteronomy 25:11-12

"That must be the fault of the pig herders. We need to make sure that they wash before they slaughter the pigs."
MannaGivers:

"I don't know. Perhaps there's more to it. Maybe the problem is something in the pigs themselves?"
GoldenIdolers:

"Well, that doesn't seem likely to me. But at least we agree that we do have a problem. People keep eating the pigs and getting sick. Did you see that worm Isaac coughed up? Man, I thought I was going to throw up."
MannaGivers:

"Yes, it was huge. And what about the children? We don't want them to get ill. Maybe we need to have the tribal leaders remind them how dangerous it is.."
GoldenIdolers:

"Oh, that never works. Hey, I've got it. Maybe if we make it a law that it is forbidden by God to eat pigs?"
MannaGivers:

"Now, that's an idea! I'm glad we can discuss things despite our differences and reach a solution together."
GoldenIdolers:

"So am I. Shalom."
MannaGivers:

"Shalom."

But as time went on each became more adamant that theirs was the correct way, and that the other side were traitors to the nation. Such as when this came up:

Question from the audience:

"Baruch accidentally killed Jacob. When he went to chop some wood, the head of the ax flew off, striking poor Jacob dead. What are we to do? It wasn't intentional. Baruch and Jacob were friends."

GoldenIdolers:

"Intentional or not, Jacob's sons are entitled to Baruch's life!"

MannaGivers:

"That doesn't seem like justice. Baruch doesn't deserve death. Maybe we can create, I don't know, places of sanctuary where he can flee and save himself from such wrongful vengeance until calmer heads can come up with a just solution."

GoldenIdolers:

"Are you out of your mind? Are you wearing your bleeding-heart cry baby diapers again? "

MannaGivers:

"Listen, you sun-addled pervert— "

GoldenIdolers:

"You brain-dead pussy! Did your mother drop you on your head at birth? It's a wonder you can figure out which hand to wipe yourself with."

MannaGivers:

"You piece of dried camel dung!"

GoldenIdolers:

"You know, maybe we'd be better off if we sent all you morons back to Egypt!"

MannaGivers:

"Your head is so far up your fucking butt—you think it's nighttime when it's broad daylight."

GoldenIdolers:

"Oh, yeah? Well, you don't even know your ass from a hole in the ground!"

And so on....

I tell you, that kind of outright stupidity makes me want to send Lucifer Mike, and Gabe down there to kick some sense into the lot of you.

However, to get back to the main problem. As I said, it looked like the Israelites were royally fucked.

The elders of the twelve tribes realized that their first order of business was to get someone in charge to lead them all and to whom they could dump the blame if things went badly. There was some thought of putting Aaron, Moses's brother, in charge, but they did not want to start the idea of a royal dynasty—they'd seen enough of that in Egypt, thank you very much.

Finally, they were able to agree that there was none so capable as Joshua, Moses' right-hand man.

Now, this is the part of the story that I am not too crazy about. Since Moses was more of a negotiator than a fighter, I had been hoping that he would lead the Hebrews peacefully into the land of their forefathers and negotiate as much as possible with the various peoples there.[118] Look, call me an optimist. Call me naïve. But, sometimes the best plans of Gods and Man just don't work out. Because Joshua was no Moses.

I guess one of the hardest things for most people in a position of power to have is compassion. Maybe it's the power; perhaps it's that when you become revered by the crowd, you can lose your perspective.[119] You get lucky a couple of times, and suddenly you think you're the greatest thing since lox on a bagel. Which I suppose leads to the megalomania of kings, emperors, self-proclaimed gods on earth with their supposed divine rights. The masses, fodder for such ambitions, are propagandized into believing that it is I who chooses these idiots, who are often the worse of the worst and

---

[118] What? Did you really think I was so petty a God that I'd get pissed off about a little misunderstanding at the waters of Meribah Kadesh back in the Desert of Zin, as it says in Numbers 20:2-13? Never happened. Just some careful editing on the part of some Priest about one thousand years later, because admitting that Moses just walked off as I told you would really have messed up the narrative.

[119] Believe me. Took me eons to chill out enough and learn to be humble. Which isn't easy when you keep telling me I'm holy, and there's no one before me, while you're praying to me to grant you this and that. I mean, it could really go to a God's head if He's not careful.

do exactly the opposite of what I stand for while invoking my name.

So, back to Joshua. Joshua didn't even really try to negotiate with the various peoples. He immediately got the Israelite troops together and crossed over the Jordan and proceeded to spy out the area. First stop, Jericho.

You may have read the Book of Joshua, filled with miracles like walls falling down, the sun standing still in the sky, and so forth. The problem is that Joshua died about 1240 BCE, but the book was written over six hundred years after the conquest occurred. An early version may have been put together during the time of King Josiah,[120] but it wasn't completed until after the fall of Jerusalem to the Babylonians and the later return of the exiles back from Babylon in 539 BCE—so how accurate do you think your history books are some seven hundred years after the fact?

Yes, I'm afraid that the version you know is mostly propaganda to remind the reader of the "glory days."

The walls of Jericho did not fall because of the priests marching around them for six days blowing trumpets, so that on the seventh day when the shofars were blown as the army shouted, the walls came tumbling down to show my glory. I never suggested any such thing. No, just a good old-fashioned earthquake

---

[120] More about him later. But right now, I may as well tell you now, Josiah, king of Judah about 640 BCE, was the ruler under whom a lot of the rules and regulation that Moss supposedly got from Me in Deuteronomy and Leviticus were actually written—again, hundreds of years after Mt. Sinai.

that had occurred years ago so that Joshua's army just marched right in and claimed the area.

I have no wish to recount the conquest story in full because it is largely the usual story of every war: The war cry calling for victory in my name. The wholesale destruction of cities. The atrocities and crimes that accompany every war: rape, the murder of innocent children. The lack of mercy that feeds off the blind assurance that this is God's will....no, it never changes. From well before Joshua and on through David, the Babylonians, the Greeks, the Romans, Muslim jihads, the Crusaders, the Ottoman Empire, to the American Civil War, the Russo-Japanese War, the Balkan Wars, the Russian Revolution, the Spanish Civil War, two World Wars, the Greek Civil War, the Chinese Civil War, the Korean War, the Chinese Cultural Revolution, Vietnam, the Gulf War, ISIS...

What, exhausted already? Why, that's just a very small amount of many, many more I could mention that the Heavens have seen over the history of the human race. You shed so much of your brothers', sisters', and children's blood that you make even me weep. And sometimes I wonder if creating you was just one big mistake. Don't you understand? How can you be called "Children of God," how can you bring forth the "Kingdom of Glory" (whatever you think that to be) when you act like the lowest of all Creation?

So, so much for Jericho.

Then, there's the story of Gibeon where Joshua defeated the armies of the Amorites and, at his request, the sun stood still in the middle of the sky and did not go down for about a full day.

Sure.   Good story, but have you even considered what would have happened if I had broken the fundamental laws of physics and celestial mechanics for this? No? Okay, let me tell you.

First of all, what it would actually mean is that the earth would have to stop rotating because it is that very fact that makes it seem that the sun rises and sets in the sky.[121] And as that happened, you would be thrown to the East at a bit over one thousand miles per hour, along with everything else in the biggest pileup in the history of mankind!   Makes getting stuck on the highway at rush hour a joke.

And the oceans also rise out of their beds coming at that same one thousand miles an hour. You think you've seen a tsunami? Imagine the mother of all of them coming right at you!

Try to survive that one! [122]

---

[121] Ah, those fun-filled days when they thought the earth was the center of the universe and that the sun revolved around it rather than vice versa. But along came thinkers like Copernicus and…. oops!

[122] For the sake of argument, let us say I did stop the sun in the sky. Then, that would directly cause me to break an earlier promise the Bible says I made right after the flood—I know, I told you the real story earlier, but let's stick with the Bible here, huh? Genesis 8:22— "As long as the earth lasts, seedtime and harvest, cold and heat, summer and winter, **day and night,** they will never cease." Do you want to make a liar out of me?

Book IX – Of Joshua, Judges, and the Coming of the Kings

As I said, this is not my favorite part of the story I am telling you. War, war, war, kingdoms whose "glory" has long vanished into sand: Jericho, Ai, Jerusalem, Hebron, Jarmuth, Lachish, Eglon, Gezer, Debir, Geder, Hormah, Arad, Libnah, Adullam, Makkedamh, Bethel, Tappuah, Hepher, Aphek, Lasharon, Madon, Hazor, Shimron Meron, Akshaph, Taanach, Megiddo, Kedesh, Jokneam, Dor, Goyim, Tizrah… Bloodshed in their founding, some of them cruel, some of them kind, each with their own gods, tales of glory---human suffering… and for what? I know, my sense of time is not the same as you humans. You see in years, I see in centuries, millennia, eons.[123]

> *""My name is Ozymandias, king of kings:*
> *Look on my works, ye Mighty, and despair!'*
> *Nothing beside remains. Round the decay*
> *Of that colossal wreck, boundless and bare*
> *The lone and level sands stretch far away."*[124]

The halls of Babylon, the greatness that was Greece, the glory that was Rome, the wonder of the Ottomans, the mysteries of the Qin Dynasty of China… All those so-proud kingdoms now but names in history books, nothing more than ruins for tourists to gape at.

---

[123] Respectively hundred, thousands, and billions of your years.

[124] Percy Shelley's "Ozymandias." And thanks, Percy, for letting me quote you here.

As shall be your kingdoms of glory soon enough as they fall to time: the United States, Great Britain, the European Union, China, Russia, Japan, and so on. And future tourists will come to stare at the glory that was yours...and the sands will remain silent.

Futility, utter futility, says the Speaker, everything is futile. What does anyone profit from all his labor and toil under the sun? Generations come and generations go, while the earth endures for ever.[125]

The bloodshed you spilt come to nothing.

Even when Joshua was old, there was still much more land to be occupied. But that would be left to future judges and kings. In the meantime, it was allotted among the various tribes. Joshua was one hundred and ten years old when he died.[126]

Eventually, all the remaining members of Joshua's generation died out, and the tribes, now unorganized and undisciplined, became the prey of raiders and plunderers. So, there arose new leaders, called Judges, to lead them in fighting back.

And the Hebrews got into a vicious cycle of their own making: while a Judge lived, they would follow him or her and fought their way to peace. But when a judge died, until a new one was

---

[125] Ecclesiastes 1:2-4. But while the monuments humankind builds to itself, the wars of today's enemies who become tomorrow's friends, may be indeed futile, there is something in the human spirit that does endure as I shall tell in its time and place.
[126] Well, that's what the Bible says anyway.

elected, the unity would dissolve into the old chaos, and the plundering would begin again. And after that new Judge was confirmed, they would follow that Judge, and all would be well. And again, when that Judge died, things went back to crap.

Othniel, Ehud, Shamgar, Deborah, Gideon, Tola, Jair, Jephthah, Ibzan, Elon, Abdon, and Samson—oh, Samson: the Hebrew Hercules, strong, but, as often the case with men, a total sucker when it came to women. It's right there in the Book: Delilah asks him the source of his strength, so he makes up something, and the next morning the Philistine try to use it against him resulting in their defeat. So, she asks him again, and once again, he makes up something, with the same result for the Philistines. This goes on for a while, and you would think the old boy would get wise that there wasn't something quite kosher about Delilah. But----no! Finally, the love-struck idiot tells her the truth—it's his long, uncut hair (or at least that is what he thinks) ---and of course, Delilah gives him the haircut to end all haircuts. He takes one look in the mirror and ZAP! —he just wilts, gets captured, blinded, and made a slave. Of course, much later when his hair grows back (along with his psyche), he gets his revenge by destroying the pillars holding up the Philistine temple, killing his enemies—and unfortunately, himself.

Yep, sometimes men are such schmucks.

And again, the people would dissolve into chaos and served many gods until Eli, and then Samuel, the final judge and also the first prophet, led them back to my ways.

But Samuel got old, and his sons, Joel and Abiah, were corrupt, ripping off the people of their sacrifices and in general attempting to profit from their positions. Eventually, the populace turned against them.

The Israelites looked around at their neighbors. And they thought, what makes us different from the people around us? Well, the various people had their gods, but the people of Israel had one too.[127] So, that wasn't it. Their neighbors had their own distinct ways of dressing, but they did, too. So, again, that wasn't it. It couldn't be the food, it wasn't the language, it wasn't the color of their skin....

Finally, they saw that all the people around them lived in kingdoms and wouldn't you know it, those kingdoms had kings! The Hebrews, on the other hand, were a loose collection of tribes, and the leaders they had had (these judges we just talked about) were really just leaders in wartime and otherwise served as a source of justice among them. That was basically it, though they did invoke their authority as given by me—but they actually had very limited power over the day to day lives of the tribes.

So, seeing this, the people went to Samuel and asked him to give them a king. Samuel, already unhappy over his children, was even more unhappy with this idea. He went off, fasted, and prayed. Exhausted by the stress, the dejected man fell asleep.

---

[127] Yours truly, of course.

And I? I was displeased as well, so I gave Samuel a dream where he and I talked about it.

"Do they know the consequences of what they ask?" I said. "They seek to replace those, who merely lead their battles against invaders and gave them justice in their disputes, with a king to rule them. Call them King, Emperor, Shah, Sultan, Great Leader, Premier, Prime Minister, President—in the end, they all become the same in their mania for power. Warn the people what their kings will claim as their rights.

"For behold your king! He will take your sons and daughters and make them serve his pleasure. Some will be assigned as officers over many of the rest, now forced to be fodder for the wars the king makes to show his power. Millions will die, your children as soldiers forced to fight in wars they do not understand, themselves killing millions of innocents, people with whom they would have no quarrel—then left on the fields of battle only to ask "why?" as their lifeblood slowly fades away. Others will be forced to serve as his personal slaves, lavishing him and his favorites with perfumes, food, and wine, and to prostitute themselves as he indulges in whatever perversity may suit his pleasure.

"Your best fields, your best vineyards, and the goods they produce will be taken by him and given to his family and courtiers. And you will be made slaves to work that very land you once called yours. He will willingly allow you to starve by the millions while he and his flatterers live fat off your labor.

"He will divide you against your brother and sister, feeding you lies so that you see *them* as the cause of your suffering, and you will gladly kill your brother, your sister, your father, your mother, your child — never understanding who is the true cause of that suffering."

Upon awakening, Samuel's face was wet with tears. He went to the people of Israel and told them what I'd said in that dream. But they refused to listen.

"No, we want a king. We must have a king to rule over us. Then we'll be like the other nations with a king to lead us out to war and fight our battles."

Samuel sighed. "Alright, you fools. But when the day comes — and it will — when you cry out against that king, don't come running to me! And don't go running around blaming God for sending you the ruler that you chose. It's your cock-up. You're on your own."

The First Book of Samuel would have it that I told him who to choose as the first king of Israel. No, no, no. I always get the blame! I wanted no part of this. But Lucifer was so fascinated by the whole idea of selecting your own ruler (rather than having him forced upon you as was the usual case) that he volunteered to go down and help monitor the whole thing. So, I'll let him tell you the story in his own words since he was there. Luce?

Book IX – Of Joshua, Judges, and the Coming of the Kings

Thanks, Lord. Boy, considering how badly I've been played over all the centuries, I appreciate the opportunity for once to stand up for myself a bit. I do get so sick of getting a bad rap. Let's get this straight: I never led a rebellion against God – are you for real? As if I would want all the headaches He has – the poor guy really deserves a good millennium or two to chill out and recharge the old batteries. Not that he's old, God forbid! – but the job does age you.

And just for your information, I don't have a tail and horns, I'm not red, I don't carry a pitchfork, and I was never throw out of heaven. And for that matter, if I were the so-called Devil, my kingdom being Hell, running around to entrap and damn wicked souls for all eternity – man, if I were evil incarnate, I'd probably be congratulating those evil ones, and partying with them. They would be my army for an eventual attempt to destroy God once and for all in a great Apocalypse such as you talk about in your Revelations and in the prayers of your more maniacal preachers and assorted crazies (you know, the very ones whose actions would be most inclined to actually bring on the end of the world). If I were punishing the evil ones with those wild tortures you can read about in Dante, for example, I'd theoretically be doing God's work!

So, kindly give me a break. There is no Hell – except for the one you humans seem at times to want to make out of the Earth.

Okay, thanks for letting me vent. I'm feeling much better now.

As the big guy said, I think it was about 1050 BCE, or so when I heard about what Samuel was going to do, I was fascinated. I wasn't sure how this was going to turn out. See, the gang and me, we're angels. We

kind of reach our agreements by something called common sense, compro-
mise, and a desire for the welfare of all — I know they are rather unusual
concepts for a lot of you mortals. But you should give it a try, it's amazing
what you can accomplish that way.

I asked God to let me go to Earth and watch the whole thing as
sort of an intellectual exercise on my part. Got to be fair though, I kind of
kept after him for a while, [128] *and I do know his weak side---no, not gonna*
mention it here (I'm not crazy you know. That's all we need — you mortals
exploiting it!). Either he had enough of me going "Please. Oh, pretty
please. I'll be your best friend" — or he actually saw that it might be a good
idea,

"Okay, okay, get your butt down there, Luce! Full report when
you get back."

When I arrived in Ramah, Samuel's town, the elders had just
gathered together. Using my powers of disguise — which allow me to im-
personate anything and anyone [129] *— was accepted as an elder named Zech-*
ariah from the tribe of Reuben, who, by some lucky "quirk "of fate, was
actually out of town attending his new grandson's bris.

A little wine, a little food, and I was comfortably settled in to
watch the show.

"The fairest way to elect our king is to have all the people vote."
This by way of Jekamiah, a member of the tribe of Judah.

---

[128] *Did God tell you that I invented the whole idea of nagging?*
[129] *You should hear me do my impersonations of some of your leaders. (Yeah, I*
know—some of you think it may not necessarily be just an impersonation!)

Book IX – Of Joshua, Judges, and the Coming of the Kings

"Sure," laughed Jedial of Benjamin. "You'd like that just fine. That guarantees that the new king will come from your tribe because it's the biggest! What about the smaller tribes like mine?"

This realization was met by a lot of grumbling – a good deal of it from Jekamiah himself as he saw his tribe's plan fall apart.

A bit more wine and everyone got more cooperative once again.

"How about this. The people of each tribe get to vote for electors who make the final decision," interjected Heman the Levite. "Each tribe gets the same number of electors. Then no one has an advantage."

"I don't know about that!" yelled Bukki the Gadite. "What's to prevent someone from messing around with the votes? What if the person who the electors choose is the least popular choice among all the people? Are we going to have rioting on our hands?"

"Before you even get to that," I said, "May I ask a question? I think there's a point you are overlooking. If you are electing someone, who is running for the job? Just who wants to be king?"

"Oy!" cried Samuel. "Didn't even think of that one. We could have hundreds of candidates for king! I guess we'd have to first come up with some way to eliminate them bit by bit until we get the list down to a reasonable few. That could take months just by itself! That's crazy!"

There was general wailing and pounding of fists on the walls. It seemed that this would never work.

Samuel said, "I'm leaving the room for a minute. Need to think without all this yakity-yak. I can't hear my own brain!"

Out he went. About thirty minutes later, he came back in, with a calm look on his face (maybe he had a secret stash of the good wine – I don't know), sat down and said,

"I thought, and I thought. I walked around tossing a pebble in my hand for a while just to calm down, and then it hit me. Why don't we leave the whole thing to chance? Here's what we will do. We will have three lots. The first lot will consist of twelve stones from which one will be picked to tell us which tribe our new king will come from. Once we know that, the second lot will consist of a number of stones, each marked with the name of one of the families from that tribe. Of course, we'll need to eliminate families where there are no adult males.[130] After we chose the family, we put all the adult males' names in the lots and pick the winner."

And again, grumbling and moaning until Samuel raised a hand for silence. He looked hard around the room with his dark eyes, almost covered by his bushy eyebrows.

"Anybody got any better ideas?"

And so, it was.

Representatives from each of the twelve tribes gathered in Samuel's tent to watch the first drawing of the lots. Twelve stone markers (or "lots") were created; each having the name of one of the tribes marked on it in chalk, having been carefully examined to ensure they were of equal size and weight, and that there was no way to tell one from the other by feel. Each representative of his tribe placed his marker in Samuel's sheepskin bag. When all twelve markers were in the bag, we each had a turn

---

[130] *I know ladies, but what do you expect from a male-dominated society?*

shaking it up so that there would be no way to rig it by knowing which one was on top.

I held the bag as Samuel was blindfolded. I gave the bag one last shake and held it out to him.

Samuel reached inside and drew out one of the lots. Removing his blindfold, he looked at it and proclaimed, "Benjamin!"

"Benjamin!" cried Jekamiah, who you'll remember represented Judah. "That pipsqueak of a tribe? Nothing good ever comes out of Benjamin."

Jedial leaped to his feet. I thought he and Jekamiah were going to come to blows, but Samuel raised his hands and forcibly separated them.

"Sit down and stop acting like three-year-olds," he said. "You all agreed. So let it be spoken, so let it be done! Jedial, gather the names of each family of your tribesmen who have sons. In two weeks, we will draw the next lot."

I thought that Jekamiah was going to start a tribal war, but he realized that the other tribes were not going to support him, and he was wise enough to know when he was out-numbered politically.

The two weeks passed swiftly, and the elders of Benjamin came to Samuel with lots containing the names of the tribesmen and the second lot was cast.

"Kish son of Abiel" Samuel announced. And of course, there was grumbling amongst the Benjamites, some, who I guess must have personally known Kish's sons, seemed rather shocked at the selection. I overheard one of them say, "Okay, bad enough it's going to be one of those Kish boys, but God, please, not Saul. Oh, he has his moments, but he's so damn full

of himself and so stubborn. And, sometimes, he's such a Gloomy Gus, there's no living with him."

The next morning, Kish and his family joined Samuel and the elders for the final casting of lots. Kish had three sons: Abner, Abinadab, and Saul, But Saul hadn't shown.

"That son of mine. I don't know what to do with him. He's not as dutiful as my two loves here. Said he wasn't interested in the whole King thing."

"Well, "Samuel sighed. "Perhaps we won't need him at all. We have three lots here, so the odds are against him. Let's do this."

Samuel reached into the bad, looked at the lot he had withdrawn, and frowned. He held it out to Kish.

"Oy vey ist mir!"[131] Kish wailed. "It's Saul! Where is that nudnick?"

"He's hidden himself among the supplies," Abner said.

Down we went to where Kish and his sons had camped and began to examine the supplies.

"Look! Why does that bag have a head of hair?" laughed Abner

"And it's moving," I added.

For Saul had forgotten one little detail in his attempt to hide. He was taller than all the others and stood out like a sore thumb.

Everyone had a good laugh, even Saul (poor fellow though, he wouldn't be having that many more), and he was carried around on the shoulders of his new subjects who were shouting "Long live the King!"

---

[131] "Oh, woe is me!" in the Benjaminite dialect.

Me, God, again. Saul's reign of forty-two years was one of war and bloodshed. His biggest enemy was the Philistines, whom he never could defeat with any finality. Perhaps it was, this continual frustration, dwelling so much on his mind, that caused his moodiness as he got older. Anything could set him off. Sometimes it seemed he didn't know where he was, or at times not even recognize his own children. When all seemed quiet and calm, his more violent side would come out for no reason. His servants would quiver in fear when he called them — for they could not be sure that they would come out of his tent without having vessels thrown at them, or even if they would come out at all.

The attendants could not decide what to do. Then, one of them, having recently returned from Bethlehem, recalled a certain young man named David.

Carefully his attendants approached the king.

"Sire, you see how an evil spirit from God seizes you.[132] Why don't you command your servants to find someone who can play the lyre? Then, when the evil spirit comes upon you, he can play, and you will feel better."

Saul cried out. "I'll try anything at this point. See that it's done."

Then, the servant said, "I have seen a son of Jesse of Bethlehem. He knows how to play the lyre so sweetly that it sounds like music from Heaven. And he is a brave man and warrior. He speaks

_____

[132] Yep, somehow you knew I'd get the blame.

well and is a fine-looking man---though not as fine-looking as you!" he carefully added when Saul frowned.

So, David came down to Saul and played for him. And, Saul felt much better. Saul put David into his service, where he quickly grew to be a great favorite of the king, eventually rising to the rank of armor-bearer. Seems like a pretty good deal all around, if you ask me.

Then along came Goliath.

Book X – Kings and Chronicles

O nce more, the Philistines gathered for war against the Israelites. They assembled at Sokoh which was in Judah. Saul and his forces came out and camped in the Valley of Eliah. The battle lines met so that each occupied a hill, with the valley beneath them.

Most people are familiar with the story of David and Goliath in some form or other. Either you've seen a version of it on television or in the movies[133] or as one of the stories told in your Sunday Schools, etc.

David always emerges as the great hero of the story, being the only one brave enough to face and defeat the towering Goliath, but as usual, there's a bit more to the story than you may be aware.

History (and often religious accounts) tend to grow more elaborate as time passes—first of all, you may have the witness accounts, but then as the legend of the "great hero" intensifies and recedes further in time, the events get politized, and you may wind up with some tales that are far too far from the truth.[134] And of course, as the saying goes, "History is written by the victors."[135]

---

[133] There have been at least two versions in the past 60 years. The 1960 version even had Orson Welles as King Saul.

[134] As you've seen numerous times in this book.

[135] Or perhaps in today's world, by the Internet.

Therefore, let's take a step back and give you the correct version.

When Saul's armies had gathered, David's older brothers joined up. David, being the youngest, had to go back and forth from the camp to help tend his father's sheep at Bethlehem.

So, he wasn't in the camp that day when the Philistine champion, Goliath, first came out of the enemy camp. Goliath was tall, certainly taller than the average man. But, here we come to the first uncertainty in the story because, depending on which manuscript of the first book of Samuel being used, your Bible will tell you his height is either nine foot seven inches — or a more reasonable six foot eight inches. What's the truth? The Dead Sea Scrolls, the first century CE Jewish historian Josephus, and other manuscripts say six foot eight inches. It is later manuscripts written after the eighth Century CE that use the nine foot seven inches. You may wonder why?

Well, Goliath would have been tall in either case because back then the average height was about five feet!! But, in later centuries, when people got taller and as the truth faded, six foot eight inches, while still tall, wasn't t as impressive! So, to make David's victory more amazing, the scribes raised the ante.

Either way, he was something to behold. He weighed about three hundred and ten pounds, wearing a bronze helmet on his head, and dressed in a suit of bronze scale armor which itself weighed about one hundred and twenty-five pounds. His legs were protected by bronze greaves, and for a weapon, he had a giant double-edged sword. His shield-bearer went before him, guiding him.

You have to imagine what it was like for the Israelites when this monstrosity came forth for the first time. I think the general reaction was something like

חרא קודש![136]

Goliath stood before the Israelites and bellowed, "C'mon you cowards. Who wants to fight? I'll take you on two at a time. Hell, I'll take you on ten at a time and not even break into a sweat. Well?"

His taunt was met with silence.

"Bah, this is the great Israelite army? I fart on this army. I laugh at the so-called might of King Saul. Tell you what. Choose a champion, one man from among you. I will fight him no matter what armor you put on him, no matter what weapon. If he can kill me, our army will surrender, and we will become your slaves and serve you; if I kill him, you will become our slaves and serve us. Come, I defy you. Give me a man, if there actually is a true man among you, and we will fight it out."

On hearing this, Saul and his army were terrified. Imagine all the crapped pants that day.

---

[136] The Hebrew equivalent of "Holy Shit!"

The next morning, Goliath came back out, once more led by his shield-bearer and repeated the same taunt. And again, he was met with silence and the faint smell of excrement coming from the Israelite camp.

This went on morning and evening for forty days.

Meanwhile, David's father loaded him up with food and clean undergarments to bring back to his brothers in their camp. He reached it about the time the army was going out once more to battle positions. War cries resounded.

David quickly delivered his supplies to the officer in charge and ran to the battle lines where he found his brothers. He was just about to ask how they were when Goliath came forth and again issued his challenge.

"What the hell is that?" David asked.

"Oh, you see that man-monster," Eliab answered. "He's been doing this for forty days. Saul has said that he will give great riches to the man who kills him."

"As well as his daughter in marriage and a tax exemption for the entire family," added Shammah.

David spat on the ground. He took a hard look at Goliath, studied him for some time, then nodded. "Bah! Just who does this Philistine think he is? He's easy pickings."

David got an audience with Saul. "Let's not lose heart over this putz. I'll fight him."

Saul laughed grimly. "Are you out of your ever-loving mind? You're still a young man mostly tending flocks, while he's been an experienced warrior from his youth."

"Your majesty," David answered. "I've been in the fields. While some were living the life of pleasure, I was out protecting my father's sheep. When a bear or lion came and carried one off, I went after it, struck the beast, and rescued the sheep right out of its mouth. And if it then turned me on, I seized it by the hair, struck and killed it. This son of a whore Philistine will be like a piece of chicken fat for me."

As his brothers would have told you, David was a little conceited, so he was a bit prone to exaggeration. Nevertheless, Saul, not about to challenge Goliath himself, and realizing there were no other volunteers, agreed.

David refused both armor or sword. He went down to the stream, chose five smooth stones, put them in the pouch of his bag, and sling in hang, approached Goliath.

Goliath came forth, yet again led by his shield-bearer, and looked David over. "What the shit is this? He's little more than a boy! Your champion is a pup. Do you think I am a dog that you come to me with sticks? Come here, little puppy, and I'll give your flesh to the birds and the wild animals!"

David stayed calm. Because he knew that Goliath had a weakness.

If you remember, I said that David spent some time studying the Philistine. And this is what he had noticed:

Goliath moved slowly, and David wondered why the Philistine's shield bearer always seemed to be leading him around. He watched as the giant stumbled a few times, and then he realized why: *Goliath couldn't see!* In fact, he was extraordinarily near-sighted and suffered as well from double-vision. As to the matter of armor, well, all that weight, the helmet, the suit of scale bronze and the greaves, David realized, weighed the giant down. Oh sure, if David ever got close enough, Goliath, with his long reach and wicked weapon, would have easily killed him, but David would make sure that was never going to happen.

But, you might object, David only carried a sling. That sling was nothing like a modern kid's toy. This baby was simple but deadly. Entire armies had been using them for years, and much as David had told Saul, they were highly effective as a weapon against bear, lion, or other beast. It was just about as potent a weapon as your modern day .45 caliber pistol. David totally knew what he was about.

So, as Goliath approached, David kept out of his range. He reached into his bag, took out a stone and put it into the sling's pouch. He twilled the sling around and around and then let fly. And hit Goliath right in the...

...space behind the greave on his right leg, as the giant bent his leg, which buckled and caused Goliath to fall forward face down on the ground.

That's correct. The stone didn't hit his forehead, as you probably were told! Remember, Goliath wore a helmet which covered his forehead and had a piece protecting his nose. How would you expect the stone to penetrate such an impossible spot and then strike through the bone there? And if Goliath had been hit like that, he would have fallen backward not forwards.

But, that isn't important one way or the other. Either way, the big guy was down for the count.

David moved quickly. He stood over Goliath, took hold of his sword and drew it from the sheath. Goliath's sword was heavy. David barely had the strength to use it to kill Goliath and then cut off his head.

Seeing this, the Philistines panicked and began to run. With a shout, Saul's army pursued them back to Philistia as far as Goliath's hometown.

And, of course, leaving the dead strewed across the land-scape, like in so many wars before, and in much too many wars since.

You might think that Saul would have been grateful to David for pulling off what he was too chicken — that is, too reluctant to do himself. And at first, he did. He kept David with him, and it seemed that no matter what mission Saul gave David, David would pull it off with great success. David rose higher and higher in the ranks, and the troops were pleased by this recognition as well. Saul's son, Johnathan, loved David as much as he loved himself, and David returned that love equally.

There has often been speculation that David and Johnathan were lovers. With the carefully chosen words that some "religious" leaders use to show that I consider homosexuality a terrible sin, let's say this. If they were or weren't, and I am NOT telling you one way or the other, who cares? It's no one's business but their own. As long as they aren't hurting anyone else, and it's between two consenting adults, I don't give a damn. Love is such a scarce, sacred thing in this world of yours. So, I say, if you find it, more power to you. Go for it!

Anyway, as I was saying, Saul was initially overjoyed with David. But one day, after David had led a successful raid against the Philistines, the women came out and began dancing before the troops, singing:

"Saul has slain his thousands,

And David his tens of thousands."

Saul heard this, and, well, let's say he was less than pleased. David had been exalted, treated like own of his own family, loved like a brother and a son—but what more could he ask for? Did he want Saul's kingdom as well?

From that time, a darkness fell over Saul, and an ever-increasing fear and hatred of David overtook him. One time while

David was playing on his lyre in another room of Saul's house, the king got so angry that he grabbed his spear and hurled it in David's direction. Luckily, it missed.

Eventually, Saul told Johnathan and his attendants to kill David, but Johnathan warned David, who went into hiding upon his advice. While he was doing so, Johnathan spoke to Saul, reminding him off all David had done for the king. Saul relented, and he and David made peace.

But only for a while. Once again, war broke out with the Philistines. David, leading the troops, struck them with tremendous force, leaving the enemy no choice but to flee before him. And when David returned to Saul's house, again the king's heart went cold when David played his lyre for him. Saul tried to pin David with his spear, but he dodged the thrust so that the spear was driven through the wall.

Fearing for his life, David escaped during the night. Even as Saul pursued him, David found shelter in different areas, and those who felt oppressed by Saul came to join him. After a while, he had quite a good size army of his own.

It may come as a shock, but for a while, David even found refuge among the Philistines – yes, the same Philistines he fought against under King Saul; the same Philistines whose hero, Goliath, had met his fate at his hands. David, in order to escape Saul, made his base in Gath, which coincidentally was the city Goliath came from and pledged loyalty to King Achish of Philistia. And

David was another one of those bloody "heroes" who then went forth and raided various towns and cities of the area, taking sheep, cattle, donkeys, camels, even clothes, not leaving a single person alive to be taken prisoner back to Gath, because he thought "They might inform on us and say. This is what David did."[137]

David and his men even marched with Achish's army against King Saul at the battle of Jezreel. However, the Philistine commanders objected to him, worrying that he would betray them to Saul. Though Achish had learned to trust him, the King felt he had no choice but to send him back to Philistia without participating in the battle.

Which may have saved him from regicide. Because in the battle, the Philistines, pursuing Saul up to Mount Gilboa, managed to kill his sons Johnathan, Abinadab, and Malki-Shua. The fighting became fiercer and desperate around Saul, and Achish's archers overtook him, and critically wounded him.

At this point, the Bible gives us two versions of how Saul died. In the First Book of Samuel, it says that the mortally wounded King said to his armorbearer, *"Draw your sword, and thrust me through with it, lest these uncircumcised men come and thrust me through and abuse me."* However, his armorbearer, very much

---

[137] 1 Samuel 27:11

afraid, refused. Leaving Saul no choice, the King then committed suicide by falling on a sword.[138]

On the other hand, the Second Book of Samuel, says that: *three days after Saul's death, an Amalekite claiming to have escaped from the Israelite camp, went to King David. Telling him that Saul and his son, Johnathan, had died, he said, "I was on Mount Gilboa, and I saw Saul, leaning on his spear, the Philistine chariots in hot pursuit. He turned around and seeing me, motioned to me to come closer.*

"'What can I do for you?' I asked.

"The King replied, 'Stand here by my side and kill me! I am dying, but I'm still alive.'

"I knew that after he had fallen, there was no chance he would survive. So, I stood beside him, and I killed him. And I took his crown, and the band on his arm, and have brought them to you."

David and his men tore their clothes. They mourned and wept and fasted until the sunset for Saul, for David's beloved friend Johnathan, and for the army of Israel who had fallen in battle.

And then, David called for one or his men to strike down the Amalekite who had brought him the news.[139]

In the course of things, it probably doesn't matter which is true. But, what about it, do you think it was the Amalekite being truthful or was he trying to curry favor with David? I will let you decide, but I will say that no matter which version is accurate, in

---

[138] I Samuel 31:4 (and I Chronicles 10:4 basically tells the same version)
[139] II Samuel 1:2-16 (Looks like Samuel couldn't keep his story straight)

the end, King Saul died bravely. Let us give that troubled monarch that much.

And the death of Saul[140] started the real power play amongst the tribes of Israel. On one side, the supporters of Saul's son Ish-Bosheth, consisting of most of the tribes of Israel, based in Mahanaim. On the other, David's supporters, primarily of his own tribe, Judah, based in the city of Hebron. You had to know this was going to be trouble

Each side had their general: Ish-Bosheth had Abner, who had also been the commander of Saul's army, while David had Joab, his nephew. The war between the two houses lasted a long time, David getting progressively stronger while the house of Saul got weaker.

Sometimes, the little stupidities change the course of history. Abner seemed to be strengthening his own position in the house of Saul. Then, for whatever reason, Ish-Bosheth accused him of sleeping with one of Saul's concubines. This really pissed off Abner.

"By the foreskin of an uncircumcised Jebusite! What kind of dog do you think I am? I've always been loyal to you when it would have been so easy to turn you over to David. I never touched her. But, if you are so worried about who fucked who, guess what—you just fucked yourself!"

---

[140] For you history buffs, this is roughly 1000 BCE

Abner met with the elders of Israel to convince them to make David their king, and he spoke to the Benjamites as well. He then went to David to tell him what he had done — and David was greatly pleased. After a great feast, David sent Abner away in peace to assemble the tribes that were now going over to his side, so that a covenant could be made between them and David.

Sometime after Abner left, Joab returned from a raid. Hearing about what his rival had done, he left David and, unknown to the king, had Abner brought back. He had Abner brought into an inner chamber as if they were going to have a private talk.

After all, as Joab told Abner, "If we're going to be friends and allied against a common enemy, we should first make sure we end any misunderstandings between us."

And then Joab stabbed him in the stomach and Abner died.

David was furious. But Joab claimed that the reason he had killed Abner was in revenge for Abner killing his brother in the battle of Gideon. Was it true? Or was Joab afraid of an ambitious general just waiting to take his place beside David?

Though David cursed Joab, he realized he needed the commander if he was to succeed in his future battles. It's the never-ending story: political expediency wins out over morality. Nothing new. Watch your leaders, and you can see it's the same thing today.

Wondering what happened to Ish-Bosheth? With Abner dead, he lost courage which alarmed the remainder of Israel that had stayed loyal to him. Two of his own men killed him while he was taking a mid-day nap. They cut off his head and brought it to David. And, as with the Amalekite who claimed to have killed Saul, grateful David ordered them executed for regicide.

The war was over. The heads of the tribes of Israel came to David and pledged their loyalty. Saying that he was the Lord's anointed — see, there they go, blaming me again! — they made him king over all of Israel.

He was thirty years old when he became king, and he would rule for forty years until his death.

Don't worry. I'm not going to go over those forty years, just a few highlights — or maybe you might say, lowlights.

Of course, a king needs a capital city. He marched to Jerusalem and attacked the Jebusites living there.

Looking up the hill, he said something that he would soon regret. "Whoever leads the attack will become commander-in-chief."

That was all Joab had to hear. Because up he went, and David smiled tightly as he was forced to honor his vow. Joab was now commander-in-chief.

David took up residence in Jerusalem, and it became known as the City of David. David built up the city and grew more and more powerful.

He had a palace built for himself, took more concubines and wives, and he sat contentedly on his throne.

He was a shrewd king, and after the defeat of the Philistines, he had word spread through the prophet Nathan that God—remember me?—had declared that He was going to make David's name great among all men. Furthermore, he claimed that I had said that *"when your life ends and you rest with your forefathers, I shall set up one of your family, one of your own children, to succeed you, and I will establish his kingdom. It is he who is to build a house in honor of my name, and I shall establish his royal throne for all time.... Your family and your kingdom will be established for ever in my sight; your throne will endure for all time."*[141]

Frankly, I need a house like a hole in the head. I'm God; I can't be contained in a mansion on the hill! And as far as establishing a royal throne for all time.... well, history may very well argue the case.

I find human history to consist of periods of incredible advancement between what are mostly the same stupid attempts to conquer and subdue each other—and no matter who wins, I seem to get the praise or the blame depending on whose side you happen to be on. If I want to watch two sides going head-to-head against each other, I'll watch the NFL—and I won't be picking the winning team, either.

---

[141] 2 Samuel 7:12-13,16

What else am I going to tell you about old King David? You can read a lot about him in some of the books of the Bible — both books of Samuel, the first book of Kings, and the first book of Chronicles. I'm not here to give you a history lesson. Still, he wasn't the first, and he wouldn't be the last ruler to let power go to his head. David lusted after Uriah's wife, Bathsheba, and, oops! got her pregnant. He tried to have Uriah take some time to be with Bathsheba in the hopes that Uriah would be convinced that the child was his own. Uriah was too loyal and honorable a man to take time away from the front lines when others could not. Then the king arranged to get rid of the cuckold by having Joab place him in the area where the fighting was fiercest and then having Joab's troops fall back, leaving Uriah exposed. And so Uriah died, betrayed by the king he honored. Really shitty, low thing for David to do — as if he could then say that it wasn't his hand that drew the sword against Uriah, that it was an act of God. After all, David was not to blame. It was just one of those things. You know, shit happens.

David later married Bathsheba, and he saw it as my punishment when their child became ill and died.[142]

And maybe it did seem like I cursed David's house. One of his sons, Amnon lusted after his step-sister, Tamar, raped her, and, his lust now satiated, threw her out of his house. Her

---

[142] Not my doing. I'm not taking revenge on innocents because someone fucked up. But once again, you see how I get blamed for everything.

brother, Absalom waited two years to avenge her; his men struck down Amnon at a feast Absalom threw for Amnon and the other sons of David. Seven years later, Absalom led a rebellion against David, forcing David to flee his capital of Jerusalem. Absalom chased him across the Jordan, and the decisive battle between them was fought in the Ephron forest. Twenty thousand men were killed that day, and at the end of the slaughter, David had won the day.

But his victory turned bitter for him. Absalom had been riding his mule into battle, when Absalom's long hair got caught in the branches of the tree, leaving him hanging in midair as the now riderless mule keep on going. When this was reported to Joab, he took three javelins and plunged them into Absalom's heart while he was still alive in the tree. Ten of Joab's armour-bearers then surrounded David's son, struck him and killed him. They took Absalom and threw his body into a big pit in the forest and piled a heap of rocks over him.

When the king heard this, his heart mourned. "O my son Absalom! My son, my son Absalom! If only I had died instead of you—O Absalom my son, my son!"[143]

But this wasn't the end of David's troubles. First a famine, then later a plague. Even another failed rebellion by his son Adonijah with Joab's support. Need I say that it was believed that I was punishing David for disobeying me?

---

[143] II Samuel 18:33

As all mortal men must do, no matter how much power and riches they accumulate in their lives, no matter how many monuments they build in their own names, David grew old and died. His son Solomon succeeded him as king in 970 BCE.

Solomon, the wise. Solomon, the wealthy. Solomon, the powerful. Solomon, the king who had seven hundred wives and three hundred concubines. Solomon, the builder of palaces and temples. Solomon, the author of the Biblical books the Song of Songs,[144] and Ecclesiastes, Solomon, the last king of the twelve tribes of a united Israel.

The Book of Proverbs is also traditionally said to have been written by Solomon, but if so, Solomon talked out of both sides of his mouth. For example, first Solomon says, "Do not answer a fool as his folly deserves, or you will grow like him yourself."[145] Which sounds like good advice, but then he almost immediately contradicts himself with "Answer a fool as his folly deserves, or he will bethink himself wise."[146] Which is it, Solly? After all, "A proverb in the mouth of fools dangles helpless as the legs of the lame."[147]

Who is the fool? I'll leave that for you to decide.

---

[144] Naughty, naughty, Solomon!
[145] Proverbs 26:4
[146] Proverbs 26:5
[147] Proverbs 26:7

The first thing Solomon did after David's death was to conduct a purge of his potential enemies, such as Adonijah and Joab, claiming that it was King David's final request.

Now Solomon was fully in control. He allied himself with the Pharaoh and married his daughter.[148] He accumulated some forty thousand chariots and twelve thousand horsemen, which may help explain the truth of why his reign was one of peace. Think about it. Remember this is the ninth century BCE. Would *you* have wanted to mess around with something that huge? David had left him a goodly fortune which Solomon then used in building himself a royal palace and a temple for yours truly.[149] Of course, that was a tall order. So, he conscripted thirty thousand men from all the tribes of Israel to travel in relays to Lebanon where they would pick up cedar and pine for his buildings. Additionally, he forced some seventy thousand men to serve as carriers and eighty thousand as stonecutters, all overseen by eight hundred foremen.[150] The damn project took up more people than his army! By the time he had finished, the king had been engaged in building projects for about thirteen years — seven on the temple, but the full thirteen simultaneously on his palace.

---

[148] My, how times change. Moses would have had a heart attack. But, it's the story of human society: Yesterday you were my friend, today you are my enemy, tomorrow you are my friend again. You people just don't want to get it.

[149] I've already told you what I think about all that, but whatever!

[150] So, marrying the Pharaoh's daughter wasn't the only idea he had gotten from Egypt.

And yes, the temple he built was impressive. Bronze, gold, magnificent carvings of fruits and flowers, great pillars twenty-seven feet high and eighteen feet around. In all, the temple was ninety feet long, thirty feet wide and forty-seven feet tall. Not bad. But consider that on the other hand, the Palace of the Forest of Lebanon (as his palace was called) was one hundred fifty feet long, seventy-five feet wide, and forty-five feet high. So, you could kind of guess which was the more important to Solomon. Seems always to be the case with your leaders. They talk about how they worship and kneel before me---but their main interest is to glorify themselves. And so many of you buy into it that you forgive them anything—because they are good, God-fearing men, of course. Excuse my sarcasm.

The man sure loved his gold, though. When it came to overdoing it, your modern con men—pardon me, leaders have nothing on him. His shields—over nine hundred of various sizes—were of gold. His throne was of gold. His goblets were made of gold. All the household articles in the palace were made of gold. Gold, gold, gold. You could go blind from so much gold! Tacky, tacky, tacky.

Funny, though. The horny fellow loved many women from many foreign lands. Guess the Pharaoh's daughter just couldn't satisfy his appetites. As I said, he had seven hundred wives of royal birth, along with three hundred concubines. And they nagged, and nagged, and nagged. Oh, he could stand it while he was young, but as he grew old, his heart became less and less devoted to me as the God of Israel, and these foreign wives eventually led him to worship other gods, He built high places where each wife could offer sacrifices to their native god.

I didn't care. But it was later said that I was angry with him because of this, and the events that subsequently occurred were my doing. You know, don't piss me off!

He began to have enemies: Hadad of the royal line of Edom, Rezon who controlled Damascus and ruled in Aram. Finally, Jeroboam, who had been one of Solomon's officials, also rebelled and fled to Egypt to bide his time.

In his later years, Solomon became disillusioned by life. As he wrote in Ecclesiastes, everything was futile. All things were wearisome and monotonous because they would continuingly reoccur. There was "nothing new under the sun."[151] The past was forgotten; the living would be forgotten as well by their descendants. Wisdom was a burden; for the more you know, the more your sorrow. Pleasures, the palace, the temple, all he had built, his riches, now seemed meaningless, "a chasing of the wind, of no profit under the sun."[152] What good was being wise when in the end, death came for the wise as well as the fool? Where there should be justice, there was wickedness. As for me, he felt that I tested humans to see what they truly are. Man has no advantage

---

[151] Ecclesiastes 1:9
[152] Ecclesiastes 2:11

over the beast: all came from dust, and to dust all returned. Meaningless, all meaningless.

When Solomon was dead, his son Rehoboam was declared king. Jeroboam returned from Egypt, and he and the assembly of Israel went to the new king. "Your father laid a heavy yoke upon us, but if you lighten it and the harsh labor he put on us, we will serve you."

Rehoboam asked for three days to consider. He went to the elders who had served Solomon and sort their advice

"Your duty is to God," they said, "and He asks that you be benevolent to your people. Treat them well. Say 'yes' to what they are asking. You'll go down as a great king, and all will be well."

But, the younger courtiers, the sycophants he had grown up with, the ones who were now jockeying for position and power in the new kingdom, said, "Oh, mighty king! You are the wise one, you are the great ruler. Your word is that of God himself. How dare they challenge you. Fuck them!"

And like many a king, many an emperor, many a president, many a dictator, he took the advice of those who flattered his ego—because, apparently, experience does not matter, and the new know better than the old. And of course, who knew anything better than he did. Just who was running things, anyway?

So, he agreed, "Fuck them!"

When the three days were up, Jeroboam and the people re-turned to hear his answer. Rehoboam snorted and laughed. "If you thought my father's yoke was heavy, wait until I get done with you. My father scourged you with whips; I'll use scorpi-ons."[153]

When the people heard this and realized that the new king had absolutely no interest in listening to them, they answered, "Go screw yourself," rebelled, and left only those who lived in the towns of Judah to stay loyal to him. Rehoboam sent out Adoram, the officer in charge of forced labor, but the Israelites stoned him to death. Rehoboam fled to Jerusalem and from that day, the kingdom was divided. Never again would there be one kingdom of all the twelve tribes together under the house of David. The people made Jeroboam king over Israel, leaving Rehoboam with the tribes of Judah and Benjamin.

This split between the House of David and the ten tribes caused many problems. Among them: since Jerusalem's temple was the acknowledge place of my worship, Jeroboam worried "If the people go up to sacrifice in the house of the Lord in Jerusalem, it will revive their allegiance to their lord King Rehoboam of Ju-dah, and they will kill me and return to King Rehoboam."[154]

He took counsel and then built two golden calves, just like the one that the Israelites had made while waiting for Moses at

---

[153] I Kings 12:11
[154] I Kings 1:27

Mt. Sinai, declaring them the gods of his kingdom. Against the rules of the priesthood, where tradition had it that all candidates must be from the tribe of Levi,[155] he appointed anyone who wanted to be a priest to the office. As long as their first loyalty was to him, Jeroboam could care less about any rules.

Supposedly, that pissed me off, and it was prophesized in my name---yes, here we go yet again — that a king would come out of the house of David named Josiah[156] who would destroy the altars Jeroboam had built and that the House of Jeroboam would be destroyed.

If I were to recount the story of every king of Judah and every king of Israel, this book would get much too long. It took two books of Kings and two books of Chronicles to handle most of it, and your eyes would glaze over from all the betrayals, power-mania, lies, murders…which sadly, make up most of the story going forward. Look, I breathed life into you, but I don't know where you got those things from. I didn't do it![157]

And every time something happens good or bad, it's supposedly my doing. Either I'm rewarding someone for following my rules, or I'm punishing someone for breaking them—I have nothing other to do but deal with you humans day in, day out. It

---

[155] The tribe of Moses and Aaron.
[156] More about him in a bit
[157] Lucifer is shouting over my shoulder. "Well, don't blame me! I had nothing to do with it, either."

seems like I'm just waiting for you to fuck up. The mean, venge-
ful, angry God—I sound like a variation of Santa Claus—I see you
when you're sleeping, I know when you're awake, I know if
you've been bad or good, so be good or get the plague!

Now, hold on for a bit because here's where it really starts
to bet messy. Let's take a few moments to mention all those kings
so I can just give you the highlights, eh?

We'll start with the kings of Israel, which was also known
as the Northern Kingdom. Starting at around 930 BCE or so, there
was Jeroboam, then his son Nadab, assassinated by Baasha—who
also killed all of Jeroboam's family—in turn, his son, Elah, and
guess what? —yep, assassinated and family destroyed by Zimri
who succeeded him. Then, you have Omri, Ahab, Ahaziah,
Joram, Jehu, Jehoahaz, Jehoash, Jeroboam II, Zechariah, Shallum,
Menahem, Pekahiah, Pekah, and the last king of Israel, Hosea who
was defeated by the king of Assyria—the tribes of Israel were
then forced into exile in Assyria about 730 BCE and disappear into
history as the Ten Lost Tribes.

As to the kingdom of Judah, after Solomon we have Rehoboam, Abijah, Asa, Jehoshaphat, Jehoram, Ahaziah, then after
Ahaziah was killed by King Jehu of Israel, Athaliah—the mother
of Ahaziah--attempted to destroy the whole royal family. However, Ahaziah's son, Joash, escaped and later became the next king
when Athaliah was put to death. And you won't be surprised to

learn that Joash was later assassinated as well, followed as king by his son, Amaziah, then Jotham, Ahaz, Hezekiah, Manasseh, Amon who was—yep, again!—assassinated and then replaced by Josiah (who we'll come back to in a bit), Jehoiakim, his son Jehoiachin, and then finally Zedekiah under whom Jerusalem was conquered by Nebuchadnezzar, the king of Babylon who destroyed the temple and carried away most of the citizens to Babylonia in 587 BCE.

And let us not forget about Doc, Grumpy, Happy, Sleepy, Bashful, Sneezy, and Dopey.[158]

Need a second to catch your breath?

If you go into the details of the various books of Kings and Chronicles, what you find is that many of these kings strayed from the worship of the "God of their fathers," where I am called "Yahweh."[159] So-called "foreign Gods" would be brought to the kingdoms of Judah and Israel by the marriage of their kings to wives from other kingdoms. Temples were constructed for the worship of Baal, or Chemosh, or Molek, or Asherah, etc. Prostitution—both male and female—was part of the rituals of some of these gods, as well as human sacrifice. Prophets of Yahweh—men such as Elijah, Nathan, Elisha, Jeremiah, and others—would go before these kings, condemn them for abandoning the "one true

---

[158] Sorry...couldn't help myself.
[159] To be precise, my name there is YHWH (which represents four Hebrew consonants called the Tetragrammaton) as Moses would have known it.

god" and for leading the people astray, and warn them of dire calamities that would occur because of this. And of course, these
prophecies turned true — especially as these books of the Bible
were written ages after these events occurred, and we all know
how it works in hindsight. Then, the people (those who survived
the punishment caused by my so-called divine wrath) would turn
back to the worship of me as Yahweh for a while, then eventually
fall away again, which would result in even greater calamities
down the road.

I know the list of kings is long, but do you remember Josiah, one of the kings of Judah, and how I said we'd come back to
him? In 641 BCE, when he was only eight, Josiah became king of
Judah upon the death of his father, Amon, who had worshipped
Baal and other "idols." Amon had sacrificed one of his own sons
in fire, practiced divination, and consulted with mediums and
spiritualists. A totally evil son of a bitch, who wound up assassinated by his own officials in his palace. And *his* father, Manasseh,
had been even a bigger bastard — it was said that he" ...shed so
much innocent blood that he filled Jerusalem from end to end," [160]
killed the prophet Isaiah, and led the Judeans away from me into
acts of such wickedness that the prophets declared that I would
"bring such disaster on Jerusalem and Judah that it will ring in the
ears of all who hear it..."[161] and ultimately cause the eventual

---

[160] II Kings 21:16
[161] II Kings 21:12

277

destruction of Jerusalem and the temple and the exile of the people.

As to Josiah, however, perhaps as a reaction to all the horrors his father and grandfather had brought to the kingdom, or to the prophecies about the future fate of Judah, he was only sixteen when he began to "revert" to what was thought to be the true worship of the God of Abraham and Moses. At twenty, he began to purge the land of the temples and altars devoted to Baal and the other gods.

But what exactly was the true worship? So many centuries had passed since the time of the Patriarchs and of Moses, so many kings and prophets had already come and gone twisting it for their own purposes that naturally the traditions were corrupted. To be truthful, by now no one really knew for sure what the religious laws were supposed to be.

When Josiah was twenty-six, he sent Shaphan, the son of the governor of Jerusalem, and Joah, the son of the Secretary of State, to repair Solomon's temple. They went to the high priest, Hilkiah, and entrusted him with the funds for the temple. Work began with Jahath, Obadiah, and Meshullam, all Levites who were eligible to assist the priests in the divine worship. They and other Levites also served as scribes.

Why am I telling you all these details? Let's reconstruct a conversation or two that occurred during this construction, and I think you'll get the idea.

As they sat around the dinner table, the high priests and Josiah's officials got into a discussion of the state of affairs in the kingdom.

"Oh, things are improving day by day," said Hilkiah. "It's good to have the one true God back."

"True," Shaphan agreed. "And once the temple is fixed up, Jerusalem can reclaim its glory days, and the proper order of things can finally be restored, with the proper respect paid to you and your brother Kohanim and us Levites as well."

"Indeed," Hilkiah raised his glass as Meshullam poured more wine. "But here's the thing, Shaphan—it's all well and good to say that, but we need to guarantee it. We need to have some final authority, something in writing that we can show the people."

"What are you proposing?" Joah asked.

"I've been thinking about this for many years, and now it looks like God or some lucky chance has created the perfect setup. You, Obadiah, and Jahath are excellent scribes. With your skills and my priestly background, why can't we forge—I mean, 'discover' a holy scroll, outlining the rules?"

"Beautiful, Hilkiah," Meshullam enthused. "We could say it was the 'Book of the Law of the Lord' obtained by Moses!"

"No one is going to fall for that!" Joah demurred.

The priest chuckled. "Oh, you'd be surprised. People are so gullible they're willing to believe almost anything they are told by someone in authority."

Shaphan nodded. "And if we say Hilkiah found the book in the temple during the repair work..."

"It just might work at that," the others finally agreed.

So, the conspirators began with each of their pet peeves.

"I really hate those male prostitutes," Meshullam began. "Always going around dressed to the nines. And some even dress like our women prostitutes! You can't even tell them apart. Do you have any idea how embarrassing that is?"

Everyone laughed. Meshullam's sexual appetites were a poorly kept secret among the ruling class.

"Fine. Let's make male prostitution a crime." proposed Hilkiah.

"Yes. Make it punishable by paying a fine equal to double what the customer paid. That stuff should only occur in the privacy of one's own house!" said Meshullam.

So, it was written down.

"You know," said Hilkiah, "we need to do something about the food offerings. The sheep and cows are okay, but the last time, someone brought in a lobster without thinking, and I'm allergic. My throat blows up if I'm anywhere near them."

"Kind of a pity. I like a good steamed lobster tail," Jonah mused. "For me, it's those damn pigs. You all have seen people vomiting and getting the shits from eating pork. It's got to stop."

Shaphan wrote on the scroll: "*And the LORD spoke to Moses and to Aaron, "Speak to the children of Israel, and tell them this is my word., You have many things you can eat. Nice roasts of lamb, sheep, cattle, they're all yours. But keep your hands off the pig, it's dirty. Don't eat it, and don't even touch a dead one. And of the creatures of the sea, have a great time with all those that have scales and fins. Have a nice pickled herring, maybe a white fish, but no shrimp, no lobster, no crabs, huh? You don't know what they've eaten – and believe me, you'd rather not know."* [162]

And so on and so forth. Many, many rules — rules about washing your hands, rules about women and their time of the month, rules about childbirth and purification, rules about clothing, rules about masturbation, rules about unlawful sexual relationships, haircuts, etc., etc. And promising death and disaster to Jerusalem and Judah for not obeying them.

You need to know that these "laws" were only the beginning of the written records that would become parts of the final Bible books of Leviticus and Deuteronomy. In later years, during the Babylonian exile, the Jewish editors of the writings would incorporate ideas from the other cultures they encountered, and so the "law" as set forth in Josiah's time, would change and sometimes would improve, and other times be made worse. Such as in this case, where the original as you saw before basically said no male prostitution with the penalty being only of a fine, when the final version you find in Leviticus reads "If a man has intercourse

---

[162] With a lot more verbiage and some editorial changes, this would form the basis of Leviticus Chapter 11.

as with a woman, both commit abomination. They must be put to death; their blood be on their own heads."[163]

And we could spend days going over these rules and why they were created, but we won't because, for the most part, I had nothing to do with them.

Not to knock them all—there are many laws that deal with compassion, and fairness, and how to treat your fellow human: ideas like not defrauding your fellow, and not slandering others; leaving the edges of your fields alone when harvesting and leaving fallen fruit and such for the poor and the foreigner; respecting the elderly; treating foreigners as well as the native-born; giving generously to the poor—all that leads to a loving heart and brings you closer to me. It's just a shame that so many of you seem not to follow them.

Shaphan read this so-called Book of the Law to Josiah, who tore his robes and wept. He was in despair. He realized that most of the prior kings of Judah, his own father and grandfather, hadn't obeyed the rules. Were he and his people supposed to suffer because of what occurred before them?

After conferring for a while, Hilkiah and Shaphan told Josiah that they had consulted the prophetess Hudulah and she said these disasters would not occur in his lifetime. Which, if you ask me, was probably the smart answer—and helped prevent panic when word got out to the populous about the Book.

---

[163] Leviticus 20:13

Josiah, as I said, really cleaned up Judah's act. It was said that there was never a king who followed the Lord (per the so-called Law of Moses) with all his heart and soul.[164]

That didn't stop him from falling to the fortunes of war, however, for he died fighting against the Egyptian pharaoh, Necho, at the battle of Megiddo, 610 BCE.

But let us to return to 587 BCE, some twenty-three years later. One hundred and thirty years or so after the Northern Kingdom had been conquered by Assyria under Shalmaneser, forced into exile, and then disappeared into history's dust. Now, with Jerusalem and Judah captured by the Babylonians under Nebuchadnezzar, and the deportation of the upper classes into Babylon, was the Kingdom of Judah doomed to the same fate?

---

[164] 2 Kings 23:25

Book XI – Of Jews, Persians, Greeks, and Romans

By the rivers of Babylon we sat and wept
when we remembered Zion.
On the willows trees there
We hung up our lyres,
for there those who had carried us captive,
asked us to sing them a song,
our captors called on us to be joyful:
"Sing us one of the songs of Zion."
How could we sing the LORD's song
in a foreign land?
If I forget you, Jerusalem,
may my right hand wither away;
May my tongue cling to the roof of my mouth
if I do not remember you,
if I do not set Jerusalem
above my highest joy.[165]

A beautiful song of longing for one's homeland that resonated down the ages. Some twenty-four thousand years later, it would inspire the great Italian composer Giuseppe Verdi's famous "Va Pensiero," the chorus of the Hebrew Slaves in the third act of his opera Nabucco.

---

[165] Psalm 137:1-6

Book XI – Of Jews, Persians, Greeks, and Romans

Happily, he and his librettist, Temistocle Solera, ignored the final lines of the original psalm:

> *Babylon, Babylon, the destroyer,*
> *happy is he who repays you*
> *for what you did to us!*
> *Happy is he who seizes your babes*
> *and dashes them against a rock.*[166]

The horror of war and the never-ending cycle of revenge.

But that isn't what I want to talk about. There'll be more of that later on, unfortunately. Let's take a look at what happened to Judaism during the exile.

The exiled Jews still had their belief in me as Yahweh; they considered their exile due punishment for not following my rules. If only they would do so now, they believed, I would redeem them from captivity. However, the very fact that they captives in a foreign land caused massive problems in doing so. First, the worship they knew required animal sacrifice performed at the Holy Temple in Jerusalem. But there was no such temple in Babylon nor anywhere else in Persia, and the actual temple had been destroyed by Nebuchadnezzar. Obviously, this was a biggie!

---

[166] Psalm 137:8-9

The elders, the priests, and the scribes thought about the problem. How were they going to keep their identity in a foreign land? Couldn't build a temple---Nebuchadnezzar would never go for that, and besides, the last one took seven years to build. Not to forget, of course, that it was supposed to be in Jerusalem, and not Babylon. And without the temple, animal sacrifice was out of the question.

Finally, in attempting to find a way to keep faithful to their Yahweh oriented religion, they came up with a method that would eventually produce modern Judaism. I won't bore you with the lengthy deliberations. Though, to tell you the truth, there is something to the old joke that if you put *two* Jews together in a room for a discussion, you'll wind up with *three* arguments. The elders replaced the temple worship with the synagogue as a house of worship, and prayers replaced the animal sacrifices—which was a much better idea if you ask me!

Trying to keep true to what they regarded as the Laws of Moses, they also emphasized the Sabbath as well as the observance of other Jewish holidays such as Passover, Rosh Hashanah, Yom Kippur, etc. However, this, they felt, was not enough to maintain their identity and keep them separate from their conquerors, so they refined the rules on circumcision (ouch!). They also began to write down the books that would eventually become the Old Testament that you know today, especially the Five Books of Moses (the Torah).

Still, they could not wholly escape the influences of both the Babylonian Chaldean culture and religion under Nebuchadnezzar nor the Persian Achaemenid ones which followed under Cyrus the Great. Stories from Babylon's national creation myth, the *Enuma Elish,* form the basis of the first Genesis creation story[167] — the very one I quoted at the beginning of this very book — but were changed to conform to the Jewish idea that there was one and only one god, instead of the multitude that was led by Marduk, that existed in Babylonian mythology. The Biblical version of the Adam and Eve story was influenced by the *Atra-Hasis* epic, but there man and woman were created from clay by the female god, Mami. The Flood story in the *Atra-Hasis* was copied into the Story of Gilgamesh from where it eventually was adapted into the Biblical one, so that where they have Ziusudra and Utnapishtim respectively, we have the person we know as Noah.

Nor can we ignore the influence of the Persian prophet Zarathustra and the religion he found, Mazdayasna, or as it is known to the non-believing world, Zoroastrianism, the Persian imperial religion under Cyrus the Great:

---

[167] "When the heavens above did not exist,
And earth beneath had not come into being—
There was Apsû, the first in order, their begetter,
And demiurge Tia-mat, who gave birth to them all;
They had mingled their waters together
Before meadow-land had coalesced and reed-bed was to be found…"
(from the First Tablet, Lines 1-2)

I'm God and You're Not

For, a long time ago, there was a man who, at first, faithfully served the ancient multitude of Persian gods. No, not Abraham—we've been through his story. Zarathustra, who is also known as Zoroaster, became a priest at the age of fifteen. But, unlike many who blindly accepted the traditions and mores that went before them,[168] Zarathustra had the type of mind that is a blessing and a curse as well—the type of mind that caused him to be dissatisfied with just accepting others' words for the truth, and to seek out different teachings and to observe through his personal experiences what was fact and what was false.

Then, when he was about thirty years old, while attending a spring festival, Zarathustra had a vision—of course, it may have been influenced by all the haoma he consumed. He looked at the river bank and suddenly saw a shining figure approaching him.

Zarathustra got down on his knees and averted his eyes.

"Oh, get up!" the being said, pulling the priest upright. "I hate being patronized like that. And don't give me any of that 'I'm a sinner and unworthy' stuff, either."

"I'm sorry, oh Lord. I—"

"I am Vohu Manah, Good Purpose, and I bring you the peace of the Lord Ahura Mazda, the Wise Spirit. Come sit with me, for I have much to tell you."

In Zarathustra's vision, Vohu Manah told him of the existence of two primal Spirits: Ahura Mazda, and Angra Mainu who

---

[168] Something that would never happen today, of course!

was otherwise known as Ahriman (Hostile Spirit). Ahura Mazda brought Asha (the truth) while Ahirman brought Druj (the lie). Or in other words, Good (Ahura Mazda) versus Evil (Ahriman).

Or, much to Lucifer's disgust, God against Satan.

Hey Luce, do you want to say something here?

Lucifer again. I just want to know what did I do to get such a bad rap. Damn that King James guy. Just because Isaiah was taunting the Babylonian king's fall with "Bright morning star, how you have fallen from heaven, thrown to earth, prostrate among the nations!"[169] and James' translators had to make הֵילֵל בֶּן-שָׁחַר (Helel ben Shachar) be" lucifer" (which was Latin for "bright morning star"), I've had nothing but grief. Look God will tell you, I'm really not such a bad guy.[170] I mean, even the author of Job kind of got it that I am a part of the Lord's inner circle, and not his enemy. It's that damn fake press!

Zarathustra also taught about a future life, a resurrection, and reward. The Jews had never thought much about that. They were more concerned about this life and prosperity in it. But, the Jewish writings, such as the Books of Daniel and Job, now began to incorporate this, and the idea of a Messiah started to evolve into something more than just a great human leader (such as Cyrus) who acted in my name.

---

[169] Isaiah 14:12
[170] I've tried to!

The changes by engendered by these contacts changed the Jewish religion so much that it was almost like a new religion.

Even after the Exile,not all Jews accepted this new concept about the Immortality of the Souls; one notable exception was the group that would be known as the Sadducees. The people who professed this new doctrine would be called the Pharisees. Yes, those Pharisees and Sadducees that would later come to play such a role in the story of Jesus — but let's not get ahead of ourselves.

And this wouldn't be the last time the nature of Judaism would change, but more about that in its proper time.

The prophet Ezekiel had predicted the destruction of Judah and the temple and now was in exile in Babylon with his fellow Jews. He now prophesized that one day I would return them to their homeland and restore the nation to its former glory.

Well, unlike some of your leaders who will remain nameless here, I don't take credit for the acts of others. After he had conquered Babylon in 539 BCE, the Persian king Cyrus the Great, believing that Yahweh was one of the good guys, allowed the exiles to return to Judah, under the lead of Zerubbabel and Joshua the High Priest, though a significant number of the deported decided to stay behind.

Under the leadership of the priests, Judah became a province of Persia. Ezra brought the Torah to Jerusalem in 428 BCE, and you could call that the date that modern Judaism began. He reorganized the Israelite state politically built the new religious system based on Torah and its study. Nehemiah, a Jewish noble in Persia, was sent a bit later as governor to rebuild the city walls and the temple in Jerusalem.

Two hundred years went by as Persia dominated the Middle East and Egypt. Then along came the Macedonian king Alexander III. You know him as the Greek conqueror, Alexander the Great. It took him ten years, but in 334 BCE he finally defeated the Persian empire, and the "civilized" world was now Greek.

In reviewing this newly conquered addition to his empire, Alexander made a triumphant march to Jerusalem. According to both the Jewish Talmud[171] and the Jewish historian Flavius Josephus, the High Priest, who was worried that Alexander would destroy the city, hurried out to meet him before he even got to Jerusalem.

To the High Priest's amazement, Alexander dismounted and bowed to him—and Alexander bowed to just about nobody. In Josephus's account, when asked by his general, Parmerio, to explain his actions, Alexander replied, "It was not before him that I prostrated myself but the God of whom he has the honor of being high priest. It was him whom I saw in my sleep dressed as he is

---

[171] The central text of Judaism developed after the later destruction of Jerusalem by the Romans in 70 CE. It was the primary source of Jewish religious law and theology until modern times.

now, when I was in Dion in Macedonia, and I was considering with myself how I might become master of Asia. He urged me not to hesitate but to cross over confidentially for he himself would lead my armies and give over to me the empire of the Persians. Since, therefore, I have beheld no one else in such robes, and on seeing him now I am reminded of this vision and the exhortation, I believe that I have made this expedition under Divine guidance, and I shall defeat Darius and destroy the power of the Persians and achieve all the things I have in mind." [172]

He was also delighted to find out that the book of Daniel had predicted that a Greek would defeat the Persians—naturally, this had meant him.

Though they had fought against him on the side of the Persian king, Darius, Alexander made an arrangement with the Jews. As long as they would be loyal to him and pay their taxes, they could pretty well govern themselves. Out of gratitude to Alexander, the Jews did a few things. First, they agreed to name every child born the next year "Alexander," which opened the door for Jews to give their children other Greek names as well. And this helped to bring in the Greek language and culture, and a mixture of Greek and Middle Eastern culture arose known as Hellenism.[173]

A mutual fascination between the Greeks and the Jews developed. For the Greeks, with their multitude of gods, the Jews

---

[172] Josephus Flavius, Antiquities of the Jews, XI.8.5
[173] Hellas being the name of Greece in the Greek language.

were something new — a people that worshipped a single God who acted throughout history, a people with a profound legal system and philosophical traditions. The literacy rate among the Jews was unheard of in those times. For the Jews, the Greek intellectual culture that had produced great philosophers like Socrates and Aristotle, a culture with a love of science, wisdom, art, architecture — this was unheard of! The Greek language was considered to be so beautiful that the rabbis even allowed the Torah scrolls to be written in Greek. The Greeks, equally fascinated, had the entire Hebrew Bible translated into Greek by seventy Jewish rabbis, thus giving the world the first translation of the Old Testament.[174]

But things were bound to change. Perhaps things would have gone much differently for the Jews and for your later religions if Alexander hadn't done one small stupid thing: In the evening of June 10, 323 BCE, the great conqueror died in Baghdad under somewhat mysterious circumstances. He was only thirty-two years old. His glorious empire, which stretched from Greece to Egypt and India, broke apart, and two Greek Empires emerged in the Middle East: The Ptolemies in Egypt and the Seleucids in Syria. The Land of Israel became the border between these two warring Empires. Initially, the Jews were under the control of the Ptolemies, but after the Battle of Panias in 198 BCE, Israel found herself in the domain of the Seleucids and their king, Antiochus.

---

[174] The Septuagint, from the Latin word *septuāgintā* " meaning seventy."

By this time, the upper classes of the Jews, along with much of the Mediterranean world, had largely embraced Hellenism. It had gotten to the point where many of them rejected their Jewish identity—even going through painful operations to undo their ritual circumcision (ouch, again!) to conform to the Greek ideal of the human body, and to remove the one physical mark that identified them as Jews. The vast majority of the Jews, however, remained loyal to their religion, and what differences had once seemed a source of exotic attraction now came to be seen as a sign of rebellion. Israel was the border state between these two rival Greek Empires, and the Jews, who refused to assimilate, were viewed as a disloyal population in a strategically vital part of the Seleucid Empire.

Hellenized Jews tried hard to bring their fellow Jews out of their "primitive darkness" and into the glories of the "modern world." This brought in the Seleucid king, Antiochus IV Epiphanes[175] who, in the mid-second century BCE, reversed all those years of tolerance and enlightenment. He issued a decree that was the breaking point: in a multicultural and basically tolerant ancient world, he ordered that the Jewish religion be outlawed. He turned the temple in Jerusalem, the temple dedicated to Yahweh, into one dedicated to Olympian Zeus, the king of the Greek gods. In horror, the Jews watched what they saw as the desecration of

---

[175] Epiphanes meaning "God Manifest"—so another asshole with delusions of grandeur. Oh well, not the first, and sadly, certainly not the last.

their holy temple, robbed of its treasures, defiled by offering a sow upon the altar and scattering its juice over all the sanctuary and vessels. Antiochus ordered the replacement of the Jewish feasts with the drunken revelry of Bacchanalia, forcing the Jews to worship Bacchus, the god of pleasure and wine.

The horrors that Antiochus inflicted on Jerusalem and its people are well-documented in the Books of Maccabees, and I would rather not repeat them here – if I just say that he was the Hitler of his time, you can probably get the idea. More weeping in Heaven.

Ever hear of Chanukah? You know, that Jewish holiday with the menorah that shows up somewhere around Christmas time? Well, guess what? That's where we're at now.

The year is 167 BCE. In the little town of Modiin, a Jewish priest named Matthias refuses to worship the Greek gods. When another Jew, one of the Hellenized, steps forward to offer a sacrifice to an idol in his place, Matthias was so enraged that he rushed forward and killed him right at the altar. Shouting "follow me, all who are zealous for the law and stand by the covenant," Mathias fled to the hills along with his five sons: John Gaddi, Simon Thassi, Judas Maccabeus,[176] Eleazar Avaran, and Johnathan Apphus, sparking the revolt against the Seleucid empire. But it was also a civil war between "Judaism" and "Hellenism," between the orthodox and the

---

[176] "The Hammer"

reformers, the Sadducees and the Pharisees. The Maccabees de-stroyed pagan altars in the villages, circumcised boys and forced Jews into outlawry. When Matthias died the following year, Judas became the leader and used guerrilla warfare tactics to victory. Ac-cording to Josephus, Mattathias's great-grandfather's surname was Asamonaios, or Hasmonean as their dynasty would be eventually known.

Afterward, Judas and his forces entered Jerusalem in tri-umph, cleaned and purified the temple, reestablished the Jewish religion there, and installed Johnathan as the high priest. Three years after Antiochus had defiled the temple, they celebrated the dedication of the new altar for eight days and decreed that this cel-ebration should be observed every year for the eight days as well. Hence, Chanukah which means "Dedication!"

So, what's with the Menorah and the eight candles? The story goes that during the dedication of the temple, the priests only found one small container of purified olive oil, just enough to burn for one day. However, when the temple lamps were lit, somehow the oil lasted eight days—enough time to produce additional oil. This "Chanukah miracle" is NOT part of the story told in the two Maccabean books; it is recounted in the Jewish Talmud which was written down about six hundred years after the temple dedica-tion—so make of that what you will.

The war was not over, however. Giddy with success, many among the Maccabean forces wanted to continue the revolt and conquer other lands with Jewish populations. Non-believers in these newly conquered lands were given a choice: to convert to the "pure" Judaism of the Maccabees, with the males being circumcised as per the ancient mark of the Jews, or to be exiled. Judas continued the fight in Galilee and Transjordan. The war kept on until Antiochus Epiphanes died in 164 BCE, when a sort of truce occurred for a while between the Syrians and the Jews, the Syria kingdom temporarily under the control of general Lysias who had bigger fish to fry while the new king was underage. But the war soon resumed. It even got so intense that Judas even sent a delegation to Roman to seek help there.

After five years of leading the revolt, Judas was killed in battle. His brother Johnathan succeeded him as general, and later, when the new Seleucid King Alexander Balas, made peace with him, Balas proclaimed Johnathan as the new High Priest in Jerusalem. This was the start of the Hasmonean dynasty in Israel. But this also started more infighting among the Jews. The divide between the Pharisees and Sadducees grew. Johnathan was not a descendant of Moses's brother Aaron the first Priest, and thus his appointment as High Priest was against Jewish law. Jonathan was assassinated by Diodotus Tryphon, a pretender to the Seleucid throne, and was succeeded by Simon, who himself was assassinated in 135 BCE.[177] The dynasty was maintained by Simon's son John, known later as Hyrcanus I.

---

[177] Sigh. Beginning to sound familiar?

The dynasty continued until 64 BCE when the Hasmonean court of law (the Sanhedrin.) appealed to the Roman general Pompey to intercede in the civil dispute between the two brothers: Hyrcanus II and Aristobulus. Pompey marched on Jerusalem and made it a client kingdom of Rome. The Hasmonean dynasty ended in 37 BCE when the Idumean Herod the Great became king of Israel.

After Herod the Great died, eventually Herod Antipas became tetrarch of Galilee.

And then there was Jesus.

Book XII – Of Jesus, Mohammed, and Beyond

hat can I say about Jesus?

Was Jesus My son? Was he indeed the true Messiah? Is Jesus (or to use his Hebrew name, Joshua) really coming back to judge the world?

Here's the problem. If I say "Yes" or if I say "No," I'd probably start a religious war, and there would be more conversions made on threat of death, institutions and civilizations might fall or gain in power — you know, that stuff you do just about every time you come up with a new religion or split one apart because of some insignificant disagreement. You've been doing that for thousands of years without any input from me, and I'm not going to start messing around now.

So, I'm going to take a pass.[178] But, I will say this to the believers, he didn't die on that cross for your sins just so you could go out and make more of them — some in his name.

You have four gospels and a bit of Acts, and even they can't agree on the details about Jesus. So, let's have a little quiz, shall we?

First question: Where was Jesus born?

---

[178] I may tell you more if (God forbid!) I have to write you a sequel. Probably have to call it "For Christ's Sake! I'm still God."

Answer: That depends. Matthew and Luke say Bethlehem, Mark is fairly quiet on the point, though he implies it is Nazareth, while John point blank says Jesus was NOT from Bethlehem.[179] You may also wonder why all the Gospel writers refer to him as "Jesus of Nazareth" not "Jesus of Bethlehem." Did you know, there were *two* places called Bethlehem — one is "Bethlehem of Judea," the city near Jerusalem that contains the Church of the Nativity, but there is another one called "Bethlehem of Galilee," right near Nazareth? Take your pick.

Second question, and this is a multiple choice just to make it easier: Assuming Judas was real[180] and that he did betray Jesus, how did he die?

    a. He hung himself

    b. After buying a plot of land, he fell, and his entrails burst out

    c. Duh?

Answer: Well, it's "a" if you believe Matthew or "b" if you believe what Luke says in the first book of Acts. Given that he couldn't have done both, I'd go with "c."

But getting back to this Jesus as Christ stuff, if you have read the rest of this book, you know perfectly well that I don't give a shit what you believe about "God" and religion — except just don't hurt anyone, huh? You can't define me by your human standards. I'm

---

[179] John 7:40-43

[180] That's a story all of itself, and I won't get into it here.

God! —I'm not, for example, some orange faced narcissist with a bad haircut who demands to be followed unquestionably no matter what stupidity comes out of his mouth. I'm not trying to force you to think a certain way, to believe only the things I tell you and ignore your own common sense and intelligence. It doesn't matter to me if you think I am one in one, three in one, one in three, zero in one, one in zero, thirteen in a dozen, or six in seven eighths. It makes no difference in your day-to-day lives, but you sure want to kill each other over it. I may have given humanity life, and I keep my eye on you, but I also gave you free will. You decide what to do with it.

I tell you truthfully—if you want to call yourselves Christians, then actually follow Jesus's teachings. Don't go to your church on Sunday, say a couple of prayers and go around with a holier-than-thou attitude. Don't go screaming because someone wishes you "Happy Holidays" instead of "Merry Christmas!" What does that have to do with anything? For Christ's sake! You turned the very holiday you celebrate his birth into the worship of material things, and he would be appalled at it.

So, one day a year you go around with love in your heart for your fellow man, and you think that redeems you while you treat him like dirt the rest of the year.[181] And don't think this lets those of you who call yourself Jews, Muslims, Buddhists, whatever, off the hook, because so many of you are equally hypocrites.

---

[181] And I won't even get into how the date is wrong in the first place!

But, at the moment, we're talking about Jesus.

Strip away all that Messiah stuff, the idea that Jesus died for your sins, original sin, immaculate conception, the Resurrection, the miracles, all the incidental stuff, and get to the essentials of what he taught. You are still left with a great religious teacher—all that other stuff is like a side salad to the entrée. Don't stuff yourself on the lettuce and miss the main meal. You do not have to believe all those other things to be able to call yourself a follower of Jesus if you choose to call yourself one. Too many of you have the whole thing backward. Too many so-called Christians have taken the name of this martyr to love and compassion and made of it a weapon for hate.

So, for them, I have a message from Jesus:

"Stop crucifying me."

Because, yes, there was a god-filled teacher in Galilee who lived and died some two-thousand years ago, and this is what he tried to tell you:

"Blessed are the merciful, for they shall be shown mercy."[182]
"Blessed are the peacemakers; they shall be called God's children."[183]

---

[182] Matthew 5:7
[183] Matthew 5:9

Book XII – Of Jesus, Mohammed, and Beyond

"Do not store up for yourselves treasures on earth, where moth and rust destroy, and thieves break in and steal; but store up treasure in heaven..."[184]

"Go and learn what this text means, 'I require mercy, not sacrifice.'"[185]

"Always treat others as you would like them to treat you: that is the law and the prophets."[186]

So many wise men, teachers, prophets, martyrs come and gone before and after him, trying to tell you the same thing and you still won't pay attention! You still don't get it.

Stop being so damn concerned with the messenger and try spending more time listening to the message! The messenger only opens the door to find me., and there are many, many of these doors. If you keep tripping around at the entrances and never step through one, you never will. Because, it's the message that's important, not who delivers it or how.

Let me repeat that. It's the message!

Three years of preaching, then came the cross. It could have ended right there. But somehow, the belief that Jesus had been resurrected from the dead and was indeed the Messiah the Jews had been waiting for, began to spread through Jerusalem, and so the

---

[184] Matthew 6:19-20
[185] Matthew 9:13
[186] Matthew 7:12

Christian movement started as a cult within Judaism. The apostles preached that Jesus's life, preaching, death, and resurrection fulfilled Jewish prophecy; they saw incidents in the Bible going back to Genesis as prefiguring the coming of Jesus. Believing that the end times were near, and that Jesus the Messiah (or Christos in Greek) could return at any moment, they traveled around the Jewish communities around the Mediterranean spreading the "Good News" and slowly winning converts to their sect.

By the tenth year after Jesus's death, this early Christianity had spread as far as Rome. But it remained a Jewish cult, its followers attending Jewish temple and following Jewish rites and the Torah, Most Jews rejected its teaching—for the Jewish idea of the Messiah was of a great human leader, not a "son of God." Why, at one point, the Jews had called Cyrus the Great a messiah. And it was a time of many so-called Messiahs anyway. How could I have a son? — "Hear O Israel, the Lord your God, the Lord is One."[187] This was the foundation of the Jewish religion. Why the very idea was blasphemy.

It might indeed have stayed that way forever, if not for Saul (aka Paul) of Tarsus.

---

[187] Deuteronomy 6:4. This is the "Shema" and remains to this day the most important prayer of Judaism. The Shema Israel is the first prayer taught to Jewish children, and it is the last words a religious Jew says before death. Over the centuries, so many, much too many, persecuted Jews, in pogroms, Holocaust, and on and on, have been martyred with these words as their dying breath.

Book XII – Of Jesus, Mohammed, and Beyond

It was Saul who brought the teaching of Jesus to the non-Jews. As more and more non-Jews began to accept Jesus as the Messiah, the leaders of the Jewish Christian cult found that they had a problem. Because they still saw the movement as part of Judaism, they wanted these new converts to fully embrace the Jewish ways: no pork, and so on. Jesus hadn't planned on founding yet another religion. As he said during his Sermon on the Mount: "Do not suppose that I have come to abolish the law, but to complete it. Truly I tell you: as long as heaven and earth endure, not a letter, not a dot, will disappear from the law until all that must happen has happened. Anyone therefore who sets aside even the least of the law's demands, and teaches others to do the same, will have the lowest place in the kingdom of heaven."[188]

But the real stickler: that little thing called circumcision (ouch!). Not only was circumcision painful, but it directly contradicted the Greek ideal of male beauty that was embraced by Rome. So, when the potential Gentile convert would hear that, it was an insurmountable problem. "Are you for real? No one's touching my schlong!"

Saul's radical, and history-changing idea was that circumcision was irrelevant, that Jew and Gentile were united in one faith in Jesus the Christ, and that Jesus had "died for our sins."[189] Saul argued that "all that must happen" had happened, and therefore

---

[188] Matthew 5:17-19
[189] 1 Corinthians 15:3

the old laws did not apply. The Cross had not been a defeat, but a triumph that absolved man from his sins and reconciled him with God. According to Saul, I had sent Jesus, my son, into the world for this very purpose, and he would return. Those who believed in him would be raised from the dead to eternal life.

The doctrines of Saul and other apostles eventually led them into conflict with some of the Jewish religious authorities, and it wasn't long before they were thrown out of the synagogues and began to be persecuted as blasphemy. Still, it took centuries before Christianity truly became a distinct religion, wholly divorced from its Jewish parent.

While this was going on, tensions were developing between the Jews and the Roman empire. When Rome began to proclaim the Emperors as gods themselves and demanded that they be worshiped throughout the Roman Empire, this of course contradicted the Jewish belief in one and only one God, and the idea of a mortal being as a god was laughable.[190] Emperor Caligula ordered that a golden statue of himself be placed in the Jerusalem temple to be worshiped, but his death at the hands of the Praetorian guards thankfully adverted the crisis for a while.

But in 66CE, a full revolt broke out.

---

[190] Despite what some of you seem to think about your leaders.

Initially, the Jewish Zealots[191] seemed successful by taking over Jerusalem, but they were perhaps even a greater enemy to their cause than Rome was. They fought amongst themselves; they had inadequate training and a lack of discipline. They even destroyed the food supplies in Jerusalem in an attempt to force me to intervene, forgetting that old injunction about not tempting your god.

The Romans laid siege to Jerusalem, and in 70CE the walls were breached. On the 9th day of the Jewish month of Av,[192] (which falls in late July or early August in the modern western calendar), a day which would become the saddest day in the Jewish year, the city was set on fire and the second temple was destroyed. And by some strange coincidence, this was the very day that the first temple had been destroyed about 655 years before. Again, mass destruction and all the horrors of war that I've discussed much too many times already. Josephus, who personally witnessed the destruction, wrote that over one million people were killed during the siege and that ninety-seven thousand were captured and enslaved.[193] All that was left of the temple was a portion of the retaining wall—the Wailing Wall that still stands today in Jerusalem.

---

[191] There were three main Jewish sections at this time: the Sadducees, the Pharisees, and the Essenes. There fourth sect, the Zealots, advocated violence against the Romans, and against any Jew who they saw as collaborating with them.

[192] Tish B'Av which has become a day of mourning to commemorate the many tragedies that have befallen the Jewish people, many of which have occurred on the ninth of Av, thus a day seemingly destined for sorrow.

[193] Josephus, The Wars of the Jews VI.9.3

If you go to Rome today and visit the remains of the forum, you can still see the Arch of Titus, commemorating the event—the south panel depicts the spoils taken from the temple, including the great Menorah. And each year, on the anniversary of the day, the ninth of Av, the Jews observe a day of mourning in remembrance of the sad events that occurred that day, and for all the horrors that they and their brethren would undergo in the 2000 years that followed.

Though Jerusalem fell, the resistance did not die out. Two more Jewish-Roman wars broke out. The last one, 132 CE was led by Simon bar Kokhba, who himself was acclaimed as a Messiah. The revolt was successful for two years until finally a Roman army made up of six full legions with auxiliaries and elements from up to six additional ones finally crushed it. The Romans then barred Jews from Jerusalem, except to attend Tisha B'Av. Although Jewish Christians hailed Jesus as the Messiah and did not support Bar Kokhba, they were banned from Jerusalem along with the rest of the Jews. It wouldn't be until 1948 CE that the Jews would have a homeland again with a divided Jerusalem, and 1967 CE before they were able to reunite Jerusalem.[194]

The gulf between Judaism and Christianity now became wider, and eventually, they went their separate ways. It happens in the best of families. The Jews would have to determine how the Jewish religion could somehow survive in a Gentile world. With the destruction of the temple and the banishment from the holy

---

[194] And the Holy City still remains a source of conflict even now.

city, the only part of the ruling group that still retained any power were the Pharisees, the rabbinical group. Through their efforts, Judaism was transformed from the temple and animal-sacrificial oriented form[195] to one centered around the synagogues. Centers of Jewish culture developed in Galilee and Babylonia where the development of the Talmud, containing a compendium of the "Oral Law" and instructions or teachings about it and the Torah, continued.

Meanwhile, the Christians continued to proselytize to the Gentiles, winning converts. But, because the Christian ritual was secretive and different from the public religion, it often aroused suspicion among the pagan majority. Judaism may have been different, too, but it was an old and established religion. Once it split from its predecessor, Christianity was no more just a bizarre sect of that religion but was something new and different. It seemed to threaten the status quo: for they worshipped a convicted criminal and refused to regard the emperors as more than just men. Rumors, misunderstandings, and lies spread about their religion—that Christians committed incest because they referred to each other as "brother" and "sister," that they were cannibals who sacrificed infants in the eating of the "blood and body" of Christ in their communion.

---

[195] Sadly, animal sacrifice had been reinstituted with the return from the Babylon captivity about five hundred years earlier.

How odd that these very same libels would later be used by the Christian church in their persecution of the Jews, a persecution has gone on for over sixteen hundred years in humanity's most protracted mass crime.

Would Christianity have eventually died out? Only God knows![196]

The year is 325 CE, and the place is Nicaea, known today as İzni in Turkey. Some three hundred theologians are gathered together in a great council called by the Roman Emperor Constantine I. The emperor "himself proceeded through the midst of the assembly, like some heavenly messenger of God, clothed in raiment which glittered as it were with rays of light, reflecting the glowing radiance of a purple robe, and adorned with the brilliant splendor of gold and precious stones,"[197] as he recalled the events of the past few decades that had led his becoming the sole emperor of the Roman Empire. He smiled enigmatically, for though still an unbaptized pagan, Constantine repeatedly claimed that he owed his victories to the "Christian" god. In 312, he had fought the Battle of the Milvian Bridge against his rival Maxentius in the name of that Christian God, Constantine claimed that the night before the battle he had seen a vision in which the Christian sign appeared in the sky with the legend "In this sign, conquer." Was it true? Well,

---

[196] Just a saying here, folks. Don't take it literally.
[197] Eusebius, *Vita Constantini*, Book 3, Chapter 10

it seemed that Constantine had earlier received a vision of the god Apollo at a shrine in Gaul. Or maybe the whole thing was just a trick of the moonlight reflecting off the clouds? I had nothing to do with it, goodness knows; I wasn't taking sides. It was an age in which every Greek or Roman believed that religion piety led to political success, so it was entirely understandable and expected that Constantine should do so as well to justify his quest for power. But vision or not, he defeated Maxentius army and triumphantly entered Rome two days later. It had only been twenty years earlier that the Great Persecution of the Christians had begun under the emperor Diocletian, in which Christians were forbidden to worship, their property seized, their scriptures destroyed, men, women, and children tortured and, in some areas of the empire, burnt alive. But as the grand champion of Christianity, a year after his triumph at Milvian Bridge, Constantine was party to the Edict of Milan, which legalized Christianity and religious toleration throughout the empires.

To be truthful, he had been a bit more concerned about social stability and the protection of the empire than he was for justice or care for the Christians per se. He was known to be superstitious and believed enough in the existence of the non-Christian gods not to want to offset the balance of good and evil.

Yet there were deep divisions within Christianity You remember Jesus, you know, the guy from whom this whole thing started? Well, there was a great argument going on about his nature and his relationship with an aspect of me which they knew as "God the Father."

Some argued like Arius, "Christ is separate from God. Why do you think we call him 'the Son'? As the Gospel says, the Father begat the Son. That means that the Son had a beginning. Therefore, he's not eternal."

Others, such as St. Nicholas,[198] argued, "No you idiot. Christ is eternal and of the same substance as the Father."

And still others, "You're nuts. Jesus was a man, a totally human man. We all agree that his mother was Mary, but his father really was Joseph! God adopted Jesus as his son and, as well, Jesus became the Christ at his baptism, not before."

There was also, "Of all the dumb ideas in the world, this one takes the Eucharist! There is only one God as it says in the Bible. Christ and the Holy Ghost are just other faces that God shows to us. They're not separate things."

This was countered by "You sons of Satan! There is one and only one God, but He is indeed three distinct entities: Father, Son, Holy Ghost. Three in one!"

"No, God is like a circle. Without beginning and without end."

"No, He's like a tree. Giving forth knowledge and good fruit for his creation to eat."

---

[198] Yes, that St. Nicholas!

"A tree? Is He an oak tree, or maybe a maple? Perhaps he's an olive tree, they have so many in the Holy Land. He couldn't be a fig tree – remember what happened to the one that refused to give fruit to Jesus.[199] You know you don't want to piss him off!"

Constantine had enough of this headache.[200] But, there had no such thing as aspirin back then, so here they were in Nicaea to settle things. Fights would break out, the meetings became shouting matches, but in the end, it was here that the Nicene Creed was created. And thus, the Trinity:

We believe in one God, the Father Almighty...and in one Lord Jesus Christ, the only-begotten Son of God, begotten of the Father before all the ages, Light of Light, very God of very God, begotten, not made, being of one substance with the Father, through him all things were made... And in the Holy Ghost, the Lord and Giver of life ... who with the Father and the Son together is worshiped and glorified, and has spoken through the prophets...

Of course, this didn't solve everything. Even the creed became a bone of contention. It wasn't until 380 CE that the Edict of Thessalonica made this Nicene Christianity the official religion of the Roman Empire, and so began the history of one group of believers in Jesus persecuting another group of believers in Jesus.

---

[199] Just in case you don't recall it, you can find it in Mark 11:12-14; 20-21.
[200] Him and me both!

As to the Biblical canon, there were hundreds of gospels out there about Jesus, hundreds of letters that may or may not have been written by Saul and the other apostles. What was canon, and what was not? Even though there were Gospels written as far back as forty years after the crucifixion, it took a few hundred years to finally come up with some sort of a list of books that would make up the official Bible (Old and New Testaments).[201] But differences occurred depending on what denomination you belong to. What a mess!

Such religious arguments, among others, vital and trivial, became so intense that the church would split into Roman Catholic and Eastern Orthodox Churches. Martin Luther would later come along and, attempting to correct what he saw as corruption in the Catholic Church, founded Protestantism, which resulted in still more sects, like Anglican Methodist, Calvinism, and Baptist—just to name a few. And then, the Catholics and Protestant sects would persecute each other; some Protestant denominations would persecute other Protestant denominations—all over the same Jesus who

---

[201] Among the works that didn't make it into the New Testament: Book of Jubilees, Gospel of the Hebrews, Gospel of the Egyptians, Infancy Gospel of James, 1-2 Clement, Gospel of Thomas, Gospel of ,Jude, Gospel of pseudo-Barnabas, The Shepherd of Hermas, The Didache, Gospel of Peter, Gospel of Matthaias, Gospel of Judas, Gospel of Mary Magdalen, Acts of Andrew, Acts of Barnabas, Acts of John, Apocalypse of Paul, Apocalypse of Peter, etc., etc.... No wonder it took so long!

preached about mercy and love. What the hell is wrong with you people?

Even with all that, Christianity went on to become the world's largest religion.

Meanwhile, in Arabia...

It is the twenty-second day of December 609 CE. We are in a cave on the mountain Jabal al-Nour, about two miles from Mecca, in what is now called Saudi Arabia. And there, Mohammed, who would often come here for prayer and reflection, has had a vision of the angel Gabriel, who commands him to

Proclaim! In the Name of your Lord, Who has created (all that exists),

Has created man from a clot (a piece of thick coagulated blood).
Proclaim! And your Lord is the Most Generous,
Who has taught by the pen,
Taught man that which he knew not.[202]

. Thus, the beginning of a twenty-three revelation that would become the Quran. Three years passed while Mohammed continues to have more visions of Gabriel. He begins to proclaim his message to the world: that I am the only God ("lā ilāha illā Allāh"), and

---

[202] Quran: Surah 96:1-5

all must submit to my will and my commandments. Although Mohammed called me Allah, he also said that I was the same God who was worshipped by the Jews and Christians ("the People of the Book"). Abraham, Moses, and Jesus were my prior messengers and to be highly respected. Unlike in Christianity, Jesus (called "Isa") was not thought to be my son, but a human prophet sent by me with the revelation of the Gospel. Mohammed was the last in the line of the prophets, sent to restore my original message that had been distorted over the years by both Jew and Christian. This was Islam.[203] All people who follow God's revealed guidance and the messengers sent with it 'submit' to that guidance and are considered Muslims.[204] Adam, Moses, Abraham, and Jesus were thus Muslims!

Mohammed's teachings were written down in the Quran. Within one hundred years of his death in 632 CE, Arabia had become Muslim, and Jerusalem, which had been under the control of the successor of the Roman Empire, the Christian Byzantine Empire, was conquered. Having completely taken over the Arabian Peninsula, the Muslim advance was knocking on the walls of Tours, France where it was finally halted. However, as the Ottoman Empire, at its maximum, it expanded westward into Europe as far as Spain, while to the East it would grow into North Africa, Central Africa, India, Russia, and as far as Indonesia.

---

[203] "Submission (to God)"
[204] "Muslim" meaning "he who submits."

From a small handful of followers, Islam would grow to become the second largest religion on Earth and the challenger to the dominance of Christianity.

So, is Islam the true religion? Again, I'm not saying. But, think of it: three great religions emerged out of the wanderings of one man, Abraham (Ibraham), who sought to know me Judaism, Christianity, and Islam.

And sadly, they've been fighting ever since.

Book XIII – The Apocalypse of God

ow then.... What? Excuse me for a second. What's the problem, Luce?...

Uh huh.... I see... You know, you're right! Would you care to enlighten the audience?

Lucifer here. My apologies for the interruption, but as it looks like God is getting near the end of this book, I noticed that He has forgotten one little thing. Do you remember way back near the beginning? God said, "All past, present, and future existed in my unchanging omnipresence. There was nothing except me, drifting in an eternity composed only of me. And this pretty well went on for oh let's say billions and billions and billions of your earth years, as I contemplated myself. And then, I had a Thought. It was quite a curious Thought, this first Thought of eternity. For it occurred to me that in all this contemplation of myself, there was one thing I did not know: what did I look like?"

He never told you, did he?

Considering that this was the first question He ever asked himself and that it's the reason why he created me in the first place, I just couldn't let Him forget. I know the Big Fella has a lot on His plate, but still!

Anyway, once He created me, the answer was right in front of him.[205] Because neither He nor I nor any of the angels He later created actually have a corporal "form." And, as God told you, your creation was

---

[205] Sorry about that one, but I am a little devil sometimes, you know?

318

*kind of an accident. Certainly, you were **not** created in His image – He doesn't have one! It was mankind that created its idea of what God looks like based on its own image. So, most of you picture Him as a human being, maybe as a bearded white man, eh? Wrong! What do you think God looks like to a cockroach? Yep, a giant cockroach! To an eagle, a giant eagle. To an amoeba, a giant amoeba. To your pet dog, a giant dog – nope, not you, even though you probably think so. And to Alpha Centaurians he's a giant version of themselves – and if you ever saw an Alpha Centaurian, you would know how utterly weird that would look.*

Get the idea now?

Again, sorry for the interruption.

Thanks, Luce, I guess I owe you own there.

To continue what he was saying, just for a moment: In truth, there are no words to explain it, no concept of what I truly am. But, strip away your human failings, the hate and the hurts in your hearts, the stubbornness of human pride and willfulness....and look what remains in the human heart. That's what I look like. That is who I am.

To get back to what we were discussing before: You've had plenty of wars between Christians and Moslems and Jews—the same old same old story again of horrors and atrocities. Crusades, pogroms, massacres, genocides, world war. Babies skewed on swords and bayonets. Pregnant women, their bellies ripped open and their children killed in the womb. Men, women, children burned alive all for my glory!

Thousands and thousands of years, and it still goes on: The annihilation of one and a half million Armenians and the genocide of hundreds of thousands of Greeks in the early 20th Century. Eleven million killed in the Holocaust, over a million of them children, six million Jews — almost two-thirds of the Jewish population of Europe! Poison gas used on masses to cause a slow, agonizing death. Bombs. Biological warfare. ISIS. On and on in a perverted dance, worshipping death over life.

Though the vast majorities of Christians, Moslems, and Jews want nothing more than to live their lives in peace and to freely follow their religions, there has been so much hate and misunderstanding over the centuries. Fanatics, blinded by hatred, pervert their religion, killing innocent people in the street, and blowing up babies while shouting how great I am. If I'm so damn great, then what the hell do I need these bastard dogs for? Murdering innocent worshippers in their synagogues, churches, mosques because of some perverted belief that there is only one way to me and all other are blasphemy. *This is how you honor my name?* Others, reacting to these horrors, would condemn entire peoples for the actions of a few — willingly treating them worse than animals, rounding them up into camps, ready to start yet more holocausts with a different cast this time. Why would I want to add to the misery? What kind of sadist do you think I am? How could you possibly worship a God like that? And how many times must you be told, mankind, you are so much better than this.

And for the love of God,[206] please stop blindly excusing your leaders from their evils just because they pay lip service to being good Christians, or Jews, or Moslems, or whatever. You cannot justify stealing food from the poor and elderly, taking away the support given to my truly innocent ones—the autistic, those made homeless and/or forced into poverty through no fault of their own, the physically or mentally disable, and others such as these—because the fools who lead your country pretend they are my servants. You excuse pedophiles and rapists because they claim to be doing my work now. What on earth are you thinking?

I don't know. Maybe when you were created by that accidental mashup of the donkey-dolphin and the pig-monkey by Ezequiel and Suruph, it also accidentally knocked your brains up, and no one realized it at the time when you were first created.

Of course, that may also explain why none of you are perfect, each of you has some flaw in your character, even the best of you. Well, I guess it's time I fessed up and admit that is by design. If all were perfect, what would be the point? I'm perfect, you're perfect, everything is perfect…no point in striving, no point in love, no point in artistic endeavor, no need to better yourself or the world…it would be just another form of death.

---

[206] No pun intended.

But the thought occurs to me: if there was nothing to do, no need, nothing to aspire to—wouldn't that be imperfect, too? I don't know. Sometimes I get too philosophical for a God—blame it on those ancient Greek guys like Socrates, Heraclitus, Zeno, Democritus, and the like. I did spend a lot of time listening to them back in the glory days of Greece, and I guess it may have rubbed off a bit. Oh well!

But, back to your imperfection. Some of you use it and aspire to make yourselves and the world better for it—people like Siddhartha Gautama, Malala Yousafzai, Martin Luther King, Jr, Mohandas Karamchand Gandhi, Tenzin Gyatso, Thomas Merton, St. Francis of Assisi, Raoul Wallenberg….and perhaps you, the very person reading this right now. Changing the world for the better does not require that you shout to the world; you can change it merely by a kind act, a heart that seeks to love instead of hate.

Others fall into a trap of desire and seek power over others, making the world a place of suffering and destruction. Some of them even pretend to be my worshippers while opposing my will in all their actions—people like Attila the Hun, Caligula, Torquemada,[207] Leopold II of Belgium,[208] Adolf Hitler and his subordinates Heinrich Himmler and Adolf Eichmann, Father

---

[207] Grand Inquisitor during the Spanish Inquisition.
[208] Founder of the African nation Congo Free State (now called the Democratic Republic of the Congo). In1885, he ordered, his men to torture, maim and slaughter close to 50% of its population

Coughlin,[209] Josef Stalin, Ismail Enver Pasha and Mehmet Talat Paşa, [210] Mao Zedong,[211] Kim Il Sung and his son Kim Jong-Il, Osama Bin Laden, Bashar Al-Assad, Donald Trump[212].... And, as you can see by some of those names, they don't even have to be murderers. Their evil can be banal; they seek nothing but their own self-glorification no matter what the cost to their fellow men and women, who are nothing more to them but pawns to be used and cast away.

And sometimes the gang and I just shake our heads in wonder at your behavior.

Take, for example, Christmas. It's supposed to be the celebration of Jesus Christ's birth---whether it is the actual date of his birth does not seem to matter, but that's not the point. Certainly,

---

[209] Up to thirty million listeners tuned to his weekly broadcasts during the 1930s in which he would issue anti-Semitic commentary such as "When we get through with the Jews in America, they'll think the treatment they received in Germany was nothing."

[210] Two of the principal perpetrators of the Greek (1914-1922) and the Armenian Genocides (1915-1922) in which somewhere between three hundred seventy thousand and seven hundred thirty-seven thousand Greek, and between eight hundred thousand and one million eight hundred thousand Armenians were murdered.

[211] Being a communist, Mao did not believe in me, of course. He is possibly the biggest mass murderer in history. It's believed that he killed some sixty million people. Most of his victims were his fellow Chinese, murdered as 'landlords' after the communist takeover, starved in his misnamed 'Great Leap Forward' of 1958-61, or killed and tortured in labor camps in the Cultural Revolution of the 1960s.

[212] Like Coughlin, he pretends to be Christian while promoting hate and fear between people, and doing everything that Jesus condemned, and ignoring what he preached.

this should be a time of reflection for all members of the Christian faith...The midnight masses and other services are inspiring, and I really do like the music—like that Silent Night song. A beautiful time of year. But, why do you turn the period from the end of November through the end of December into such a frenzy? First, there are the lights—blinding, flashing—what does that have to do with the birth of a baby in a cave in Bethlehem? Some candles in the window are a nice touch, but all that stuff in your yards and over your houses? It's not a competition, folks. And what does a tree covered with lights, bulbs, and tinsel have to do with Jesus anyway? —The damn thing is a Yule log; it's pagan! But that's okay...we up in Heaven never understood what a bunny rabbit had to do with him either.

Then in the United States, there's that annual bullshit of there being a war on Christmas, and that you can't say "Merry Christmas" but have to say, "Happy Holidays," or something like that. First of all, the last time there was a real war on Christmas in America it was courtesy of the Pilgrims—yes, *those* same Pilgrims that came over on the Mayflower in...oh, come on, you used to be taught this in your public schools in the US...1620!! Along with other groups, they considered Christmas to be an abomination— heck, it wasn't even legal to celebrate Christmas in New England until 1681 and even then, public pressure frowned on it. It didn't become a national holiday until 1870 (thank you, President Grant). Secondly, no one is stopping you from say "Merry Christmas" if you wish. But, it's also the time of Chanukah, of Mawlid el-Nabi,[213] the Winter Solstice, Zarathosht Diso,[214] Rohatsu (Bodhi Day),[215] Festivus, Kwanzaa, Yule, Saturnalia...The point is that—now read my lips very carefully because I'm only going to say this once: *IT'S NOT JUST CHRISTMAS TIME!!!!* Do you hear Buddhists going around complaining that they can't say "Happy Rohatsu!"? Look, if a non-Christian wishes you a "Happy Holiday," or for you non-Christians if a Christian wishes you "Merry Christmas," just lighten up. How about trying to understand the spirit in which the greeting was meant—one of brotherhood, peace, and inclusion? Still, I'm glad you don't concern yourself with such trivial, unimportant things after all—you know, like war, starvation, poverty...that sort of thing Jesus preached about! That would really be horrible!

And joy of joys.... the mad dash where you will practically kill for a parking space, so you can run into an over-crowded mall, so you can push and shove and kick your fellows so that you can get that special hot toy or that seventy-five inch UHD Smart TV that they just knocked down in price.[216] Because it isn't the thought that counts, it's the fucking present!

Then, you have the endless holiday specials...carols and seasonal songs being sung ad nauseum, by the same old overly worshipped celebrities that shall be forever left nameless here in

---

[213] The birth of Mohammed.
[214] The death of Zoroaster.
[215] The day the Buddha achieved enlightenment.
[216] The one that you just gotta have today even though the price will go down AFTER the holidays.

the Spirit of Good Taste. Oh, speaking about spirits...I have to admit that Christmas Carol still gets to me. Give me Allister Simms any day. Luce and I always choke up and start to blubber when Tiny Tim dies. Damn, that Chuck Dickens sure can write!

You know, every so often I speculate on what would happen if the Second Coming did occur—and then I realize that Jesus would just get crucified again—this time by those who most loudly and self-righteously proclaim themselves to be his follows. After all, they know his message better than he did!

I don't want to think I'm just picking on Christians, because pretty much every group has got some issues where I'm concerned. For instance, let's take Orthodox Judaism. You know that bit about remembering the Sabbath day, and keeping it holy by doing no work, and so forth? Well, because of how "work" was interpreted by the rabbis and such, this creates a major problem because carrying anything outside the home is considered to be work! That means, no keys, no wallets, hell, you can't even carry your baby or push it in a stroller outside of your house. So, to get around this, there is the concept of an Eruv, which is an enclosure that some Jewish communities construct in their neighborhoods as a way to permit Jewish residents or visitors to carry things outside their own homes. It must be made of walls or doorways at least roughly three and a third foot high. In public areas where it is impractical to put up barriers, doorways are constructed out of wire and posts, even

Book XIII – The Apocalypse of God

PVC pipes on utility poles where necessary to make the enclosure. Now, I'm a pretty reasonable God, I think. I'm not trying to make it hard for you humans. So, let me ask you — don't you find this a bit much, just a bit specious? If you interpret a rule to state that I would forbid you to carry your baby around, maybe something is wrong with your interpretation? And do you really think that you're fooling me with that sort of thing anyway? C'mon — I'm not a virgin at this kind of stuff---I've been around, you know? I've seen it all, and again, this is one of those what the fuck?! things you do that kind of blows our minds up here.

I can keep going... Do I even have to mention that perversion of Islam called ISIS? Most Moslems just want to raise their families and live in peace with their neighbors while these worthless dogs want to kill anyone who doesn't conform to their sick vision. Suicide bombers! Shooting, blowing up even their fellow Moslems at the very moment they are bowing in prayer to me. And they do these horrors invoking the greatness of my name! They disgrace their prophet; they disgrace my name. And just wait until they see the reward they are going to get after they "martyr" themselves. Oh, are they going to be surprised — and not in a nice way either. I'll give them virgins alright! Damnit! As I said way back at the beginning of this book — if I wanted to kill anyone because they didn't worship me in exactly the right way, I'm God, and I would do it myself! What kind of a God would be so weak as to need you

327

puny humans to do it for him? Remember, I'm supposed to be all-powerful?

And there are Hindus attacking Moslems and Buddhists attacking Hindus and this, that, and the other---and it makes me sick.

Sorry I kind of got on my high horse here, but there are times I want to come down there and knock some sense into you.

Of course, this seems like the state of the world — so much evil, so much hate, so much pain and suffering. You would think I'd give up in despair. You think it's been getting worse and worse — that it is a sign of the coming of the end times. Let me tell you — it's not getting worse. Because you have better, instantaneous communication via television or Internet that no other age has ever had, these things scream at you twenty-four hours a day. And I guess you feel helpless — so you react by despair, or with a horrid fascination with such things (much like how drivers slow down on the highway to rubberneck a crash). Or you go mindless — and try to find meaning in things that have no meaning, like your latest teenage idol, or imagining the life of the insanely rich celebrities you create. Or you turn it all off and go batshit over a sports team, almost having an orgasm when they win and almost dying when they lose. Hell, if Jesus did indeed come back, straight out of the sky from Heaven like many of you imagine, the news coverage would be interrupted because they needed to announce the winner of the World Series or the World Soccer Cup! And just think of the riots if he interrupted the last five minutes of the Super Bowl!

But this is NOT the world, I promise you. No, I don't despair, though even a God is allowed to have moments of doubt. Because then I see such wonders, such beautiful reminders of the human spirit that one's faith in humanity can only be restored. You've been told so many lies; you've been taught to hate, to fear — and yet, that darkness is continuously pierced by light. And that light comes from the best part of you, from your true nature.

There are profound examples all through history, such as a person protecting the victim of persecution, knowing that to do so can cost their own life. But, it isn't required that you make yourself martyrs or wander the world in poverty seeking enlightenment.

Simpler things illuminate the human soul, and make the Angels rejoice:

❖　　　A poor man gives his last twenty dollars to help a stranded woman he doesn't know who has runs out of gas; she, in turn, starts a social media fund that raises over three hundred thousand dollars for him from over ten thousand donors.

❖　　　Greek Islanders fishermen, housewives, pensioners, teachers — people of a country suffering through terrible economic times — respond to the tragedy of the refugee

329

crisis by opening their homes to those children, men and women fleeing war and terror, often risking their own lives to rescue thousands from the freezing sea — without regard to race, nationality, or religion.

❖ Hearing about the crisis of starving people in Puerto Rico after Hurricane Maria, an internationally-known chef lands on the island a few days after the storm and recruits a team of chefs and volunteers, who together serve more than three million meals.

❖ Teachers spending money out of their own pocket for school supplies to help their students get an education when the government won't provide enough funds.

❖ A parent of an autistic child, coming home from work, gives up the use of the only television to that child can watch beloved reruns of The Wiggles and Barney, over and over. On his only spare time on the weekend, that parent (who much rather be doing anything else) takes that child to the same mall each time, to do the same routine of lunch, Ferris wheel and carousel. Why? Because it makes the child happy.

❖   An overworked social worker volunteers her time and talent to help a lonely elderly woman from out-of-state find care when she can no longer care for herself, even though that social worker has no responsibility to support anyone from another state.

❖   Doctors volunteering their talents gratis to save the lives of poor children overseas.

❖   A person walks from his house to a friend's in the middle of a major snowstorm while the friend is away just to make sure that friend's cat is getting its medicine — walking 40 minutes each way in an act of love and compassion.

❖   People, themselves of limited means, find the time and resources to gather toys and gifts for refugee children.

❖   Two cars collide, and strangers offer comfort and food so that an elderly passenger doesn't go into diabetic shock.

❖   In the middle of a major highway, cars stop so that a mother goose can cross the road with her goslings.

❖ A child pays for an ice-cream cone, trips and drops it and the vendor gives him another one for free.

❖ People of all faiths, of different color, of different sexual orientation, of different nationalities, band together to fight against prejudice.

This is why I love mankind.

Do not forget that spark of divinity within you, humanity! Do not give in to the animalistic side of your nature. Remember that you are also Light that seeks to quell the Darkness. And when you look around, and it seems that mankind is going back-ward...don't forget that for every one step taken back in the eternal dance, humanity then takes two steps forward.

So many of you crave a better world. It doesn't matter what religion you follow — it doesn't matter if you follow any religion at all, whether you take your inspiration from the Bible or Quran or Gita, or from Harry Potter. It doesn't even matter if you believe in me or not.

So, for a change, let me ask you a question: *What kind of world do you want help to create? — One of Hope or Despair? Of Love or Hate?* I hope you are proud of your answer. I hope *I* am always proud of your answer.

Meanwhile, many of you wait for a Messiah to come save you, or Mahdi, or for Christ to return and usher in the kingdom of God. But, the wait has been so, so long. You wonder: why does He tarry?

Don't you see? You are asking the wrong question. You should be asking "Why do *I* tarry?" Think about what you've been told by the great teachers of your kind:

The kingdom of God is within you.[217]

And We have already created man and know what his soul whispers to him, and We are closer to him than [his] jugular vein.[218]

He who is rooted in oneness realizes that I am in every being…[219]

By your own efforts waken yourself, watch yourself. And live joyfully. You are the master.[220]

I am a stranger to no one; and no one is a stranger to me. Indeed, I am a friend to all.[221]

You see, what you are waiting for is already inside you. You want justice, you want peace, you want children to live happy and free. You want an end to hunger, an end to poverty, an end to mothers and fathers crying to me in the night for their sons and

---

[217] Luke 17:21
[218] Quran 50:16
[219] Bhagavad Gita
[220] Dhammapada.
[221] Guru Granth Sahib, p.1299

daughters destroyed in wars that are fought over nothing! I can hear the human cry for meaning in the face of destruction.

The power is in you! I breathed a spark into you at creation: the ability to choose, to make your world a Heaven of your own, or to make it a Hell. Look inside. For if you truly want that kingdom to come, it's you who has to start building it.

And the question for me has always been: *What does it mean to be God?* For all the years since humanity was created, I have watched you, and observed my own reactions to the things you did and still do. You taught me about the dark side: anger, you taught me about fear, you taught me about hate. But I also learned about the light side: compassion, sacrifice, and love. I discovered that all these qualities are mine as well as yours and that I needed to learn how to grow from the dark into the light. And that is where you helped me.

And if you should choose not to believe the Genesis story that I made man in my image, that's fine. Because as you grow, as the human race matures and grows wiser, you keep making me over in yours.

So, thank you, humanity, for making me a better God than I was at the start.

And there is so much more for you to learn, so much growth that it would astound you to know the details. And perhaps there is still more for me to learn as well.

Together. Human and God.

THE END

About the Author

Michael Zelig is a long-term religious pilgrim, and has been involved in Judaic, Episcopalian, and Buddhist studies and rituals. He baptized himself and others in the Jordan River, and is ordained in two churches. Although Michael has worked in a variety of positions in Information Technology, he is now a full-time stay-at-home-father and is devoted to his wonderful son. This is his first novel, and he is currently working on his next one.

Follow Michael Zelig at

www.MichaelZelig.com
www.ImGodandYoureNot.com

and on Facebook: MichaelZeligAuthor

www.ingramcontent.com/pod-product-compliance
Lightning Source LLC
Chambersburg PA
CBHW031612100726
47898CB00006B/1755